THE PUPPETEER

HARROW FAIRE: BOOK TWO

KATHRYN ANN KINGSLEY

Copyright © 2020 by Kathryn Ann Kingsley

First Print Edition: September 2020

ISBN-13: 979-8-68303-622-5

ASIN: B08HCWF5WR

All rights reserved.

No part of this book may be reproduced in any form or by any electronic or mechanical means, including information storage and retrieval systems, without written permission from the author, except for the use of brief quotations in a book review.

This is a work of fiction. Names, characters, places, and incidents either are the product of the author's imagination or are used fictitiously, and any resemblance to locales, events, business establishments, or actual persons —living or dead—is entirely coincidental.

ACKNOWLEDGMENTS

Thank you.

No, really. Thank *you.*

Thank you for reading these silly stories that I put together and mash out onto the page. Publishing is exhilarating, terrifying, gratifying, and incredibly stressful all at once. But what makes it worth it is knowing that there might be a few people out there who get as much of a kick out of reading my stories as I do when I'm writing them.

To Michelle, Sylvia, Amanda, "Ziph," and Aza, my growing cheerleading section of alpha readers who keep me motivated to keep going.

To Kristin, who dutifully reads these monstrosities and reminds me that it's *sank* not *sunk.* Someday I'll figure out the whole lay/lie/laid/lying thing. I swear I will. Today is just not that damn day.

To Lori, my editor, without whom these things would be a nightmare to read.

To Evan, my ever-patient husband who puts up with me while I spend hours working on these things.

Again, to all of you, I say thank you.
And enjoy.

The Family

0. The Contortionist
1. The Magician
2. The Flyer
3. The Aerialist
4. The Ringmaster
5. The Catcher
6. The Twins
7. The Zookeeper
8. The Strongman
9. The Bearded Lady
10. The Juggler
11. The Firebreather
12. The Rigger
13. The Clown
14. The Seamstress
15. The Puppeteer
16. The Soothsayer
17. The Diva
18. The Barker
19. The Mechanic
20. The Maestro
21. Mr. Harrow

1

MADNESS IS AN INSIDIOUS DISEASE.

We do not see the danger until it is too late. It creeps into the cracks and crevices of the mind and makes itself at home, like carpenter ants in the framing of a home. We do not know the floor has rotted away until one ill-timed step destroys the façade of normalcy.

But carpenter ants do not destroy a home. They change it. As matter cannot be destroyed, they consume the structures we have built and rearrange it for their own use.

While a home beset by such insects might seem uninhabitable for those who look at the situation from the outside, to the ants it was the intended outcome. We might inspect the foundation and find it derelict and dilapidated. We might scoff and say that anyone who lives within such a place is idiotic, and that they should have not neglected it in such a way. And, in extreme cases, they should move.

Consider this metaphor in relation to one's mind. That place in which we spend the entirety of our mortal lives. What happens when your home is beset by insects then?

One cannot move out of one's own mind, try as we might. We are trapped within these structures of ours, for better or worse and come what may. We must make do with what we are given and what we have left. Whereas you or I in our daily lives might seek a new homestead in such an infestation, in this labyrinth of the psyche, we cannot.

There are different ways that a consciousness, once gnawed and riddled with holes, might come to adapt to such a state of being. Consider three men with this dilemma, if you will.

The first man may seek to repair the damage—replace the eaten portions and shore up the foundations. This man is pragmatic, but shortsighted. He treats the symptoms, but not the cause.

The second may seek to exterminate the infestation—to seek the illness at the root and rip it out. This man is wise, but must need act quickly before the house collapses around him.

The third man merely laughs—he accepts his new state of being and does nothing to repair his home. He declares himself King of the Ants, lifts up hammer and sledge, and tears the remaining walls apart with his own two hands.

You might think that man the fool. You might think him a harmless, laughing lunatic.

It is a mistake that leads to ruin.

For that man is the most dangerous of them all.

-M. L. Harrow

CORA WOKE up from a dreamless sleep. She had expected to be troubled by nightmares or at least her usual tossing and turning. Or, which had been the pattern the past few days more often than not, to be pestered or terrorized by Simon. But it seemed she had been so exhausted that her mind couldn't even summon up nightmares from her day. Which was pretty damn impressive, as she had plenty of fuel for her mind to burn.

Being haunted by a man-eating murder-circus, almost being turned into an inhuman and monstrous meal-via-porcelain-doll by an undead psychopath, and now being trapped inside said man-eating murder-circus with said undead psychopath.

An undead psychopath to whom she was mildly attracted, but that was another stupid problem entirely.

It took her a solid couple of seconds to remember where she was. The linens smelled fresh and clean, but not like home. Despite a slight chill in the air from the early spring weather, the blankets were thick and warm. She could hear the click of a heater going on and off occasionally.

The room was streaming with morning sunlight. It hadn't even occurred to her to pull the blinds around the large bed at the back of the boxcar. But the light didn't bother her. She was lying there...basking. And it took her a long time to realize why.

She didn't hurt.

She was...comfortable.

There was no ache in her back or her hips. There was no tenderness in her joints. There wasn't that background hum of pain that had plagued her for the past decade of her life.

She stretched and waited for the pain to start. It was too good to be true. She waited for the familiar pang to stab into her hips, her shoulders, her elbows, anything.

Nothing.

She rolled her wrists. She arched her back. She waited for the sound of popcorn and crunching and the mild ache that went along with it. Nothing happened. She rolled onto her stomach and pushed up onto her hands, waiting for the agony to start. There was none.

She fell onto her stomach and let out a small, disbelieving laugh. She flopped onto her back, stretched out her arms and legs wide, and let out a long, contented groan.

She didn't hurt. For the first time in years...she didn't hurt. She felt like she had slept. Really, honestly *slept.* She wasn't exhausted, beaten down, and feeling like she had woken up after being dragged behind a runaway truck. She felt good. Honest-to-god good.

It wasn't possible.

None of this is possible.

She looked up at the wood paneling of the ceiling. It was stained a rich cherry, and it was clear the whole space was very old, but well maintained. *No, this place is alive. The Faire is keeping it this way with the bits and pieces it eats from people. Remember?* She sat up and ran her hands through her hair. It felt stringy and gross from having been out in the rain last night for hours.

She looked down at her hands. She remembered nearly tearing off her fingernails clawing at the invisible wall. She should at least have bruises from what had happened. She bruised so easily ever since she was a kid. But nothing was there. Touching her nose, she remembered bloodying it when she ran into the invisible wall. But it wasn't even sore.

Simon healed.

I healed.

I...Am I really one of them now?

No.

No, she refused to accept that she was trapped. She refused to accept that she was trapped in this damn place. A monster and a circus freak. This was all some wild illusion.

It was a trick. She'd get dressed and get the hell out of here. Simple as that.

She slipped out of the bed and the little demi-room in which it was partitioned in the back of the boxcar. Going into the bathroom, she pulled the t-shirt up and over her head to look for the purple blotches she was certain would be on her shoulder.

After spending hours trying to get through the invisible barrier that was holding her prisoner, she should have *something.* Some mark of what she had done. She should hurt somewhere. She always hurt *somewhere.*

Nothing. She didn't even have bags under her eyes. She looked...better than she had in a long time. She furrowed her brow at her own reflection, confused. Letting out a sigh, she didn't know what to do about it. Be mad that she wasn't in pain? That she didn't have puffy marks under her eyes? That she looked...healthy?

Glancing over at the tub and shower combo with the old-fashioned brass wall-mounted showerhead, she was too tempted. If she were going to try to escape this place, she might as well do it not feeling gross. She pulled her still-soggy clothing out of the tub and threw them over the towel rack and flipped on the shower. It got hot after a minute, and she stripped out of her borrowed nightclothes and stepped in.

It was amazing how cathartic a shower could be. Hot water seemed to make everything better. She found some shampoo and went about scrubbing her hair. She had a lot of it—it went down well past her shoulders—so it took a while. It didn't help that she had knotted sections while being out in the rain having a breakdown.

Combing conditioner through her hair with her fingers gave her time to think.

She played over the events of the past few days in her head, right from the very beginning, and tried to piece it all together. No matter how many times she thought it through, it all came down to one thing.

Black magic was real. Or at least some kind of dark supernatural power. It certainly didn't seem benign.

The Faire was alive. It ate parts of people's "seity," and so did the men and women—the *things*—that lived inside it.

But what she couldn't accept was the possibility that she was now one of them. That was where she drew a hard line. But all the evidence pointed to the opposite. The invisible wall that had kept her trapped last night. And then there was what happened with Trent.

He hadn't recognized her. They had been best friends since grade school, and he had looked at her like a stranger. There wasn't even a flicker of recognition in his eyes when she had desperately begged him for help. Nothing.

Even if they had paid him off, she wasn't sure he was that good of an actor.

She decided it didn't matter what was real and what wasn't. She could sort it all out when she was safely at home, in her own bed, and talking to the cops filing a report about kidnapping and harassment. She'd leave the "black magic, occult, man-eating murder-circus" out of the police report.

Her thoughts swung back to Simon. Those puppets of his...what he had said he was going to turn her into. She shivered despite the hot water and went about scrubbing herself with a washcloth and soap. Now Simon claimed he couldn't hurt her without hurting himself, and so therefore, she was safe. She didn't know if she would ever be *safe.* He was a lunatic.

Why had he come out in the rain for her? It didn't make any sense. He was all over the map with her. His compass spun wildly and without warning. One moment, he was kissing her. The next, he was terrorizing her, screaming in a rage about how she was his property. If Aaron and Jack were to be believed, he had dumped her out in the grass like garbage. Then he...came out into the rain to drag her inside. North, south, north, south, and back again.

It didn't matter. Simon was dangerous. It was more than a little likely that everyone else in the Faire was just as murderous, but they just hid it better.

Her next steps were simple. Get dressed, find a car, and drive it through the invisible wall. Get home, call the cops, then cry into a bottle of whiskey. Simple. Right?

Probably not. Nothing had been simple all week, and something told her that it sounded easy, but she might as well be trying to climb the outside of the observation tower with two suction cups.

I will not accept the fact that I'm trapped here. I'm not going to just accept this.

She turned off the shower and dried herself off. Her clothing was still soaking wet, so she dug around in the closet until she found what she needed. She wound up with underwear that thankfully fit her, along with black jeans, socks, boots, a tank top, and a simple gray linen coat. It was all stuff she would happily wear.

As though someone had picked it out for her.

She shuddered at the idea that this could all have been planned in advance. More and more evidence piled on the half of the scale that said she was now part of this place. But on the other side was an ounce of hope. And hope was very hard to kill.

When she had finally finished brushing out her hair, there was a knock on the door. She blinked and debated not answering it. She went through the options of who it could be. Best case scenario, it was a pack of cops coming to rescue her. Worst case, it was Simon coming to kill her.

Santa Claus, Darth Vader, and Einstein could also be standing there, with how her goddamn week was going. After the second knock, she went to the door and cautiously opened it.

And immediately had to jump back as two women plowed into the room. "Wh—"

"Good morning!" the first one exclaimed. She was about Cora's height, with shoulder-length blonde hair and a bright, shining smile. It was the woman she had seen performing on the metal hoop the other day. She was effortlessly beautiful. She was also carrying a tray with a plate heaped with scrambled eggs, bacon, and hash browns.

It wasn't until Cora noticed how good it smelled that she realized she hadn't eaten since breakfast the day prior. Her stomach grumbled, not caring that the invaders might be dangerous. "Uh..." She just watched as the other woman followed the first.

The second woman was a tiny thing. Maybe five foot even, or just a smidge more, with short dark hair. Both women looked like athletes. The blonde looked like she could rip off a car bumper with her bare hands.

Cora blinked. "Hello?"

The blonde with the tray put it down on the table in the little kitchenette. "I'm Amanda. This is Donna. You missed breakfast, so we figured we'd bring it to you." Amanda shot her another award-winning smile. Weirdly, it didn't seem faked, like those kinds of smiles usually did.

"I...um..." Cora shook her head, not sure what to do. The two women were just standing there smiling at her. Amanda was looking at her with happiness and excitement. Like it was Christmas morning.

Donna, the little dark-haired one, waved Cora over to the table. "I know this's been rough for you. Come on, sit, eat. You'll feel better with something on your stomach."

"I, thanks, but..." Cora chewed her lip and shook her head. No, she shouldn't feel like the awkward one. These people were kidnapping her. "I need to go home. I need to find a way out of here."

Both women sighed and cast knowing glances at each other. Donna moved from the kitchenette to Cora and put a hand gently on her shoulder. "I didn't come willingly either. I didn't know what was happening. Juggler just picked me out of the crowd, and before I knew it, I was trapped here too. Just like you. I spent *days* clawing at the walls, trying to get out. I snapped off my fingernails and didn't understand why they just grew back. It took me a month of running through the Inversion before I realized I wasn't going to get home. I don't want to see that happen to you."

"The Inversion?" Cora brushed off the woman's hand. She didn't want to insult the woman, but she was a little confused at how touchy everyone at Harrow Faire seemed to be. "I don't know what you're talking about."

"So, sit, eat, and let us explain." Amanda smiled and motioned to the chair. "Please. And then, when you don't believe us, you can go back to running at the gate trying to get out."

Cora rubbed a hand over her face and sighed. "Fine." She went over to the kitchenette table and sat down. It only had two chairs. Donna took the one across from her while Amanda propped herself up against the counter.

She picked up the fork and began to eat. It was good. Very good. And she was starving. After taking a bite, she remembered her manners. "Thank you. I'm Cora."

"We know." Donna smiled. "I'm the Flyer, and this is Amanda, the Aerialist. And now, you're our Contortionist."

Amanda sighed happily, almost dreamily, as if she was picturing something grand in her mind. "It's so nice to have a woman in the role. Imagine the triple acts we can do now! Hernandez was great, but he was afraid of heights. He was so skittish. So jumpy." She chuckled. "Are you afraid of heights?"

Cora hovered her fork over the pile of hash browns. "No?" She felt like she was standing on the side of the road just watching traffic fly by. "I don't think so."

"Great!" Amanda clapped, giggled excitedly, then motioned for her to keep eating. "Don't let me interrupt. You must be starving."

She wanted to escape. But she could at least ask a few questions while she ate, she supposed. Maybe try to make sense of the madness they were all trying to get her to believe. "Everyone here has the weird titles?"

"Everyone. There are twenty-two of us," Donna answered.

"There are definitely more than twenty-two employees here." Cora pointed out the immediate hole in the story. "I've seen dozens more than that."

Amanda chimed in. "They're not real. Not...really real, anyway. They're more like ghosts. People we collect or dream up. Zookeeper and Bertha the Bearded Lady both take in people who come to see them. But they aren't...I don't know. Big enough—full enough—to be one of us. I don't know how to explain it. They're not complete. You met Simon's puppets, right?"

"Seeing as he tried to turn me into one against my will?" Cora cringed. "Yeah. I have. Are they really...people he's trapped like that?"

The expression on the women's faces were a mix of disgust and anger. "Yes," Amanda muttered. "They're very real. He's a sicko."

What a horrifying way to live. And a horrifying fate she barely escaped. She didn't know if she should exactly thank Turk for stopping Simon since it had landed her here, but she still felt like she had dodged a bullet.

But maybe she had side-stepped a small projectile only to get hit in the face by a cannonball. "I might have a hard time believing a lot of this, but Simon being a sicko I won't argue with," Cora said with a faint smile that didn't stay for long.

They sat in silence for a long time. She finally couldn't let it last any longer. "Are you all really trapped here?"

"Yes. And you are, too. I..." Donna looked out the little window for a moment. "I hope you don't think about it as being trapped. I know you're scared. I know you want to go home. But this is your home now. We're Family, and we can be friends. You can be happy here."

Cora snorted incredulously. "After the week I've had? Have you *met* Simon?"

The two women laughed, and Donna nodded. She reached out and gently put her hand on Cora's. "Ask us anything you need to know. And anything we can do to help you, we're here for you. We're Family."

It was the second question she was dreading to ask, because she didn't know if she could accept the answer. Not if accepting it meant she was never going home. "What happened to me last night?"

Donna combed her hand through her hair, scratching her scalp and ruffling the short, dark strands. She was beautiful, in that I-could-probably-break-your-arm-without-trying-but-I'm-just-so-cute-you-won't-be-mad-about-it kind of way. Like a spunky bartender. "There are twenty-two of us. We're not complete unless someone is in each slot. It doesn't feel right for any of us when someone is missing. It's like there's...a hole. The zero—the Contortionist—had been empty for a long, long time. Thirty-eight years. Longer than it's ever been empty before."

"Why?" Cora kept eating. The hash browns were amazing.

Donna's expression was troubled as she talked. She fiddled with a little saltshaker on the table. "We weren't sure until this morning. After Simon mutilated Hernandez—after he turned him into one of his dolls—we were sure we'd get another Contortionist the next time the Faire returned. But we never did. It wasn't until Simon killed what was left of the old Contortionist that...you came to join us."

"Why did Simon kill Hernandez?"

"Which time?" Amanda grunted in disgust. "Doesn't matter. Sorry. He claims Hernandez asked for it. The poor man wasn't cut out for this life. He...wasn't ever happy here, no matter how many years had gone by. He wanted to be free, and he got desperate. And Simon takes advantage of desperate people."

Cora could attest to that. She ran her hand over her face and thought it all over.

In the silence, Donna continued. "So, when we have a gap to fill, another one of us can opt to Sponsor a new Family member. We can take a chunk of ourselves—our seity—and give it to the recipient. It makes them like us."

"Simon didn't want anything to do with it." Cora sipped the coffee again. Thank God for caffeine. "Ringmaster made him."

"Yeah." Amanda shook her head. "We didn't even know that was possible. It's one thing when the new Family member doesn't want to be here. It's another thing when the Sponsor doesn't want to be a part of it. Simon's been sulking in his boxcar all morning. No one's seen him since he dumped you in the grass last night."

He came out in the rain to get me. I still don't understand why. "So, he...can't hurt me, without hurting that part of himself?"

"Right. He could make you into one of his dolls, but he'd permanently lose that part of himself in the process. Ringmaster's betting Simon won't do it for that reason alone. My guess is the mad fuck thinks he can get that bit of himself back someday." Donna rolled her eyes. "Egotistical shit hasn't ever once Sponsored anyone."

"Why not?" Cora asked. "I mean. I lost a piece of myself when I came here. Ugh...I can't believe I'm actually saying that." She pinched the bridge of her nose. "But whatever. I don't feel any worse for it."

"You lost a tiny bit of yourself. Like a hair." Donna spun the saltshaker idly. "He lost a finger. It's a much bigger part, and...we only have so much to go around. Think about seity like a wick on a candle. We can add to our wicks with what we take from patrons, but once we're out? We're out. We start to fade away like poor Ludwig."

"What's wrong with Ludwig?" She furrowed her brow. "He's still alive."

"But not for long." Amanda let out a sad sigh. "The poor man. He's been here so long. He's Sponsored so many people. He just doesn't have the will for it anymore, and he has so little left to him. If you talk to him for too long, you'll notice that there's...just not much there. He used to be such a big, loud, boisterous man."

Trent said he was calm and quiet. "That's heartbreaking." Cora chewed her lip. No wonder Simon didn't want any part of it. He very much seemed to have the will to live. She didn't blame him for not wanting to "Sponsor" her.

The two other women nodded. Amanda seemed the most upset. "It is. I'm not looking forward to when he goes." The blonde folded her arms across her chest and leaned against the side of the fridge. "But he's been with the Family since, what, 1826? It's his time."

Cora blinked. It was all still so hard to believe. "How old are you two?"

Donna smiled. "I came here in 1977. Amanda's been with us since 1859. The youngest of us is Firebreather, who joined the Family in 1992."

Cora looked up at the woman with a raised eyebrow. "The Faire was here in 1992? That was two years before I was born. I remember my dad taking me here when I was little, and it looked like it had been abandoned for years. He never mentioned it being back."

"It always looks abandoned when we're Inverted." Amanda said it like it made perfect sense. "And a lot of times there's no record of us coming or going. It's only when we're here for a long time that it leaves enough of a mark that people remember. Otherwise, we're wiped from their minds."

"I...don't...understand." Cora was going to get a headache from this.

"I know. Not yet. But you will." Amanda gestured for Cora to keep eating.

Cora took another large swallow of her coffee. She hoped it wasn't drugged. But the caffeine was worth the risk. "Magic is real. I accept that. I can't deny it anymore. I've seen too much weird shit this week. But I...I can't accept that I'm trapped here. I need to try to get out. I'm not one of you. I can't be. I just *can't.*"

Amanda and Donna looked at each other for a long moment.

Amanda nodded.

Donna shook her head. "No. It's too gruesome."

Amanda shrugged. "It'd get the point across."

"What'd be too gruesome?" Cora shifted back in her chair.

"Oh, it's an old trick to break people in. Coming back from the dead usually does it. I was going to see if you wanted us to break your neck." Amanda smiled sweetly, like it was no big deal at all. "It's not so bad. Doesn't hurt."

"No!" Cora shot up from her chair and went for the door. "That's it. I'm out of here."

"Wait—"

She didn't know which of them shouted for her to stop. She didn't care. She threw open the door and bounded down the stairs. They were going to hurt her! Everyone here *was* a murdering psychopath—

And she ran right into a tall, skinny wall of red and black stripes. "Good morning, cupcake!" He beamed cheerily down at her, a smile plastered on his face. But, like it always was, it was filled with cruelty and edged in madness.

Simon.

"Fuck, no!" She pushed away from him and went to run. She made it ten steps before her limbs froze in place mid-stride. She sobbed in defeat.

"Where're you going, Cora dear?" He sounded honestly confused.

"Let her go, Simon!" Amanda shouted from behind her. She twisted her head to watch.

Simon bowed. "Oh. Hello, ladies. I didn't know you were here. I see you beat me to it. I was going to take Ms. Glass to breakfast."

"Let her *go,*" Donna snarled angrily at him as she stormed down the steps. The little woman stood close to the Puppeteer, trying to get as much in the face of a man who was well over six feet tall as she could from more than a foot lower. Simon only smiled like he found it adorable. "Whatever sick games you think you're going to play with her, I won't allow."

"Sick games?" He put his hand to his chest in mock hurt. "Me? Hardly. I can't touch her now, as well you both know. Someone has to show her around. Teach her about her new life. I figured it might as well be me. She is mine, after all."

They were talking about her like she wasn't there, stuck in mid-running-stride, frozen like she was only a frame of a piece of film. "Hey, ass-clown!"

All three looked over to her. Simon sighed. He flicked his hand, and whatever was holding her like that—his strings—dropped her to the ground in a heap. She groaned from the impact. When she got up, he was already standing there next to her. He placed a hand on her shoulder. "I'm not the Clown, darling. I'm the Puppeteer. Did you hit your head last night in your pathetic attempt at escape?"

She yanked free from him, and backed away slowly, not turning her back on him. "I'm getting out of here. Screw this. Screw you. Screw all of you."

"Careful what you ask for. They'd probably take you up on that offer." Simon shrugged. "All right, well, I'll find you when you tire yourself out." He gestured like he was shooing a child out of the room. "Go on. Do your best."

She didn't need to be told twice. Ignoring the calls from Donna and Amanda to stop, she turned and ran. Again.

She was going to find a way out of here.

She was going to go home.

2

WHEN CORA GOT to a break in the fence that surrounded the fairgrounds, she knew better than to run into it headfirst like she had last night. She reached out and placed her hand...directly on an invisible barrier.

"Fuck!" She pounded her fist into it.

Picking up a rock from the ground, she threw it at the barrier. It passed through it without a problem. She threw another rock, and then touched the same spot. The rocks had no problem, and yet something was keeping her in.

She picked up a stick. She held it out in front of her like a wand and stepped forward. The stick passed through. Her fingers touched the barrier, and she couldn't go any farther.

"Donkey cock!" She kicked the invisible barrier then swore again when she hurt her toe. "God damn, monkey-fucking piece of shit!"

She heard someone laughing behind her. A sadistic cackle she was already starting to recognize because of how it made goosebumps explode across the back of her neck. She turned her head to see Simon there, propped up against the back of the nearby storage building.

He was eating a bag of popcorn, smiling as though she were providing the best show in the world.

"Oh, screw you." She glared at him. "Go sit and spin on some barbed wire."

"What'd I do?" He looked down into the bag then back up at her. "I'm hungry." He waved at her, motioning for her to go back to what she was doing. "Don't let me interrupt. I'm having a blast watching you play Sisyphus."

"I have a hard time turning my back on you."

"Then you're smart." He smiled and munched some more popcorn. He held the bag out toward her. "Want some?"

She shook her head and turned back to the gap in the fence. Looking around, she saw a box and began dragging it over to the fence.

"You're mad at me, aren't you?" He sighed.

She rolled her eyes at his asinine question. "You were going to turn me into a doll against my will. You were going to eat me." She kept shoving on the box. "Why the fuck wouldn't I be mad, Simon?"

"That's fair." He paused. "You really think you can escape, don't you? You're not just making a show of this. This is a real attempt."

"Of course it is." She growled. "I'm getting out of here."

"You can't. You're one of us now."

"No, I'm not! You're all just fucking around with me again."

"How do you feel today, Cora?"

She huffed as she tugged the crate. It was heavy and hard to move. She had to dig her heels into the dirt as she yanked on it. Simon didn't offer to help. Not like she'd want his help, but still. More proof he was a douche. "Pissed off."

"Mmhm. Besides that."

She stopped dragging the box to stand up and glare at him. "What the hell are you asking me?"

"Your pain. Your OCD."

"EDS." She corrected but suspected from his broader smile that he was teasing her.

"Whatever. How is it today? Did you sleep well last night?" When she didn't answer, he tilted his head to the side slightly. "Well? Don't believe me all you want, but...how about your own body?"

She should be a wreck right now. Tugging on the box as she had been, she had run the risk of pulling something out of place. Running away from him and the two women should have left her knees a sore mess.

But she felt no pain. No bruises from yesterday. She had actually *slept well* for the first time in...she couldn't remember. She sat on the edge of the box. "If I drag this over to the fence and try to climb over, what happens?"

"You'll hit the same invisible wall. If you crash a car into it, you'll wreck the car and yourself in the process. You'll die temporarily, and then you will wake up a little while later back in one piece. I'd prefer you didn't do that." He wrinkled his nose. "I apparently feel when you're in physical or emotional pain, and I don't terribly look forward to finding out what it's like when you're a twisted heap of mutilated flesh." He scratched at his chest under his tie.

"You...what?" She furrowed her brow.

He groaned in frustration and took off his glasses to rub his hand over his closed eyes before replacing them. "Are you just dense? Please tell me you're not an idiot."

"Don't call me names, you overdressed crimson pimp. I'm well past my limit, and I'm done taking shit from somebody who looks like they fell out of the bargain bin at a Halloween outlet."

He cackled at her insult. "I love it when you get mouthy! Good. I was hoping you weren't an utter wet noodle." He sat on the edge of the box next to her. She fought the urge to jump up, but she was sick of running away from him. It was clear he enjoyed it, and it didn't do much good when he could snatch her with his strings.

So she gritted her teeth and just glared at him. He held the bag of popcorn out to her. When she ignored it to continue trying to set him on fire with her mind, he shrugged and went back to eating it.

He talked through a mouthful of popcorn. "You're cured of your disease. And anything else you could catch. And aging. And dying. You'll weaken over time and fade like a spent candle just like everyone else, but that's the only way you're getting out of this mess. Unless you can't handle it anymore and ask for a way out like your predecessor." He paused and furrowed his brow. "I'm not even sure how that would work now that you have a piece of me. Maybe I could consume it back? Or maybe it'd be gone forever. I'm not sure it's worth the risk."

She ran her hand through her hair. She didn't know why she was entertaining any sort of conversation with him. She should try to find a shovel to bash his face in. But with his size and strength advantage, and the weird freaky string thing he could do on command, trying to attack him wasn't going to do her any good.

And something...felt weird, sitting next to him. Like she was supposed to be there. She had always been strangely drawn to him—he was beautiful, even with his wickedness. There was a sultry sinfulness to him, even if he was a murderous psychopath. But something had changed. It felt...like there was a pull.

Like I have a piece of him in me, and it's drawn to the rest of him. No! No. No, she was not one of them. She was *not* stuck here!

Simon was oblivious to her internal debate. "I can't very well hurt you now, can I? Not with the piece Ringmaster tore out of me and stuck inside you. You can feel it, can't you? Sitting here with me. You wanted me before, even if only just a little bit. But you were too afraid of me to give in. Now..." He traced his fingers through her hair, tucking a strand of it behind her ear. "I feel it too." She yanked her head away from him. It didn't bother him. "I don't see terror. You know I'm safe." He hummed and grinned. His voice lowered, and he purred out the next words in his thick British accent like the syllables were coated in hot wax. "As safe as I can be."

"Don't touch me."

"Suit yourself." He shrugged a shoulder and ate another piece of popcorn. "What's the plan, then, Cora dear? Crash a car into the edge of the Faire? Burn it all down? Find a knife and go on a killing spree? Try to find your friend who no longer knows you and try again? I fear it's all been tried before."

"What do you expect me to do? Sit here and just accept all this bullshit?"

"What would it take to convince you? I could kill you—stab you or break your neck—and you could come back from the dead. Would that do it? Or why don't we go get Juggler, and I'll rip his arm off, and you can watch it grow back? What kind of impossible feat would it require? Say it, and I'll go get the bone saw."

"Why do you even care?"

"Because you have a piece of me, buried inside you, and this is a travesty! And the last thing I'm going to stand for is to have some little simpering, weeping, broken thing cowering in the corner when at the very least she could be a useful, *functional* facet of this admittedly small society. I have my dignity to uphold. If I'm going to have you foisted upon me, then I insist you not be a burden."

She stood, cracked her neck, then turned to face him. She slapped him. Hard. Right across the face. The impact turned his head to the side and knocked his stupid vintage sunglasses off his face.

He chuckled and stroked a hand over his cheek where she'd hit him. He might feel her pain, but she didn't feel his. That was a bonus. When he turned to look up at her, his strange and freakish eyes were filled with everything except the anger she would have expected. "Ow."

"This is your fault, Simon. All of it."

He rolled his eyes. "Here we go." He bent down and picked up his sunglasses from the grass and, plucking his pocket square out of his breast pocket, began to clean them off. "You were given a choice whether or not you wished to explore the Dark Path. Barker is a conman and a worthless turd of a human being, but he told you the cost. You chose to ignore it. The Faire gave you a choice to come and save your friend, and you came knowing you would likely never leave. Ringmaster ripped my seity from me and forced me to Sponsor you." Simon stood, moving gracefully for someone his size. He slipped his glasses back on. "Explain to me how any inch of that is my fault."

His shadow—that freakish, disembodied thing of his—was cast high up on the wall behind him, despite the fact that it was nine in the morning. His shadow grinned at her sadistically.

"You should have left me alone."

"The Faire still wanted you. I tried to turn you into one of my dolls, yes." He sighed sadly, like someone mourning a missed opportunity. "You would have been a masterpiece." He lifted a hand to trail the backs of his knuckles down her cheek. She yanked her head away from his touch. "But that would have been a kinder fate than what you are now. You are one of us. And you can *never* leave. Even when you finally give up the ghost and fade away, you will never set foot outside the Faire again."

"No! You're wrong. There has to be a way out of this. I'm going to find out how. Screw you, and screw that stupid-ass shadow of yours. I'm not going to let this happen." She whirled to storm away from him to the tune of Simon's peal of hysterical laughter.

She had made it clear across the fairgrounds before she had to stop because she was shaking too badly. She leaned against the back wall of a ride, still shut down until later that afternoon when Harrow Faire reopened. She slid to the ground and put her head in her hands.

If this is true. If I'm really one of them, then I have to find a way to be un-one-of-them. The Ringmaster made me. He'll know how to un-make me. I have to convince him this has all been a terrible mistake.

When she felt calmer and like she wasn't going to cry, she pushed up from the ground and headed back toward the staff only area of the fairground. The first person she saw was Jack, strolling down a path with a large coil of rope over his shoulder. Good. Someone she didn't want to light on fire. "Hey, Jack, wait up."

"Good morning, Cora." He stopped and smiled at her. "How're you?"

She shot him a venomous look.

His expression turned sheepish, and he glanced down at his feet. "Right...stupid question. What can I do you for?"

"Where's the Ringmaster?"

"Oh. Probably in the big top." He pointed toward the large structure close to the lighthouse-looking tower. "I'm going there anyway. Let me walk you there."

"Sure." He seemed nice enough. Not as stab-happy as Simon, or as smarmy as Aaron, so she'd take it. They started off toward the large tent.

"And it's just 'Ringmaster,' by the way. No 'the.'"

She raised an eyebrow at him. "I don't really care."

His expression fell. "I'm sorry. I'm trying to be helpful."

Now she felt like she had just kicked a puppy. She sighed and put her hand over her face. "I'm sorry, Jack. I really am. I'm just at my wits' end. I don't mean to be a bitch."

"It's okay. I get it. I came to the Faire looking for Mom. I kinda knew what had happened, but I still wasn't prepared for it. I didn't want to be here. Not really. I had a real hard time accepting it."

"Your mom?"

"The Soothsayer. Our fortune-teller." He shrugged again.

She blinked. The Soothsayer sounded like she was from Eastern Europe. Jack sounded like was born and bred American. That didn't make any sense at all. But nothing did, lately.

Jack was talking again, and she tucked that question away for another time. "I had a choice. I could either leave my only family behind in this place, or I could take the spot that was offered to me. So here I am."

"Do any of you realize how insane all of this sounds?"

He chuckled. "Yup. I didn't believe any of it either. Not at first. Nobody should have to be like this unwillingly. How long did you spend at the gate last night?"

"I have no idea. I lost track of time." She tucked her

hands into her coat pockets. "At some point, Simon came and talked me into getting some sleep."

Jack went silent for a long time. "Don't trust him, Cora. Whatever you do, don't trust him."

"I don't plan on it. I don't trust any of you right now, seeing as I'm being held here against my will."

Jack nodded sadly. "If you ever need help, come get me. I don't know as I can do a whole lot to stop that nutcase from doing anything he wants to do, but I'll at least get in between you and him if he tries to hurt you."

"Why would you try to protect me?"

"You seem like a nice girl who got dealt the wrong hand, that's all. I saw you here with your friends two days ago. Ain't right to tear you away from that. If I could set you free, I would. But nobody can."

"Not even 'Mr. Harrow?'"

"Nobody talks to him except Ringmaster."

"And nobody talks to the Faire except Mr. Harrow. But I could. So, things have been weird for everyone lately."

Jack smiled faintly. "I suppose."

When they reached the tent, she found herself marveling at the size of it. The pennants on the ropes flapped in the breeze. The whole thing looked so harmless against the blue sky. Vintage, sure. A little eerie, fine. But not like a dark magic, murderous, soul-eating, monster park.

"I gotta get ready for the acts this afternoon." He patted her on the shoulder. "You need me, you come find me. To talk, or if you need to get really drunk, anything you need."

She did her best to smile at him. "Thanks, Jack."

"Anytime." He left with a wave, off toward one of the narrow rope ladders that went up into the rafters of the tent. She saw the Ringmaster—*just Ringmaster, whatever*—standing in the center ring, talking to a man wearing a strange green and black outfit. It almost looked like layered animal print. Cora headed toward them.

The man was the strange looking, almost feral one she had seen the previous night out in the rain. He had scruffy, slightly-too-long red hair that looked neglected more than anything else. She could tell he was ripped, even with his weird animal-print outfit. The man was pointing at spots around the large, sandy circle. Seeing Cora approach, the man nudged Ringmaster in the arm and motioned with his head. As she got closer, she saw that the man's eyes were... weird. Very weird.

They were goat's eyes.

Holy shit.

Her steps hitched on seeing them. He glowered at her, and she shrank back slightly, not sure what she had done to make him angry.

Ringmaster turned to see her, and he smiled warmly. "Cora! Hello. How wonderful. I had half a mind to come find you this morning, but I thought you might fancy sleeping in." He looked down at the man next to him. "Rudy, I'll talk to you later."

The man nodded and left without saying anything. Cora couldn't help but watch him, worried that she had done something to offend the severe looking man with the freaking *goat's eyes.*

"Don't worry about Rudy. He's better with animals than people. That's our Zookeeper."

"Ah," she replied as if that explained anything at all. "Um. I feel like we need to talk."

"That we do." He pushed open a gate in the wall that separated the sandy pit from the stands. He clicked it shut behind him and gestured for her to follow him. "It's a beautiful day. Let's go for a walk."

She felt like she was strolling next to a mountain. A big, squishy, mostly friendly mountain. "I want to go home, Turk. I need you to let me go."

He sighed. "I know you do, Cora. I'm sorry. But I can't do that."

"Who can? What about 'Mr. Harrow'?"

"He only tells me what the Faire wants. I don't think even he gets to really make the call. And the Faire has never released anyone it has taken. I'm not even sure it's possible. You're...not the same as you were when you came here. You're not human anymore."

"That's a load of shit."

"I know it sounds that way." He patted her on the shoulder. "But you'll come to understand. Sooner or later, you'll accept your new reality. I just hope you come to be happy here. Everyone here will help you to sort all this out. We've all been through the same mess you're in now. We get it."

They stepped out of the darkness of the tent and into the sun, and she squinted at the sudden change of light. "You just need to be patient."

"Me? Patient? Never."

The sudden new voice made her blink in surprise. Simon. He was standing in front of her...and pointing a gun straight at her. It was her .22 from the day before. It might be a glorified pop toy, but it was a glorified pop toy that could kill.

She squeaked in shock. She didn't get the chance to do much else.

Simon grinned. "Boring!" He pulled the trigger.

Bam.

Pain exploded through her chest. She placed her palm against the spot, and it was instantly hot and wet. Looking down, she saw blood blooming into the fabric of her shirt.

Simon simultaneously snarled in pain and grabbed his own chest, dropping his head and muttering curses.

Ringmaster shook his head and pinched the bridge of his nose. "Simon...you damnable idiot."

Cora collapsed to the ground, feeling her limbs starting to go numb. He had shot her straight in the heart, and everything was getting tingly and strange. Shock was setting in quickly.

He'd killed her.

She was going to die.

Ringmaster knelt at her side and helped her lie on her back. "Lie still, Cora. It'll be over soon. Just let it pass. I'll have a glass of gin ready for you when you wake up."

Wake up?

He had to be kidding.

She was shivering. Shaking. Her body was shutting off her mind from the rest of it. It might take a minute or two before she died, but there was no saving her now.

There was no waking up from—

3

Cora woke up in her bed.

Well, a bed, anyway. It wasn't her bed in her condo. She could tell by the smell and the feeling of the pillow beneath her head. It was the boxcar. She jolted awake all at once. It wasn't the groggy kind of transition from awake to asleep that she would have expected if she were in a hospital after being *fucking shot in the chest.*

It was more like someone flicked the lights back on.

She reached for her chest, trying to find the wound. But someone caught her wrists. "Whoa, whoa, easy now. Easy. You're okay." Jack was sitting on the edge of the bed next to her, trying to calm her down.

Screw being calm!

She scrambled to sitting and pressed her back to the wall that served as a headboard. The bed was surrounded on three sides by windows, and the one wall that wasn't had two shelves and the doorway that led to the bed. She felt the mullion of the window at the back of her head. She was tempted to try climbing out through the glass and escaping that way.

Looking down, she pulled her shirt away from her chest. It wasn't the one she had been wearing when she'd been shot. There was no hole, or blood.

"Amanda changed you. Don't worry." Jack smiled sheepishly again, rubbing the back of the neck. "She kicked all the rest of us out of the room."

There wasn't any blood on her anywhere. Simon had shot her. Straight to the heart. She checked down the front of her shirt. And there wasn't a wound.

"I'm losing my mind..." It was the only explanation. She was going insane. This was all a psychotic break.

"No, Cora. You're not. That really happened." Jack reached out and placed his hand on her arm, rubbing it gently. "He shot you. You died. But you just...came back."

"No, I couldn't have. People don't come back from that!" *I saw Simon heal. And now I did, too.* Tears welled up in her eyes. *I can't be trapped here. I can't!* "It was a squib, or he missed, and I just panicked."

"I'm a terrible shot, but I'm not *that* bad."

She went rigid at the sound of his voice. She looked up and saw Simon leaning against the counter in her kitchenette.

He took a swig from a brown glass bottle and smiled at her. "Welcome back, Cora dear."

"You shot me!"

"Wait. Did I or didn't I? Now I'm confused." He scratched his head with a finger. "You really must make up your mind, cupcake."

"Why is he in here?" she half-yelled at Jack, who shrank back at her volume.

"I can't get him to leave. He's insisting on staying. I don't know why."

"Ah—" The Puppeteer lifted his finger to stop Jack in his

explanation. "Correction. You didn't ask me why. You just whined at me about how pissed Cora would be when she woke up and saw me here. You told me to leave. I just refused, is all."

She shot him a glare, and Jack did the same.

Simon shrugged idly. "Just making a point." He sipped from the bottle. "As to why? I shot you, dear, to rip off the proverbial bandage. Watching you panic at the gate was adorable, but now I'm done with it. I got bored. I'm here because I wanted to see if my little expedited explanation worked. If not, I have a few more periods"—he held his fingers up like a gun at her and mimed pulling the trigger—"that I can put at the end of the sentence before I have to go reload."

"Get out," she ground out through her teeth. "Get the *fuck* out."

"Nope." He smiled sweetly. "I have a vested interest in this."

"You shot me! You—" Her words caught in her throat, and she put her hand over her heart. She had felt it. She had seen it. *I died. I was really dead.* "You...you killed me."

"Mmhm. And now you see it doesn't quite stick, does it?"

"You said you couldn't hurt me."

"I didn't. I slammed your hand in the proverbial car door. That's all. You're better now." He paused. "If it's any consolation, it felt like I'd been kicked in the chest by one of Rudy's horses." He scratched his shirt over his heart. "I didn't come out unscathed."

"It ain't the same, Simon." Jack sighed. "You can't just go around shooting people."

"I couldn't stand there and watch Ringmaster pat her on the head like she's some frightened sheep. She's the Zero. She's the Contortionist—and she has a part of *me* inside her!" Simon snarled and stepped toward them, his mood instantly flicking into anger. He seemed to ride the line between manic amusement and violent fury like the edge of a razor. "And I won't have any part of me crying in a corner like a child. I have my dignity to maintain."

Cora moved to the edge of the bed and nudged past Jack. He watched her go with a confused expression but didn't stop her. She headed to the kitchenette and started fishing through the cabinets.

Simon watched her, equally confused. "What're you doing?"

She didn't answer him. Reaching into the cabinet when she finally found her goal, she pulled out a cast-iron skillet. She spun it in her hand, twirling the handle around as she turned it over to get a feel for it. Good. It was nice and heavy.

Simon smiled. "Finally, you're grateful! Making me something to thank me? Glorious. Oh! How about an eggy in a basket? I haven't had one of those in years, and I—"

Cora pulled back with the skillet and, with everything she had in her, she swung for the fences. She cracked Simon clean across the face with it. He crumpled to the floor in a heap, holding his face, moaning loudly in agony.

She didn't feel anything. She looked over to Jack. "He feels my pain, but I don't feel his?"

The Rigger—or just "Rigger," no "the," whatever—stammered in shock for a moment before he finally sputtered out his words. "He Sponsored you. Not the other way around." Jack was staring at her in complete surprise. And maybe a little bit of awe. He laughed once in astonishment.

"You broke my nose!" Simon sat on the ground with his back against the cabinets. His glasses were shattered and laying on the wood floor next to him. He held his face in his hand. "You broke my damn nose."

"Get up." She held the skillet tightly in her hand.

"Why, so you can hit me again?" He shot her a glare through his fingers, the freakish color of his eyes shining in the sunlight of the room.

She smiled. "Yes."

"Then I'm fine staying right here on the floor, thank you very much." He shifted his hand, crunching his nose back into place, and groaned again in pain.

She lifted the pan to hit him again anyway. He threw his arms over his head to protect himself, pulling his knees into his chest. For someone who was so terrifying—so cruel—it still felt wrong to bash him when he wasn't willing to fight back. With a beleaguered sigh, she threw the skillet onto the counter with a loud clang. She went over to the bed and slumped back down onto it.

"I've never seen anybody hit him like that before," Jack murmured to her. "I'm a little jealous."

"Please, go away. I need some time to think. I'm sorry."

Jack stood from the bed and patted her on the shoulder. "I understand. I'll see you later." He headed down the train car toward the door and stopped at Simon. "You. Out."

"No." Simon glared up at Jack. "I do what I like, Rigger. And she's my responsibility."

"So act like it." Jack stepped over him and opened the door. "You better not hurt her again."

"I think she can handle herself." Simon rubbed his nose. He touched his finger to it to see if it was bleeding, but since it came away dry, he reached down and picked up the broken remains of his glasses and tucked them into his coat pocket.

Shaking his head, Jack left and shut the door behind him. Cora was left sitting on the edge of the bed, looking at the man in the red and black suit on the floor some ten feet away from her. They sat in silence for a long time, just looking at each other.

"Get out, Simon." She glared at him.

He smiled. "Make me."

She figured she could try to drag him out of the boxcar, but he had a foot of height on her and at least eighty pounds. She also knew for a fact he was stronger than he looked.

They went back into silence for a long time, just watching each other.

Finally, she said the four words she dreaded. She didn't want to admit it. It felt like she was giving something up—accepting defeat. But there wasn't any way around it that she could see. "I'm one of you."

He smiled. It wasn't cruel, it wasn't manic. It was just a simple, normal expression. He rested his head back against the cabinets. A few curls of his wild, dark hair had fallen over his forehead and across his freakishly colored eyes. If it weren't for his eyes, he really would be quite pretty. "Yes, Cora."

She put her hand over her mouth and looked out the window. She didn't know if she wanted to scream, to cry, to beat him up some more, or just throw herself off the tower in the center of the park. Then again, it wouldn't matter if she did, would it? She'd just hit the ground, die, and come back.

Biting back the tears, she put her hand back down. She shifted on the bed, pressing against the window that ran along the side of the mattress, and pulled her knees up to her chin. She felt small, so she made herself that way. "People will notice I'm missing. My work. My family. They'll call the cops. They'll come looking for me." She didn't realize she'd spoken out loud until Simon responded.

"No, cupcake, they won't." Simon stood from the floor, brushed himself off, and straightened his clothing. He went to the fridge, pulled out two brown glass bottles, and popped the caps off using a hook on the wall. Heading to the bed, he offered one to her. "Cora Glass was erased from that world yesterday. You only exist here."

With a trembling hand, she took the bottle. Sniffing it, she determined it was beer. She couldn't tell what type, and she honestly didn't care. She took a swig anyway. Simon sat down on the edge of the bed, turned to face her, and was watching her with an uncharacteristic amount of sympathy. He scratched at his chest over his heart.

"Still hurting from before?" She was hopeful he was.

"Not from the gunshot, no. It's like when you were in the rain. It itches, and I don't like it." He frowned.

"Wait. The only reason you're being nice to me is because you don't like feeling my pain?" She narrowed an eye at him.

"Yes?"

She put her hand over her eyes and sighed.

"Would it help if I said I'd like to do dark and sinful sexual acts to you, as well?"

She groaned.

"Was I not supposed to say that?"

"Points for honesty, I guess." She put her hand back down and took a swig from the bottle. The beer was pretty good. She could use some alcohol. "My poor fish. What happened to them?"

"They either don't exist anymore, or they are living out their little fishy lives in whatever alternate path that would have occurred without you in it. It's all very existential. I'm afraid none of us really know for sure."

"I liked my fish." It was a stupid thing to complain about, but she felt the need to bitch about something.

Simon chuckled. "We can get you more fish."

"How do you get anything around here, anyway?" She held up the bottle.

"The Faire provides anything we need to be happy. It wants us to survive as long as possible. We lure in more people for it to feed on." He sipped his own beer and then rubbed his face. "You hit me hard."

"You deserved it."

"Are we even, then?"

"For what part? Terrorizing me, trying to turn me into a doll, or shooting me?"

He thought about it for a long moment before smiling hopefully. It was a bad attempt at innocence. A very bad one. "Is it too much to ask for all of it?"

She chuckled despite her mood and shook her head. "What do you want from me, Simon?"

"A few things. I want back the thing inside you that Ringmaster stole from me. But I don't know how to do that. Not yet, anyway. If I can't be whole, then I'll keep that part of me under close watch. Technically, by our 'laws,' I'm responsible for you. Not that I give a rat's ass for what their rules say." He took a drink. "Other than that? I think I've made myself quite clear on the topic of what I would like to do to you."

"No."

He shrugged. "Suit yourself. Maybe you will let me show you the ropes. Teach you how to perform. You could be a part of my act."

"I'm not performing."

"Of course not. Not yet. You'll need to train. Just because you have the raw talent now doesn't mean you have the discipline required to be the Contortionist." He fiddled with the bottle as he talked, leaning his back against the jamb of the door that led to the bed.

She decided not to argue with him about how she was never, ever, going to put on some stupid spangly outfit and perform with him or anyone else. She still couldn't wrap her head around what the hell had happened to her. But the impossible things she'd seen and experienced were all adding up to too much.

He was sitting there, looking for all the world like a normal man, save for the freakish clothes and the bizarre eyes. He was just...talking to her. She had the sudden urge to reach out and toy with one of the wild strands of his dark hair, and she stamped the impulse dead as quickly as it arose.

"At least no one will miss me." She furrowed her brow as she realized something. "Wait. Jack told me he came here to find his mother. If she was"—she cringed, not believing she was saying any of this—"taken by this place first, how's that possible?"

"He's an interesting exception to the rule. Jack came here with her when he was a child. Mr. Harrow marked him for collection at that point. Jack remembered his mother when no one else did, and so he came here to find her. He never left again. Quite the droll story, really. You'll have to ask him for the details. I'm afraid I wasn't paying attention." Simon leaned back on his elbow, shifting to half-lie across her bed. He was so damn tall. He took up a good portion of the bed without trying. She didn't like how at home he was making himself. But her weapon of choice was still laying on the counter across the room, and she had more desire to drink her beer than smash the bottle over his head.

And there was something strange about him. Something

that made her feel...drawn to him. *Like I have a piece of his personality stuck somewhere inside of me.* "What part of you did I end up taking?"

"I have no clue. I don't know what I'm missing in the same way you didn't notice you had forgotten your favorite color until we pointed it out. It certainly wasn't my charm or devilish charisma, that part is clear." He smirked teasingly into the lip of his bottle.

They sat in silence for a long time. It was oddly comfortable. She hated that it felt...normal. She asked a question that had been bugging her for a while. "Why are your eyes all fucked up?"

"They are not *fucked up.* They're a little strange, perhaps, but we all have our problems." His jaw ticked. "If you hadn't broken my glasses, you wouldn't have to stare at them, so this is your fault."

"You didn't answer my question."

"We are what we eat. And I eat a lot. And the more we take, the less human we become. Have you met Clown, yet?"

"The one with the skull paint on his face?"

Simon smiled knowingly. "That isn't paint, Cora dear."

She shivered. "I don't...I don't want to turn into anything like you two."

He actually looked offended.

"Nothing personal." She smiled faintly and sipped the beer. She felt the need to get a little drunk, but she wasn't going to do anything of the sort with Simon around.

"If you don't feed on the seity of those who come through our gates, you'll fade away. And if you do, you take that piece of me with you. I can't have that." He grimaced. "I won't turn into a shell of a man like Ludwig."

"Amanda and Donna were telling me about him. How there isn't much left."

"He's got all the personality of a brick at this point. He's sponsored and lost too many. Including Hernandez. I'm afraid he doesn't really like me." Simon grinned wickedly. "Although hating me is not a difficult task."

"I can't imagine why. You just seem so lovable."

"I know! This is what I keep telling people. But still, they persist." He either missed her sarcasm or was playing along with it. At the gleam in his strange black-red-white eyes, she knew it was the latter. "I'm hungry. And I've died enough times to know that it works up an appetite. Come, darling. Let me finally give you a tour of Harrow Faire." He popped up from the bed so quickly that she jolted in surprise. He was fast for someone so tall. He downed the rest of his beer, chucked the bottle into a trash can in a cabinet in the kitchenette, and started for the door all before she moved.

He turned to look at her and raised an eyebrow. "Do I need to drag you along? You know I can."

Disgruntled, she finally moved from her spot by the wall and finished her own beer. She threw it alongside his empty bottle with a clank. The last thing she wanted was to be tugged around on his freaky strings.

Freaky magic strings.

Magic is real.

She accepted it, but her mind still skipped over it like the needle on a scratched record.

There had to be a way to escape. Some way to give the Puppeteer his piece of "seity" back and let her return to her life. There *had* to be. She could finally admit that this place was what everyone said it was. But she didn't have to accept the fact that she was stuck here.

"I need to find a way out of this, Simon."

He reached out and ran his hand over her hair. She shivered at the unexpected touch as he curled his fingers under her chin and tilted her head to look up at him. He took a step closer to her, backing her against the wall. He lowered his face to hers, and for a moment, she wondered if he was going to kiss her.

She wasn't sure if she wanted him to or not.

When he spoke, his voice was a low rumble, but smooth like velvet. "You need to understand your cage before you can try to pick the lock."

She fought the urge to grab the front of his coat and pull him closer. *This is not okay.*

His mis-colored eyes flicked to her lips, and she was certain he was going to close the distance between them. But instead, he tapped his finger on the end of her nose. "Boop." The action made her jump, and her startled reaction spread a smile over his sharp features. "Step one, food. Step two, a tour. Step three remains up to you."

Without anything else to do, she followed him out of the train car and shut the door behind her. He was already whistling to himself as he strolled along the path, his fingers tucked into his pants pockets.

I need to get out of here.

4

SIMON LOOKED DOWN at Cora as she walked along next to him. He was happy she came along willingly for once. Not that he didn't enjoy tugging her around on his strings—he would never, ever get sick of that—but this made for a lot less fussing.

Truth be told, he wasn't angry that she had clobbered him with the frying pan. He was anything but, in fact. He was impressed. He was pleased. He hadn't seen much personality out of her, besides being terrified for her life, and he was happy to see just a little bit of that fire come up to the surface.

He'd known exactly what she intended to do as soon as she pulled the slab of cast iron out of the pantry. He wanted to see if she had the gall to do it.

Better she be shouting and swinging her fists than hiding in a corner. It made his heart hurt less, at any rate. Not that he was happy about his shattered nose or glasses, but one was already mended and as for the other, he had duplicates.

She was such a pretty thing, with her smoky gray eyes.

He couldn't wait to see how she performed as the new Contortionist. He realized how eager he was to see her bent into strange shapes. He wanted to help put her there.

His body reacted to that mental image of her, and he tucked his hand into his pocket to keep himself from becoming...well, more socially awkward than he already was. *Down, boy. Down! Sit!*

This is going to become problematic.

He tried to focus on one thing at a time. First, she had to accept her new life in the Faire. *Then* he could convince her that he was the right person to train her. And after that, he could convince her that he was the right person to invite to her bed and let him do—

He shoved those thoughts away. Distractions were dangerous. Besides, Cora had already let Jack near her. She had probably already been suckered in by the sweet smile and handsome features of the Rigger, just like every other girl who wandered through the park. He was tanned, buff, kind, gentle, and *sane.*

Just about everything Simon wasn't.

Simon was no slouch in the looks department, and he considered himself far above the average bar, but he certainly didn't take every opportunity to work in nothing but a white sleeveless shirt and jeans in broad daylight. The simpleton loved to show off and had already taken pity on Cora. If Simon wasn't careful, the Rigger would have her between his sheets before the week was out.

Jealousy roiled in him. It was another dangerous thing. Distractions, jealousy, they weren't what he needed. What he needed was to focus on the task at hand—ripping his stolen property back out of Cora and then devouring the rest of her whole.

Or maybe not whole. Maybe he'd keep her for a while.

She was wonderfully sarcastic when she wasn't weeping in a pile on the floor. She would be fun to play with. Especially when she was a bit more obedient and didn't shrink away from him every time he touched her.

He remembered their kiss in her dream. She had enjoyed it; he knew she had. There had been such a wonderful flush to her cheeks when he parted from her. Her pulse had sped beneath his thumb resting on her neck. Her gray eyes had smoldered and grown dark like the storm.

But something made her push him away. Fear. But not of him.

He could use that. He could pull on that thread. And little bit by little bit, she would let him inch nearer. She already was becoming accustomed to him. She could be fleeing from him now, screaming and whipping fists at his face. Just yesterday, he had tried to turn her into a doll. Today, he had shot her.

But she stayed at his side, moody and pensive. She must feel some kind of pull toward him. It was the only reason he could fathom that she let him stay in her boxcar with no other supervision. Or why she let him sit on the edge of her bed and sprawl out near her.

He was mid-stream on an effortless tour of the park. He had never given one to another Family member—he had never bothered—but he knew this place like the back of his hand. And he did enjoy being the center of attention.

Simon snatched a hot dog for each of them from a stall. She took hers, eyed it for a moment as though it might attack her, then took a bite out of it. "Thanks...I think."

"You can get food from any of the stalls whenever you like, free of charge," he explained. "There's also a cafeteria tent back in the staff area that serves three meals a day if you want something that isn't deep-fried or made from reprocessed dead raccoons."

She paused. "What the hell do you idiots do with all the money?"

"Honestly? I'm not quite sure. I'm sure it's all in a big bag somewhere." Simon shrugged. "We can't very well *not* charge admission, can we? It'd be suspicious."

"I suppose. It's still weird." She wrinkled her nose at the idea of her food being made from dead raccoons but still took another bite from the hot dog. "Can you starve to death?"

"We," he corrected.

"What?"

"The question is, can *we* starve to death. You're one of us now, darling. And no. But you can still suffer from hunger. So why bother?" He slung his arm around her shoulder and pulled her into his side. She went along for the ride, shockingly, and only went just a little bit rigid. He walked with her to a bench and sat down, patting the spot next to him. She seemed too lost in thought to argue with him.

He disliked seeing her like this. She wasn't in a panic anymore—but she was *sad.* It bothered him. He reached out and poked her in the cheek. "Cheer up, cupcake."

She looked over at him with a raised eyebrow and swatted his hand when he went for a second poke. "Are you kidding me?"

That was better. Fighting with him was fully acceptable. "Think about it. You'll never age or get sick. You have a new Family. A new place to belong. And you get to spend time with *me.* You should feel honored."

"You're a douchebag."

He lifted a shoulder dismissively. "I like your other insults better."

"You're an evil, demented, twisted, fucked up douchebag. You've tormented me, tried to turn me into a doll, and you just shot me. I shouldn't be here with you."

"Then why are you?"

"I don't know."

"I wanted to turn you into a doll because I want *you*, Cora. I wanted to keep you. I shot you because I want you to accept what you are now. My crimes are covetous, but they don't come from malice or spite."

"What about terrorizing me?"

"Okay, that part I do for fun."

"Do? Present tense?"

"Did you think I was going to stop?" He snickered.

She slapped him hard on his chest. He caught her hand in his and kissed her fingers before she tugged and freed herself. She looked away from him shyly. "Stop."

"Never." Simon knew he was tall, but sitting next to her, she looked positively petite. He wanted to scoop her up and plant her on his lap. But she'd probably scream, hit him, and cause a fuss. He tipped his head back and looked up at the blue sky and clouds overhead.

This is incredibly problematic.

Cora was gazing off into the park, watching the guests wander around and enjoy the rides. It was late afternoon. The hot dog wouldn't serve as a real dinner, but it'd be enough to tide them both over before he brought her to the cafeteria after their tour. He wanted her in his lap. Straddling him. He wanted to feel her body—

Bad Puppeteer! Bad!

Luckily, she distracted him from his thoughts that were swirling to dark and terrible places. "I need to talk to Mr. Harrow. Get him to change his mind."

"Were it so simple." He draped his arm over the back of

the bench behind her. She sat forward an inch. He tried not to take it personally. “Only Ringmaster talks to Mr. Harrow.”

“No. That’s not acceptable. The Faire talked to me, and you said it only talks to him. Maybe he’ll make the same exception.” She stood from the bench and turned to him. The look of resolution on her face was...incredibly attractive. Her gray eyes were stormy and dark. “Take me to him. I’ll make him talk to me.”

He tilted his head to the side and watched her silently. He was too busy taking it all in. She kicked his foot, and that snapped him out of it. “Why should I?”

“Because if I convince him to reverse this, then you get that piece of yourself back.”

“Clever. You’re learning. Use my needs against me. I can take you to his train car, and you can pound on the door all you want, Cora dear.” He smiled and slid lower on the bench, showing he had no interest in getting up to obey her. “But he won’t answer. He never does. Trust me, I’ve tried. I’ve done everything I can to break the door down. Do you think you’re the only one who has ever wanted their freedom?”

“I have a hard time believing that. You seem to like it here just fine.”

“I do now. I didn’t when I first came here. That was a long, long time ago.” He didn’t like to remember those days. He had ripped his fingernails out clawing at the door of the train car labeled twenty-one more than once. He had scratched his fingers down to the bone and did it again as soon as they grew back. He shook away the memory and tilted his head to watch the lights of the Ferris wheel in their slow and lazy rotations.

“How did it happen? How did you come here?”

He pulled in a breath and looked back to her. She wasn’t

angry anymore, or even belligerently determined. She seemed curious—and about him. He was almost flattered. "A story for another day. I dislike thinking about it, although I appreciate the attention."

She shrugged. "Suit yourself."

"Well, let's continue our tour, shall we? So much more to see, so very much time to see it in." He rose from the bench and slung an arm around her again. Suddenly, Cora's steps hitched. She froze and went rigid. He watched her eyes go wide. Simon furrowed his brow. "What's the matter with you now? I haven't done a damnable thing—"

"Lisa! Emily! Trent!" Cora took off in a dead sprint.

Simon looked up to the skies and groaned. "Here we go again."

IT WAS HER FRIENDS! All of them. Trent, Emily, and even Lisa, her husband Robert, and little Jane and Thomas. Cora tore up to them at breakneck speed and skidded to a halt in front of them. "Guys! It's me. You won't believe what's happened, and I need your help and—"

They were all looking at her in horror. Trent was clutching Emily, and the two children were cowering behind their parents. "Not you again." Trent glared at her. "Get away from us, you freak!"

Tears welled in her eyes, but she refused to let them fall. She looked down at Jane, Lisa's little girl. She sank to her knees on the pavement in front of them. "Janey, remember me? It's Cor-Cor. I'm here. Remember when we used to go play at the waterpark together? Remember that time I took you to the zoo, and you were so scared of the sheep until one of them nibbled on Tommy's shirt, and then you were so jealous you didn't want to leave until one came over to you?"

"Momma!" Jane ducked behind Lisa, who moved to block Cora's view of her child. "What's she saying?"

"Look, lady," Trent stepped in front of them, glaring angrily down at her. "Get away from us. Leave the kids alone!" For a moment, Cora wondered if her best friend in the world, who now was looking at her like she was a stranger, was going to hit her. Trent looked up as someone approached, and color drained from his face as he shrank back in fear.

"I apologize deeply for her behavior." A hand picked her up from the ground under the armpit, and she looked up at Simon. He still wasn't wearing his sunglasses, and his monstrous eyes were on full display. "She isn't quite well, you see. She has delusional episodes. She is perfectly harmless. She believes you are all her best friends in the world, and now is quite heartbroken that you do not know her." He smiled warmly at her friends and pulled her close to his side. "Once more, I apologize. She means you no harm."

"It's—it's uh—" Robert, Lisa's wife, was the first to respond. "It's all right. No harm done."

"How did she know our names, Mommy?" Jane asked, clinging to her mother's pants.

"I don't know, sweetie. It's just a silly game they're playing."

"Come along, Cora dear." Simon tried to pull her away, but she dug in her heels. He looked down to her, sighed, and lowered his head closer to hers. He murmured to her, but it was loud enough that she was sure the others could hear. "You're scaring the children. Look at the little girl. There is no way to fake the fear in her eyes. They do not know you, Cora. They never will."

"No..." She let out in a broken squeak.

"It does not matter if you accept it or not. This is the truth you see before you."

She felt weak. She felt empty. She pulled her arm out of Simon's grasp and walked away. She couldn't look back at them and couldn't even bring herself to say goodbye.

And it was goodbye.

She headed behind one of the rides, somewhere off the main drag, and she buried her head in her hands. She wanted to cry. She wanted to scream. She wanted to burn the place down. Her friends had stared at her like she was a monster. Like she didn't matter.

"Cora."

"Go away, Simon! Fuck you. Fuck this park. Fuck your rules, fuck all of it. I'm going to go find them. I don't care what you say, I'm going to find a way to get them to—"

Hands snatched her arms and reeled her around, and suddenly she was staring up at Simon's very angry face. He shook her hard, and the rattle to her brain stunned her to silence.

"Do you think you are the only one here who has ever lost anyone? Do you think you are the only one who has stared into the face of a loved one and seen nothing in return? You selfish, foolish girl! I was ripped out of my life. I proposed to my fiancée here in the park, on the carousel. And as the former Soothsayer rammed a piece of themselves into my body, I was forced to watch as her expression of love and devotion turned to one of *fear and horror.* She looked at me—at these eyes, and she screamed and ran away from me! I didn't earn these eyes. I was *forced* to be like this." He shook her again, his grasp on her arms tightening. "Tell me how you have lost so great a gift. Tell me how this burden is too much to bear!"

It was too much. She broke down. She sobbed, and the tears streamed down her cheeks. "Simon…I…"

He sighed, and all the rage fled from his face at seeing her pain. He pulled her over to a tree nearby and sat at the base of it, pulling her down with him. She didn't have the strength to fight. She was crying too hard. She found herself sitting in his lap sideways, her head tucked against his chest. He wrapped his arms around her and rested his chin atop her head. He began to hum to her softly, a quiet and melancholy waltz.

After a long few minutes, her tears quieted down. He smelled like cologne and antiques. He smelled just a little bit like paint and wood shavings. It was a comforting mix, and it came along with the warmth of his body. Whether she liked it or not, he was easing her pain. She sniffed. "You said you got the eyes because you ate too many people," she muttered.

He chuckled quietly, a rumble in his chest. "I lied." They sat in silence for a long time before he spoke up again. "When I wanted you in my lap, I wasn't expecting this was how you'd wind up there."

"Go fuck yourself with a corn dog."

"Sounds squishy. But I suppose if you're into that, I'm willing to try anything once." He snickered as she slapped his chest. His arms tightened around her just a little.

She fought the smile. She lost. She was glad he didn't see it. "I'm sorry about your fiancée."

"We've all lost our lives. Magician lost his younger brother. They were inseparable, those two. They performed together for years, and he watched him turn away like they had never known each other. Those who are spared seeing their life vanish are the lucky ones. But soon, your friends will be gone, and the pain will fade."

"Gone?"

"They will age and die. You won't. We're your Family now. We can be your friends. We can be even more than that." He kissed the top of her head.

She shivered. "Don't push your luck."

"I'm afraid that's all I ever do." He hummed. "But you're hardly in the mood. I understand." He tilted her head to look up at him and tutted. "I prefer you angry. I hate to see you like this." With the pad of his thumb, he carefully wiped her tears away. "Never mind the terrible heartburn it gives me."

She should hate him. She should be terrified of him. He was only helping her in order to get what he wanted. But in those awful, frightening eyes of his, she saw more depth than that. She saw a man who had also lost everything.

None of this should have happened. Not to me, not to him, not to anybody.

Mr. Harrow is to blame. The Faire is to blame.

He cradled her cheek in his hand, and for a moment she hoped he might lean in and—*no, bad Cora! He shot you today. He tried to eat you yesterday.* She pulled back from him, and his lips twinged in a faint smile. He kissed her forehead instead. He sat back and, pulling a handkerchief from his pocket, held it out to her. "Now, unless you want this moment to grow incredibly awkward for both of us, I do recommend you get off my lap."

Her face rushed with heat, and she knew she must have been blushing the same color as his suit. Just a little too quickly, she took his handkerchief and stood, wiping her face with it. She did feel less distraught, even if her heart was shattered into a million pieces. Now she was just looking down at all the tiny shards and wondering what she should do to start putting it all back together, or if it was useless to try.

"I know that look." Simon brushed himself off as he stood. "That's the look of someone staring at the empty void and wondering if they should just jump into it. But I know what will fix it."

"What?" She shot him an incredulous look as she handed him back his pocket square. He folded it deftly into a complicated pattern and tucked it back into his breast pocket.

He smiled effortlessly, like he always did. "Ice cream, of course!"

And with that, he snatched her hand, and they were off, whether she liked it or not.

5

CORA WALKED along beside him as Simon finished giving her the grand tour of the fairground. He insisted on completing the tour before they went to get the ice cream he promised. Figured. He was a jerk. But she wasn't as frightened when he was around as she was when she was alone. And that...that was deeply troubling.

When he wasn't chasing her, yanking her on strings, or *shooting her,* he wasn't totally insufferable. He was egotistical, snarky, sarcastic, and utterly self-centered, but he wasn't miserable to be around.

She found herself smiling at his jokes. Or sometimes even—the horror—laughing at them. There was a strange debonair flair about him. He was funny, and she couldn't help it. He had a shockingly quick wit, and he was always ready with some clever comment. He kept her on her toes and was easily keeping her distracted from what she had gone through. That, and he was answering her questions. If she could believe his answers, at any rate.

And he had held her while she cried. He had comforted her. It was only because he was trying to help himself and, by his own omission, he wanted into her pants. But one way or another, he was helping her. She had to give the man points for at least being honest. Most guys would lie and claim they felt something for her. He was very clear about what he wanted and why.

Unfortunately, it didn't fix her problems. It didn't fix the fact that she was stuck there, and it added to her need to escape a heaping pile of confusion over what to do with the Puppeteer who seemed unwilling to leave her alone.

She needed to find a way to talk to Mr. Harrow. She needed him to set her free. But, for all of Simon's suspect stories about his life and what was happening, she believed him that she couldn't simply pound on the man's door and have him answer.

But there was also no harm in trying. What did she have to lose? Her life? That was already gone.

They stopped to look out at the lake that sat adjacent to the park. A few people were sitting out on the sandy area, despite it being too cold to swim yet. It was growing dark, and the lights of the park were on full display. It was beautiful, in a strange and eerie kind of way.

This might be my permanent new home.

She shuddered at the thought.

"I'll be right back." Simon wandered off.

She took the opportunity to lean against the railing that separated a few food stalls from the main path and promptly got lost in her thoughts. She didn't mind the momentary break in the conversation.

What she did mind was the weird oppressive feeling that his absence created. Being alone brought back all the fear that his presence had been keeping at bay. She pulled her coat tighter around herself.

Not because he didn't scare her. Not because he was safe.

But because she felt alone.

"Ice cream makes everything better!"

She yelped in surprise. Simon moved silently, and he had come back with two cones of soft serve, vanilla and chocolate twist ice cream. He held one out to her. She blinked at him, stunned.

That ever-present grin didn't falter. "I know you haven't eaten dinner yet, but...hey, you can't get fat now either. I say celebrate. Eat ice cream whenever you want."

She took the cone from him and looked down at it, puzzled, then up to him. "You're cheering me up for your own self interests."

"Of course, darling." He leaned against the railing and licked at the ice cream. "Why does anyone do anything?"

She looked down at the ice cream. It was tempting. She loved soft serve. It was probably a sin against nature, but she preferred it to hard ice cream most times. She licked it.

"Good girl." He turned his back to the railing, kicking his leg out to rest his elbow on the top rail. "So. What else is there to know about you? You enjoy owning fish, you love to take photos, and you're incredibly flexible. What else?"

"I'm not flexible."

"Oh, trust me...you are now." He grinned.

She didn't know why he was looking at her like that. She couldn't tell if it was sexual, predatory, or just plain evil. Maybe all three at once. She turned her attention back to the ice cream. It was safer. And it was, stupidly enough, cheering her up.

When she looked back up at him, she blinked and took another step back. His expression hadn't changed.

His shadow had.

And his shadow was...touching hers.

She couldn't feel anything. But the strange and

monstrous shadow that stretched off him onto the wall beside them was...petting the hair of her shadow. She grimaced. "Oh, God. Tell him to stop."

"What?" Simon followed her horrified stare. "Oh. Ah. Yes. Right. Shoo! Go away. You're ruining the moment." He gestured with his hand, trying to swat his shadow away like a fly. The shadow didn't move, and instead just stuck its tongue out at Simon and gave him a comical and exaggerated raspberry. Its tongue was too large and out of proportion, like everything else about the deranged thing.

When it was clear the shadow wasn't going away, Simon rolled his eyes. "Don't worry about it. He's harmless. He can't do anything to you." Simon looked back at her with a smile. The freakish, warped, and twisted shadow of his was still stroking the hair of her own. When she moved away, it followed her.

"Tell your subconscious to stop petting me."

"It's really more of an id, ego, superego thing." He waved his hand dismissively. "It doesn't work that way." He licked his ice cream. "Don't let him trouble you."

She shuddered and tried to look away. His shadow shifted to hers each time she moved. Stroking at her arms, or her hair, or curling around her. She wanted to run away, but she knew it was hopeless. Where was she going to go? Where could she hide?

"It means he likes you." Simon smiled helpfully.

There's so much to unpack in that statement that I don't know what to do with it. She opted to eat her ice cream and try not to watch the grinning, nightmarish shadow as it snuggled—straight up *snuggled*—against hers.

"Why do I get the feeling the fact that you have a fucked-up Peter Pan shadow is one of the least messed up parts of this place?"

"You'd be very right about that, dear. You haven't even seen Bertha's darker freaks or Rudy's monsters yet." He fished a pocket watch out of his coat and flicked it open. With a grunt, he straightened from where he was against the railing, and his shadow snapped back to where it should have been the whole time. "I have a show in an hour. I fear I'll have to leave you to your own devices."

For some reason, that bothered her. She didn't want to be alone. She didn't necessarily want to be with him—she didn't trust him—but the idea of being on her own made her nervous.

As if he could see it written on her face, he ticked his head in the direction of the main path. "Amanda is likely practicing in the big top. I am sure she'd be thrilled to entertain you for the remainder of the evening. She seemed to take a shine to you. *Ooor,*" he drew out the word, "you could come help me set up for my own performance and stay to watch."

"I—" His shadow was grinning hopefully at her again. Christ, that was screwed up. Simon's eyes startled her a lot less than they used to, but she wasn't sure if she'd ever get used to his shadow. "I think I'll go talk to Amanda for a while."

"Suit yourself." He picked up her hand and kissed the back of it slowly. Then he grinned and licked the side of her finger.

She yelped and pulled her hand back. "Hey!"

"Sorry. You had a little ice cream on your fingers. I couldn't resist." He winked at her. "Come. Let me walk you to the big top."

Her face was warm. She knew she was blushing. She took a step back and shoved her hand in her pocket, as if to hide any evidence of what he'd done. He chuckled, shrugged, and strolled away from her, beckoning over his shoulder for her to follow.

She wished she could drown herself in the lake. She sighed and followed him wearily. She felt so tired. It had been a long, emotionally trying day. *And hey, I died. That was exhausting.*

She wanted to go talk to Mr. Harrow, but she...was also a little afraid at the same time. It was going to be a massive disappointment. There was no way in hell that Mr. Harrow was going to set her free. It was partially his fault she was here, after all. If not entirely his fault. The whole chain of command in the Faire still made no sense to her.

She wasn't ready to have more of her hopes dashed to pieces. She hung her head and resigned herself. She could talk to Mr. Harrow later. Or try, anyway. Tonight, she needed company. She just couldn't stand to be alone.

Amanda and Donna were willing to snap her neck to show her she wasn't human anymore. But Simon succeeded, and with her own pistol. If she wasn't mad at him, she couldn't be mad at them. And any company was better than no company right now. *Present company included, I guess.*

Halfway to the big top, she froze. She knew the people on the path in front of her. She cringed. It was Trent, Emily, Lisa, and her family. She shrank against Simon. They hadn't seen her yet, and she didn't know if she could take it again. She snatched him by the hand and dragged him off the main path. She pulled him into the shadows and used his tall frame to hide hers from her friends as they passed.

"Hm? Oh—I see—and—well, hello. I've never missed a performance, but I suppose this is as good reason as any." Arms circled around her and pulled her against his chest. Firm, strong, and covered in soft fabric.

"This isn't about you." Her voice cracked.

"For shame. Then why?" He must have seen her friends. "Ah. You did the right thing, avoiding them."

Her shoulders shook with her silent tears, and she tried to force them to stop. She struggled to bite it all back, and she shockingly managed.

"That's it...good girl. Ssh..." He stroked her back slowly. "Let them go. Let your old life go."

"I can't."

"You'll have to, sooner or later. The Faire won't give you a choice. It's just about how much of your sanity you lose in the process." His head tipped down, and for a moment she wondered if he was smelling her hair. "Trust me on that one."

She pushed away from him, remembering that he wasn't a friend. While he might not be an enemy, it was only because she had part of him hostage.

Simon smiled, a wicked gleam in his strange eyes. "Go talk to Amanda since it's clear you cannot be alone at the moment. Once again, my offer stands—train car fifteen. Come see me tonight if you need someone to hold you in the dead of the night." He winked. "I'm sure my shadow would be quite thrilled for the company."

"We aren't friends, Simon—"

"Quite true."

"—and we aren't lovers, either."

"I wouldn't be so quick to make that call." That fiendish smile spread over his face as he bowed. "Until tomorrow, Cora dear. Unless you change your mind."

"Go f—"

"Careful, Cora. We've only just met, and you're already running out of things for me to have sex with. Pretty soon, I'll start thinking you're jealous. Or...what's the word?

Projecting?" He cackled as he left, waving over his shoulder at her. "See you soon, cupcake."

As soon as he was gone, she felt the tears prick her eyes again. She looked up at the night sky and took a deep breath. Holding it for a second, she slowly let it out. She should go find a crowbar and try to pry the door to Mr. Harrow's train car off its hinges.

Something told her it wouldn't be that easy.

With a beleaguered shake of her head, she headed toward the huge, striped, "big top" tent that held the main ring. The staff let her in without a problem. They all seemed to know her. *They're ghosts,* she remembered. *They aren't real.*

She felt on the verge of a breakdown. Like at any point, the tiny threads that held her together were going to break and she was going to plummet into a pit of insanity.

"Cora!"

Someone called her name. Someone not at ground level. She looked up and blinked. Amanda was sitting in a hoop of steel suspended by a rope over the sandy pit, some twenty feet off the ground. She was wearing a mismatched pair of leg warmers, and her leggings clashed violently with her leotard. It looked like practice clothing. She waved. Even in her ridiculous outfit, the woman was beautiful. She sat up there like a natural. "Jackie, let me down, will you?"

"Sure thing," Jack called from somewhere high above in the tent. Easily a hundred feet up. She wasn't afraid of heights, but that was something else entirely.

The ring began to lower to the sand. When it was five feet from the ground, Amanda jumped from it and rushed up to her.

And hugged her.

Cora didn't know what to do. She just shyly hugged her back. "Um...hi."

"You poor thing. Stuck with *Simon.* I heard what he did to you—shooting you! What a terrible way to teach you a lesson. He is such an ass. Are you okay?"

"Yeah...I mean no. But I guess."

"Oh, kitten, I understand." She pouted. "What can I help you with?"

"I just—I don't know if I can sit in that boxcar by myself right now." She felt small. Alone. Afraid.

Amanda petted Cora's cheek and smiled as though she were about to cry herself. "I felt the same way when I came here. I'm sorry this has been so rough on you. But you're home now, sweetie. You have people you can rely on. And I can see it—you're meant to be here. Jackie told me what you did with the skillet." She giggled.

"Really?"

"I'm afraid everybody knows now. Clocked him with a frying pan! That bastard has had that coming for a long time. Something tells me you're just a little spitfire waiting to spark up." Amanda pulled her by the hand down the aisle and into the sandy pit in the center. She let her go and went up to the metal hoop. "Mind if I practice while we talk?"

"Sure."

She took a small hop and grabbed the ring with both hands, and in what looked like an effortless display of I'm-secretly-so-jacked-I-could-kill-a-moose muscles, she inverted, hooked her knees over the bar, and sat right up into it like it was the most natural thing in the world to do.

At Cora's expression, Amanda giggled. "I'm the Aerialist, silly. It's what I do. I bet you'd be great at lyra! Being so bendy at all."

"Lyra?"

Amanda patted the metal ring. "This is a single-point lyra. I prefer double-point, personally. But this one is much spinnier, and the crowd loves when I really get it going. Even if it does make me want to hurl sometimes."

"Oh." Cora sat down in the sand, not knowing where else to go. "You look gorgeous up there."

"Thank you." Amanda smiled down at her. "I can't wait to see you perform. It'll be nice to dust off the old Contortionist tent and see what you can do. I'm sure the guys'll go crazy for you." Amanda winked at her. "They always do love a girl who can put both legs behind her head.

Cora laughed. "I can't do that."

"Have you tried recently?"

She blinked. Sitting in the sand, she looked down at her legs. She had always been flexible—her joints being able to hyperextend in ways they shouldn't. But it had always come along with so much pain, and usually a dislocation or two for her trouble.

"Go on. Try." Amanda seemed like such a sweetheart. Like such a warm, friendly butterfly of a human. What the hell was she doing trapped in some freaky man-eating murder-circus? "I promise I won't laugh."

"Right." With a shake of her head, she picked up her ankle, and...put it behind her head. "Huh." There wasn't any pain or anything. A bit of a stretch, maybe. Like she just hadn't used a muscle in a while. She bent her other leg up behind her head. She laughed and immediately unfolded herself. "What the fuck?"

"Do you think I was able to do all this before I came here?" Amanda was hanging from the top of the metal ring by her knees, smiling down at her. "Do you think Puppeteer had his strings or awful dolls? You're the Contortionist. You can contort."

"I don't want to perform."

"Neither did I. You'll get there in time. Besides, once the Faire Inverts, you won't have much else to do but practice."

"Inverts?"

Amanda sighed. "I'm explaining this all out of order. We come and go. The Faire isn't always like this. Sometimes it looks, well..."

"Abandoned."

"Right. And then, when the Faire hungers, we come back. And when we're not here, we're in the Inversion."

"Where do you go?"

"It's really hard to explain."

"It's a bit of an alternate reality," someone said from nearby. When she looked up, she saw Ringmaster heading into the center ring. Turk was without his tailcoat, but he looked no less official. He went up to the lyra and stopped Amanda's slow spinning rotation. He bent his head down and stole a kiss from the upside-down Aerialist. "Hello, love."

"I'm keeping our new friend company."

"Better you than Simon." He kissed her a second time then let her go back to her routine. Amanda was going from move to move with an easy grace. And Cora couldn't help but notice how Ringmaster watched her with equal parts attraction and adoration.

Aw. That was cute. The big Turkish-looking man and the tiny beautiful blonde. Good for them. She almost smacked her forehead. *I'm an idiot. Turk. He said people call him Turk, and that he can't remember his name.*

Cora looked up at him. "You said the Inversion is like an alternate reality?"

Ringmaster sat on the railing of the ring. "Or a pocket dimension. I've read a few books on the subject. Wherever we go, it's not very large. It's not very pleasant. I'm afraid you'll find out sooner than later. I hate to ask this...but did Simon's uncouth display of shooting you work at convincing you that you're one of us now?"

"Yeah." Cora sighed. "I guess it did. But I want to talk to Mr. Harrow. I want to get him to undo this."

"He has never once reversed a decision. For anyone. Ever. And I'm afraid your story is hardly the most tragic. Simon himself came here under the worst of circumstances."

"He told me some bullshit line about his fiancée. I thought he was lying."

"I'm afraid not." Ringmaster folded his arms across his chest. "He was nearly broken in mind before he came here. He was shattered after that. If Mr. Harrow didn't set him free, he won't do it for you."

Cora played with the sand by her thigh, lacing her fingers into it and letting it drop away. "I can't accept that I'm stuck here. I need to find a way to talk to him. With your help or without it."

"I won't stop you. It'd break my heart to see you fall apart like him. With a piece of him inside of you, I worry that he might infect you. You're a sweet, strong soul, Cora. I think we will all be better for having you here. All of us." Turk wasn't wearing his top hat, and he ran his hand over his gelled hair. He had an odd, knowing expression, but he didn't explain what he meant.

"Well, I say I get down from this ring," Amanda said cheerily, "and we all get shitfaced! Nothing fixes a problem like alcohol."

First ice cream, now booze. Well, they were certainly checking all the boxes on the list of things-to-cheer-Cora-Glass-up-with. She laughed. "How can I argue with that?"

6

CORA WAS SITTING on the pier that stretched out over the lake. She had her back against one of the posts of the wooden decking. The lamps overhead made the water around her sparkle and shimmer. She wasn't alone. Amanda and Turk were on a bench nearby, with the blonde Aerialist contentedly relaxing on Ringmaster's lap.

Jack and Aaron were there as well. Aaron had provided a bottle of his moonshine, although currently Cora felt safer with the beer.

Donna, the tiny dark-haired woman, had also joined them. She brought along her husband, Rick. Rick was also muscular, but lithe. It was clear he was an acrobat. He had introduced himself as "Catcher," and at her odd look and giggle he explained that it was the term for the person who hung upside-down in flying trapeze and "caught" the "flyer" who usually did the fancy tricks.

He claimed he did all the hard work.

Donna had smacked him in the arm for that.

The group was all smiling and laughing, telling stories, recounting the day or some "remember that time when—"

kind of tale. Every single one seemed to have a long and funny story to tell about everything.

It was clear they were a Family.

Jack settled on the pier next to her. "How're you doing, Cora?"

"Um. Not great." She looked down at her beer. "This is helping. But I have a feeling as soon as I go to bed, it's all going to sink in all over again."

"What's going to sink in?"

"The panic and existential dread of being stuck in a man-eating murder-circus that deleted my entire life, Jack." She shot him an incredulous look. "What do you think?"

He chuckled. "That's fair. Sorry. Well, hey. When Seamstress came, she locked herself in her room for a month and wouldn't come out. You're handling it better than she did."

"Not for a lack of trying." She looked out over the lake. "I don't think Simon would let me lock myself away. Something tells me that a door with a deadbolt doesn't keep that whack-job out."

"No, it doesn't." Jack ran his thumb over the glass of the brown bottle he was holding. "He hasn't hurt you, has he?"

"He shot me. Define hurt."

"I saw you walking around the Faire with him. He wasn't making you do that, was he? Those damn strings of his."

"No, no, it was fine." She took a swig from her beer. It was her second one. She had a decent alcohol tolerance, so she knew it would take more than that to get her drunk. But she was planning on getting a little fluffed around the edges. She figured she'd earned it. "He was...I mean, he's a creep. I don't think he's ever going to be 'nice' or 'fine' about anything. But he wasn't hurting me. Apparently, when I'm in emotional pain, he feels it, so he's only being nice to me to get it to stop. Well, that, and he wants the stolen part of him back." She shook her head. "I still can't believe I'm saying this shit."

"It's a lot to absorb. No pun intended." Jack smiled. "I'm glad you're out here with us tonight."

Cora nodded. They were still laughing and having a good time. The Faire had closed about an hour before, and so there weren't any more guests bustling around the park. The hurdy gurdy of the rides were silent, and it was just them and the rustle of wind in the trees. "I want to find a way to convince Mr. Harrow to let me go."

"I know. You can knock on his door, you know. Maybe he'll listen to you. But I doubt it. He's never listened to anybody before." He nudged her arm with his elbow. "Maybe you'll like it here. You should give it a try. We're not...bad people."

"You say that in a way that makes me not believe you, Jack." She chuckled and looked over at him. "How many people have you killed?"

"Me? Nobody."

"How many people have you eaten bits from?" She shot him an incredulous look. When he scratched the back of his neck nervously, that was all the answer she needed. "Great."

"We all do it. We have to. We don't really have a choice. It'll happen to you, too. You'll just be minding your own business, and then suddenly it happens."

"So, the circus is just randomly baby-birding us bits of people. Oh, joy. That's just charming." She pinched the bridge of her nose. "And you're all perfectly fine with this?"

"We don't have a choice. Can't commit suicide. Not... unless you wanna go out like Hernandez. Or become one of Bertha's freaks. Or Rudy's animals."

"Bertha and Rudy kill people too?" She looked over at Jack in shock. Bertha seemed like such a nice person.

Rudy, she hadn't really met, but he hardly seemed friendly.

He looked like he was caught in the headlights of a truck, but it was too late to back out of the conversation now. "Well, a few people here can... *collect* people. Bertha, Rudy the Zookeeper, even Maksim the Maestro. They can take people kind of like Simon can, but...they're not nearly as much shit at being a human, though. They don't do things like he does."

"What makes Simon a monster, if others can do the same thing?"

"Some people raise chickens. Some people laugh as they pluck the feathers off the bird as it cries." Jack glared off into the darkness. "Simon is a sadist. Bertha, Rudy, and Maksim give peace to those they collect."

She avoided the mental image. Mainly, because it made too much sense. There were humane and inhumane ways to go about things. She changed the subject. "There are way too many of you to keep straight." Cora had almost finished her beer. It was time for a third. They had been out here for a while, though, and she was being careful to pace herself. The idea of stealing a bottle of Aaron's moonshine and taking it back to the train car was tempting, however. She wanted to get fluffy, but she had no interest in getting hammered in public. "You're going to have to wear nametags."

Jack chuckled. "You'll get up to speed."

"So...he can't remember his name?" She pointed at Ringmaster.

Jack hesitated before answering. "No. Not at all."

She looked at the Rigger, surprised. "How does somebody forget their own name?"

"He volunteered to Sponsor someone, way back when.

Probably almost two hundred years ago. He lost his name in the process. When that person faded away, it went with them. Nobody remembers it now."

Ringmaster was watching them, having caught their conversation. "Turk suits me just fine, and I rather enjoy it." He smiled warmly. "I prefer not to be called 'fat man' or 'tub of lard' or 'overproved loaf of bread' like Simon insists on doing."

"I didn't mean to pry. Sorry." Cora felt sheepish and tucked a leg underneath herself.

"No offense taken." Ringmaster wrapped his arm around Amanda. "It's all ancient history. I honestly don't mind not knowing. The one nice part of losing seity is that it isn't like losing a limb—you don't really miss it when it's gone. Besides, you have every right to be curious."

"I suppose." She still felt awful for having opened her fat mouth on the subject.

"This is your home now. We're your Family. There's happiness to be found here. If I had the choice to leave, I promise I wouldn't even consider it for a second." Ringmaster hugged Amanda to his side. "I don't think any of us would."

"Really? Not a single one of you would go back to your old lives?"

Silence. The group looked around at each other, and then everyone nodded.

She let out a long breath and finished the rest of her beer. "You're all freaks."

They all laughed, and she found herself smiling along with them.

Aaron lifted his flask to her in salute. "Cheers to that."

"I have a question—where do you get all this?" She

motioned at the Faire. "The popcorn, the food, the supplies. The Faire just...creates it?"

Ringmaster nodded.

Cora raised her eyebrow and looked at the Barker. "Then why the hell do you make moonshine, Aaron?"

The Barker laughed again. "What, I can't have a hobby?"

"Too bad you're terrible at your hobbies, old boy," Rick, Donna's husband said with a grin. "That stuff is shit."

"Hey! My shine is great. Not my fault you ladies can't handle it. No offense, ladies."

"Your 'shine' tastes like paint stripper," Cora teased. "And I like my hard alcohol."

"Psh," Aaron snickered into his flask. "More for me."

The conversation drifted naturally for another hour. They were just people chatting. She told them a little bit about herself—her degree in photography, the illness she had suffered, and so on. She still felt...fine. Her pain really was gone. It was weird not to have a constant reminder that her knee was twinging or her ankle was aching or her shoulder was not quite fully in its socket. It was weird to just...be. It was kind of like floating, except she was on solid ground.

It was sad that it was the lack of her chronic pain that almost made her believe in her new inhumanity more than the disappearing gunshot wound to the chest.

After three beers, she felt comfortably fluffy. When she was tired enough to call it a night, she left the group to head back toward "her" boxcar. The group waved goodbye and all wished her a good night.

The carnival was quiet as she wandered aimlessly through the closed rides and shuttered games. It was quiet. She felt alone. She hadn't realized how much she enjoyed sharing laughter and conversation with the others until the moment it was gone. It had also postponed her having to really try to wrap her head around what had happened to her.

When she reached the staff-only area, she looked at the array of boxcars arranged in the grass. Some had lit windows, but many were dark. It was well past two in the morning. She passed through the rows until she found the car labeled with a gold number twenty-one on the door. The one that belonged to Mr. Harrow.

The lights were on, but the curtains were drawn. She didn't see anyone moving around inside. She sighed. It was worth a try. Cautiously going up the stairs, she knocked.

She held her breath and waited. When nothing happened, she knocked again. There was still no answer. "Mr. Harrow?" Silence. "Please, Mr. Harrow. I need to talk to you."

Silence.

She rested her head against the door. "I think you made a mistake. I don't think I belong here."

Silence.

"Please, Mr. Harrow...I just want to go home."

Something rustled by her foot. She looked down and saw a folded piece of paper had been shoved under the door. She reached down and picked it up. The paper was faded and old, yellowed and stained like it had been left in a basement for too long. When she unfolded it, there was a note written on the inside.

"Dearest Cora,

No one believes they belong here when they first arrive. Though you may not feel like it, this is where destiny has chosen you to be. I encourage you to seek happiness in this new life of yours. Should you dismay, you have a Family on which to rely.

All my kindest regards,

-M. L. Harrow"

Well, it was a response. It wasn't the one she wanted. But at least it was something. She didn't know why he didn't just open the door and tell her that to her face, but beggars shouldn't be choosers. He could have just ignored her like everyone insisted he would.

"Thanks, Mr. Harrow..." She tucked the note in her pocket and turned away. She knew that kicking and screaming at the door, begging him to change his mind, wasn't going to work. She'd write him a note in reply and send it back to him. Maybe he'd see reason.

What was that old adage about wishes, beggars, and horses?

Stepping up to the door of "her" boxcar—it was going to take a long time for her to accept that it was anything of the sort—she pushed it open. She flicked the lights on. There wasn't anything waiting to hurt her. Nothing in the shadows lurking to jump out and rip her to pieces.

She was tired. Emotionally worn out. And while today certainly hadn't gone as poorly as the previous day, it was almost tied for last place. With a long sigh, she shut the door behind her, hung her coat on the hook on the wall, took a shower, changed, and crawled under the covers.

The bed was so goddamn comfortable. And she wasn't in any pain. Those two things plus the three beers meant it took her less than five minutes to fall asleep for perhaps the first time in her life.

She hoped her dreams would leave her alone now that she was part of the Faire. Unfortunately, it seemed there was still someone who wanted to talk to her.

She was standing in the living room of her condo. She looked around and cringed. It wasn't *her* condo anymore, was it? Not unless she could convince Mr. Harrow to change his mind. She moved to go see her fish. They might be memories of her sad excuse for pets, but she'd take what she could—

Something tackled her. Full on, football linebacker tackled her onto the sofa. "Cora!"

She screamed and landed hard on her back on the soft surface. The cushions bounced with the impact. Someone was on top of her, hugging her around the waist, pinning her down with all his weight on top of her. She smacked at the black fabric of their back. "Get—get off—"

"Cora, Cora, Cora, *hi...*"

That voice. She knew it. But...she also didn't know it at the same time. She looked down and recognized the man. "Simon? What're you—"

The man picked up his head. It was Simon, but it wasn't at the same time. He was wearing all black instead of red, and his eyes were normal. White, cyan, and black. The man smiled at her beamingly. "Kinda! Kinda not really. Mostly, maybe." He tucked his head back down onto her chest, snuggling into her, and settled his weight down onto her ribcage. "I'm Simon, though."

She let out an *oomf* as he did. "—can't breathe."

"That's stupid. Why can't you breathe?" He had his cheek pressed against her.

"—you," she wheezed.

"Oh. Oh!" He rolled off her just enough that she could gasp for air, but he could still use her breasts for pillows. He had one elbow underneath her now, supporting his weight. "Sorry."

"Get off me." She tried to push him off, but he just gripped her harder against him. Her legs were trapped under his, and he had her well and truly pinned.

"No-*pe.*"

It was Simon. But it was a weird, messed-up version of Simon. If such a thing was actually possible. She sighed heavily. "Who are you?"

"Simon, clearly."

"What do you want?"

"I'm gettin' it now." He squeezed her in a hug and tilted his head to kiss her chest, just above the swell of her breast. "Hi, Cora."

Her face went hot as blood rushed to her face. She stammered uselessly and pushed at him, but it didn't do any good. He looked at her, cyan eyes meeting hers. He smiled. It lacked the malice that it usually did. He was gazing at her with happiness, excitement, and hope. There was real affection in those blue eyes.

And a very large heaping of lust.

He leaned his head down and kissed her skin again, slower than the last time. "I like you." He kissed her again and let his tongue snake out to drag along her skin. "I like you a lot. No one ever comes to play with me. No one ever *talks* to me."

"Simon...?" She felt breathless. Confused. His embrace was coiling something deep in her body.

"Yes and no. I'm not who you think I am. Not anymore." He slid one of his hands from around her to run up and down her arm. She broke out in goosebumps and shivered underneath him. "Cold? I can warm you up."

"Who—what—" When he slid his tongue up to her neck, she gasped and tried to push his head away. "Stop—"

"Stop?" He pouted. "But why?"

"Who the hell are you?"

"You know me." He smiled. "Did I scare you? I didn't mean to." He nestled in close to her, his hips against hers, and she felt something—she felt *him* pressed against her. Her eyes went wide. He frowned again. "That shouldn't be scary. That should be exciting. Why does everybody get scared of me? And now when I can finally touch somebody, they're afraid? That's not fair!"

"Wait. Wait. You're—you're Simon's *shadow*?"

He furrowed his brow. "Shadow." He frowned, sighed, and sank his cheek back onto her chest. "Everybody calls me that, and I don't understand *why*. I just want someone to *touch me*. Or hug me. Or talk to me. Or—ohh," he moaned, and shifted his hips against hers. She whimpered. "You feel so good, Cora."

"Stop—"

He sighed and stilled his movements but didn't get off her. "Fine...but you're no fun." He sniffled.

Was he actually upset? "What...what's going on?" He sniffled again. She felt dampness on her chest. He really was crying. And here she thought Simon was all over the emotional map. "I...don't cry, please." She didn't know what to do. She just wrapped her arms around the man. The shadow. Whatever.

"I've been so alone, and he's so mean to me, and nobody talks to me, and they barely even see me. And when they do, they run away, or they tell me to leave them alone. I don't even try to scare them!"

"You tried to scare me in the mirror maze. And you terrified me."

He paused. "Yeah..." He snickered. "But it was worth it, and you were so cute, but then you screamed and ran away and hurt yourself and I felt so terrible and I couldn't even hold you and say that I was sorry! But I couldn't touch you. I can't touch and I can't feel anything! I can't feel anything *ever.*"

Holy shit, and here she thought Simon talked at a million miles an hour.

"But now I get to say it—I'm sorry. I didn't want you to get hurt." He picked up his head and plopped his chin on her chest. His head bobbed up and down as he talked. "I hope you believe me."

"What do you mean, you can't feel anything ever?" She had a hard time believing that.

"Do you forgive me for scaring you?" He pouted. Literally *pouted.*

She laughed quietly at his childlike expression. Simon's shadow smiled hopefully at her laugh. She moved a hand from around him and, although she wasn't sure why she did it, she placed a hand against his cheek. He leaned into her touch, sinking into it like it was bliss. "I forgive you."

He nuzzled into her palm, groaning low in his throat, and his expression was of a man who had found Heaven. It was the visage of someone who had been about to die of thirst in a desert but had been given a glass of cold water.

Now she believed what he said. She stroked her thumb along his cheekbone. He looked just like Simon, but his expressions came fast and wild, and he shuddered in her arms. He pressed his hips into her. She felt his need, and her face grew warm again.

"Thank you, Cora." His whisper was thick. "I...I need to ask you a favor."

Oh no. She was afraid to ask. But she didn't see a way around it. "Yeah?"

He shifted, sliding up her body until his face hovered over hers. She looked into those wild, unfettered blue eyes, and saw every emotion on the rainbow reflected back at her. Hope, despair, hate, joy, jealousy, greed, happiness. Love and lust. "He kissed you. I was so mad when he did it...can I have one too?"

"Are you going to want to do everything he gets to do?"

She meant it as a joke. What she got was a wry twist of lips that looked much more like the man she recognized. *"Maaayybe."* It was the whisper of a madman, but it stole her breath away. He lowered his head to hers, his lips grazing there, just a hair's breadth away. "Please?"

He smelled like cologne. Of paint, and an antique store. Of dust, of aging leather, of a warm place to explore. He was so beautiful. Even like this, he was awe-inspiring. She didn't know how to tell him no. So she told him, with her own, barely-audible whisper, "Yes."

He kissed her. Where Simon had been slow and sensual, his shadow was wild and unrestrained. He was a mad dog released at the door of a greyhound track, and he wanted to devour her whole. His lips worked over hers with a fervor that left her stunned and unable to respond for a long few moments before she found herself kissing him back, if far less impressively than he had started. She closed her eyes and let the kiss wash everything else away. She let him take over the whole of her awareness.

Finally, after a long few moments, he broke away with a loud moan and buried his head in the crook of her neck.

She still lay there with her eyes shut, unable to process what had just happened.

"Cora...Oh, Cora, I think. I think I love you!" He laughed joyfully.

A familiar voice broke into her dream. A voice that was already there. But this one was seasoned by rage. *"She's mine!"*

Her dream broke like a glass thrown against the wall.

7

SIMON COULD FEEL IT. He didn't know how. He didn't know why. But he did. And he was *furious.*

Someone was kissing Cora. Someone was in her bed, and it *wasn't him.* And that sent him into a rage the likes of which he hadn't known in a very, very long time. He picked the lock of her boxcar. He was barely able to still his shaking hands long enough to do the deed. But he wanted to catch the lovers unawares. He wanted to sneak up on them, so he could snap his wires around their necks and rip her would-be paramour to smithereens!

He would string them up by their feet and shatter every finger on their hands, one at a time. He would break their toes, and every little bone they owned, and then the bigger ones, and then the biggest ones, until they were a puddle of goo. He would reduce them to *pulp.* He would turn them into a decorative jelly mold that had long since been put out of fashion and arrange them with a cherry on top as a warning to anyone who dared try to have her.

She's mine!

His heart was pounding, and his vision would have been

red even without the aid of his sunglasses. He pushed the door open—the poor girl hadn't remembered to set her deadbolt or her chain, not that it would have stopped him—and crept into the room. He wanted to catch them in the act.

The thought of seeing Jack, or Aaron, or Ludwig between her thighs spurred him on. He shut the door silently behind him and stormed to the edge of her bed. He blinked in confusion. She was alone.

Sort of.

His shadow was on the wall beside him, smiling and utterly pleased with itself. His shadow cupped his hands over his heart, and made a comedic heart beating motion, and Simon watched in disgust as his reflection's eyes turned into hearts.

It hadn't been anyone else here in the boxcar with Cora.

It had been *himself*.

He'd been betrayed by his own shadow.

He never did cease to disappoint himself. "Get out," he hissed at the thing on the wall. The creature frowned, its eyes turning into an expression of sadness. *"Out."* He pointed at the wall, not daring to shout.

His shadow pouted, stuck out his tongue in a raspberry at him again, made a rude gesture, and then slunk away to lurk in some dark corner somewhere. Good. Simon turned his attention to the woman he had expected to find in the arms of one of the other Family members.

Instead, he found her lying in her sheets alone.

It hadn't been his stolen seity that had made him feel her in the embrace of another. It was because it was his own deranged Id, his unruly subconscious, that had been the source of the sensation.

His anger faded quickly at the sight of her. She was tangled in her sheets, having tossed them away. Her nightclothes were thin and rumpled, riding up as she must have tossed and turned in her dreams. So close to revealing her body, and yet doing too good of a job of obscuring it from him.

Her dark hair was splayed out around the pillow beneath her. Her eyes were shut, still caught in a dream, and her lips were parted. Her breasts rose and fell in rapid patterns, as if excited by whatever had transpired in her mind. Her cheeks were just a little flushed.

His body reacted instantly, blood surging through him, his heart pounding in his ears for another, completely different reason than anger. She was so beautiful. So soft. So sensual. He wanted her, and now, seeing her like this—he had to have her. He had to.

Knowing that his shadow had been in her dream stealing affection from her wasn't right. He wouldn't be outdone by a second-rate shard of himself. He shifted closer to her, like Prince Charming over his Sleeping Beauty, and let his lips ghost over hers.

Then came the two words that sealed his fate. Whispered, barely audible against him, but echoing like church bells calling him to worship. *"Simon, yes..."*

His heart seized. Something else in him leaped to attention. He had never heard those words uttered before—never once. Not even from his fiancée of years gone by. That was a beg. A plea. And far be it from him to deny her.

He kissed her.

And it was better than he could have dreamt. And that was something, because he had kissed her there once before.

Or maybe twice.

But neither mattered anymore. She moaned against his lips, furtive and unsure, still trapped in the dream. He lowered himself onto his elbow, moving over her. He cradled her face in his palm and answered her small noise with one of his own. As she chased his lips, answering his embrace, he let his hand slide down her throat and to drift over the swell of her breast.

"Mmff—!"

She pushed her hands against him. He chuckled. Oh, no. He wasn't going to take some false show of dignity seriously. He heard her. She called his name. She wanted him, just as much as he wanted her.

When she slapped her hands hard on his chest, he pulled back and laughed down at her. She was awake now, looking up at him with feral gray eyes that seemed almost black in the darkness. "Wait!"

He laughed.

HE LAUGHED AT HER.

The figure in the darkness over her *laughed.*

"You can't—" She pushed on his chest. He didn't budge. If anything, he got closer.

"I'm not about to be undone by that broken piece of myself. You can't possibly prefer him to me. That's unacceptable."

She heard the words, but they didn't sink in. Panic was overwhelming her. An old and terrible trauma welled up inside her chest. She whimpered in fear.

"Now, now...no need for that. I thought we might spend some *quality* time together." The figure over her slid onto her bed, slipping a leg between hers, caging her in. Trapping her.

Memories of an old horror that she had worked so hard

to forget started to break down the dam in her mind. The sensation of hands in the darkness. Of the fabric of a bed that should have been safe, biting painfully into her cheek. Of the agonizing sting. Panic broke over the surface of the wall she had put up around those images in her mind. They flooded back to her like a tidal wave.

"What's—" The figure over her grunted as if something hit him. He moved away from her an inch, and an inch was all she needed. She reached up and dug her fingernails into his face, raking down his cheeks. He howled in pain, and she shoved him away with both her hands. He let go of her to place his hands over the wounds as he fell back, toppling off the edge of the bed to the floor.

Her heart was racing. She was hyperventilating. She felt faint.

Everything began to blur together. She sat up and shoved herself into the corner of the bed, wedging against the windows she barely registered. She curled herself into the smallest ball she could.

She wasn't sure when it all went black. But her mind once more opted to pick darkness over the reality of what was happening.

SIMON WASN'T sure what hurt worse. The feeling of panic—of sheer and utter agony—that had suddenly been gripping his heart, or the stinging cuts on his face. His little hellcat had claws, and she had no problem using them.

Sure, he had been a little abrupt in his actions, but he had figured her for a girl who liked it a little rough. What he had expected was her to beg him to slow down, then to beg him to speed up. She was already pleading to be touched. She had whispered his name.

But her reaction had been instant, the moment she woke up. Whatever he had done triggered something in her like pushing down the plunger of a dynamite fuse box. Okay, maybe he had come on too strong. But it wasn't anger that he got from her. It was *sheer terror.*

He thought he had felt her fear before. Now he knew he hadn't even scratched the surface. She had cowered in the corner of the mattress and the wall, trying to make herself as small as possible. No amount of talking seemed to register with her.

"Cora, stop. Please, stop." He dug his fingers into his chest, under his shirt, scratching at the skin with his nails. He might have been bleeding, but he didn't care. The cuts on his face stung badly enough, what were a few more? "Please, Cora. It's okay. I'm not going to hurt you."

But she didn't answer. She just kept whimpering, *"Duncan, no,"* before her short and quick breaths couldn't sustain her and she fell unconscious, slumping onto the surface of the bed.

Every second of her agony had stabbed at him like knives and sent him to the ground in turn. Now that it was over, he could finally pick himself up. He had half a mind to leave her there.

But this was his fault.

It was one thing to cause her trauma when he meant to do it. He hadn't given a shit about shooting her in the chest or leaving her in the grass yesterday. But this had been an accident. He had wanted to kiss her. To hold her. To make love to her. He thought she wanted the same.

Clearly, he had been wrong.

Stupid shadow, always getting me in trouble. He pulled her from where she had collapsed in the corner of the bed and positioned her more comfortably. Flicking the lights on, he walked to the kitchenette table and slumped down into a chair.

Shutting his eyes, he waited.

But shutting his eyes was a mistake.

He knew bits of his mind didn't work like maybe they should. He knew he was a little broken. *Maybe more than a little.* But all geniuses were insane. He never let it bother him. But once in a while, one of those cracks opened wide.

Maybe it was her panic that had done it. Maybe it was the twist of the knife in his heart. Either way, it opened up like a chasm.

He loved his darkness.

But damn if it didn't pick inconvenient times to come for him.

THUMP.

Thump.

Thump.

Cora woke to an unexpected sound.

She jolted awake again and thrashed her hands, trying to attack whatever was making the noise. But there was no one there. The instant rush of adrenaline had set her heart pounding, and she sat up to try to find the source of the thumping. She was in bed, over the covers. She still wore her pajamas. She didn't hurt—but that didn't say much when she could apparently heal from a gunshot in a few hours.

Thump.

Thump.

Thump.

After looking around for a few minutes, she found where the thumping was coming from. The source was the man who had given her a panic attack. But not in the way she'd expected.

Simon was sitting on the floor of the train car by one wall.

And he was bashing his head into it.

Thump.

Thump.

Thump.

Blood was pouring down his temple. He must have cut his head on something on the wall, but she couldn't tell what. There were still nail marks on his cheeks. She couldn't have been out for long. His eyes were shut, and he just kept ramming his head into the wall.

Thump.

"Simon—"

Thump.

"Simon, stop it—"

Thump.

Standing, she cautiously approached him. He wasn't answering her. There was a good chance he couldn't hear her. He was just thunking his head into the wall over and over again. The right side of his face was a mask of red.

"Hey, stop it."

She pulled a dish towel off the front of the drawer in the kitchenette and knelt at his side. She didn't know if she should care—she didn't, really—but she couldn't leave a psychopath sitting on her floor bashing his head open. She stuck her hand between him and the wall and pressed the cloth to his head.

"Simon, stop. You're hurting yourself."

"Suzanna, I'm sorry—" He clutched at her. "Don't leave me—" She watched him in stunned silence as he hissed in a sharp breath through his nose. He slid back away from her like she was on fire and rocketed to his feet, leaving her kneeling there.

Simon pressed his hand to his temple, and seeing it come away wet, he growled. He went to the kitchenette and started the sink. Leaning over it, he pulled off his glasses and cupped water in both his hands, washing the blood off.

"Simon?" She stood slowly, keeping distance between them. She suspected he was insane, and now she had her proof. He could snap and round on her at any time. "Stupid question...you okay?"

"Who is Duncan?"

Wincing as if she'd been slapped, she put another few feet between them and put her shoulder against the wall. "You attacked me."

"That isn't the answer to my question. And no, I didn't attack you. I was flirting with you."

"You broke into my boxcar and snuck into my bed in my sleep. That isn't flirting."

"To you." He straightened and took a paper towel off a roll. Wiping his face with it, he inspected it for fresh stains. The marks she had seen on his face had just been the remaining blood. The gash on his temple was already healed. "You were having relations with my shadow in your sleep. I figured the invitation applied to the authentic product, not just the bad replica."

"I—that—how did you—"

"Are you claiming he wasn't there?"

"He kissed me."

"He has lips?" Simon wrinkled his nose. "Even more reason I had every right to kiss you without you trying to claw my eyes out." He wiped at his face again. "You really are a panicky one."

"I have goddamn good reasons, you piece of shit." She glared at him. "First, I get abducted by a fucking murder-circus, and second, you try to—" She broke off from saying the words. "You attacked me."

"You panicked less when I had you on my strings in my tent. You fought back. Here, you tried to claw my eyes out and then collapsed in a heap after hyperventilating." He put his glasses back on his face. His hand was shaking. "Who is Duncan?"

"Who's Suzanna?"

He grimaced. "My fiancée. I would appreciate it if you did not tell the others about my...eh...lapse."

"Fuck you."

"That is precisely what I was trying to accomplish, believe it or not." He glared at her. His expression was a mixed bag of anger, confusion, and pain. For once, he didn't seem manic. She kind of preferred him smiling. This version was too serious for her. "I'll ask for a last time. Who is Duncan, and what did he do to you?"

"Why the hell should I explain anything to you? I don't owe you anything."

"Because I didn't want for this to happen!" He snarled and slammed his hand into the counter. The silverware rattled in its drawer.

"What did you want to have happen? How did you expect this to go? You attacked me! What, did you think I was just going to lie there after you broke in, in the middle of the night, and go 'oh, please, harder, daddy?'" She answered his anger with her own.

"Yes, actually! I see how you look at me."

"I'm terrified of you, you stupid, egotistical sack of donkey shit! Get out."

"Not until you explain to me who Duncan is." He took a step toward her.

She shot up from the chair and took a step back. She didn't have a whole lot of room to avoid him. "How do you even know that name?"

"You were begging him to stop before you collapsed in a catatonic heap." He scrunched up one half of his nose in disgust. "I had hoped you were stronger than this. I think I am beginning to see how weak you really are."

"You don't know what you're talking about. Not a fucking thing. And don't you *dare* pretend to try."

He straightened himself to his full height. His expression remained dour. "Then explain it to me. For the last-last-last time...who is Duncan?"

Gritting her teeth, her jaw twitched. She stayed silent.

"I'm not leaving this spot until you tell me."

She wanted him gone more than she wanted her privacy. "He was my boyfriend."

"And?"

She turned her back to the wall to avoid having to look at him, and also so she had something to support her. She put the heels of her hands against her cheekbones under her eyes and rubbed them. "We lived together. We were out at a party, and we came back. I had a few drinks, and we were both a little drunk. I remember him throwing me down to the bed. I remember him pinning me there. I begged him to stop. I begged him to let me go. He just laughed at me. No matter what I did, he wouldn't—"

Her voice hitched, and she took a moment to breathe and focus. She could get through this. She could say the words. "He held me down and raped me. He wouldn't stop. I remember the pain. The next morning, I threw him out. I filed a report with the cops, but they said that because of the drinking, my story wasn't reliable. Said I didn't have 'enough' bruises to prove assault. He denied everything. A lot of our mutual friends took his side. He got away with it."

Silence.

When she heard a cabinet door open and shut, she finally looked over to him. Simon was standing a few feet away from her, holding a cast iron skillet out to her by the lip, offering her the handle.

Something about it made her laugh.

Finally, his serious expression cracked into a small smile. It faded. She shooed his hand away, and he put the skillet down on the counter. "I wasn't going to rape you, Cora. I never would."

"You shot me. You tried to turn me into one of those fucked-up dolls of yours. How the hell was I supposed to know that?"

He looked out the window thoughtfully, his brow lowered. "It's kind of a strange world we live in where I would have no problem brutally murdering you, yet I am rather offended at the notion that you think I would stoop so low as to hurt you in that way." He looked back at her. "That makes no sense. Society is rather odd, isn't it?"

She shrugged. "In one instance, the victim is around to care about the problem. In the other, they aren't. I guess."

"Hm." He took in a breath and let it out. "I don't say this often. If ever. I hope you appreciate it, as you won't likely ever hear it again. I'm sorry for scaring you."

She nodded once, accepting his apology. She believed him, strangely enough. She jolted as she realized there was a shadow on the wall next to her. That nerve-wracking sentient shadow of his was looming over her, its comical smile looking like it was quite literally flipped upside down as it hovered over her. Like it was concerned. No, it looked worried sick.

"I'm fine." She didn't know who she said it to. Simon, or the shadow. Or, honestly, to herself. It was to all three. "I just...I haven't thought about that moment in a long time. You hit a nerve."

"I would have stopped if you told me to." He opened the door. The shadow on the wall next to her snapped obediently back to where it should be. "Even monsters like me have to have some standards."

It makes you better than a lot of people, and that's terrifying. She opted not to flatter him. She didn't reply to him at all. She felt wrung out. She needed sleep. She hoped she didn't have nightmares again like she used to, but she didn't have high hopes.

"At some point, I am going to need to speak to you about my shadow appearing in your dream. But...now is not that time. Goodnight, Cora, despite what is left of it being ruined." He didn't wait for a reply and left, shutting the door behind him with a click.

Sinking down onto the bed, she opted to sleep with the lights on.

8

THANKFULLY, the old nightmares didn't come for the remainder of Cora's night. And neither did Simon or his shadow. She woke the next morning to someone tapping on her door. Pushing up from the mattress, she grunted. She felt like an absolute wreck. She probably looked like a disaster. Glancing at the old-fashioned clock on the wall, it was nearly noon.

She fought the instinctual reaction that she was late for work. Nope. She wasn't. If they were to be believed, she didn't have a job anymore. She didn't have a life.

The tapping came again. "Let me just get some clothes on." She went to the closet and quickly dug out something. She wasn't going to answer the door in her pajamas. When she was done, wearing yet another outfit that looked like she had picked it out the contents of her closet, not the Faire, she went to the door and swung it open.

"Good—"

She slammed it shut again. Shutting her eyes with a beleaguered growl, she really debated leaving it shut. The person who had been standing there was, naturally, Simon. Holding a tray of food.

Am I ever going to be rid of him? Ever?

Probably not by leaving him on her doorstep.

She opened the door.

"—morning." He was grinning as though nothing had happened. "Hungry?" He held up the tray. "You missed breakfast and lunch."

She went to reach for the tray, but he pulled it out of her grasp. "Ah-ah, it comes with a price."

"Which is?"

"Letting me in."

"Why?"

"To talk."

She raised an eyebrow.

"Just talk. I promise." He smiled.

She put her hand over her eyes. He was impossible. Absolutely impossible. She rubbed her hand over her face and took a step back into the train car. "Fine. Whatever. You can let yourself in anyway, apparently."

"Indeed! I'm afraid to say the deadbolt and the chain won't stop me either." He stepped inside and placed the food down on the kitchenette. It was a salad and a side of what looked like garlic bread. She hadn't seen anything not fried or on a stick since she got there, so it was a nice change of pace. "I would have let myself in again, but I thought that might not be the best way to make friends, twice in a row and all."

"I wasn't aware you wanted to be friends."

"Well, I'd prefer to be passionate lovers, but after last night, I think we should start over at the beginning."

She shut the door and sat at the table. She was starving.

She hadn't really eaten dinner the night prior—just the hot dog and ice cream.

He took the spot across from her and propped his elbows on the table, watching her curiously. "Did you sleep?"

"Yes."

"Not well, by the looks of things. Did I just wake you up?"

She shot him a glare. "I had a bad night."

"Mmh. Yes. I suppose you did."

He didn't apologize. He'd warned her that she was only ever going to get the one "sorry." She picked up the fork and started eating the salad. It had strawberries and tangerines in it. It was actually pretty damn good. "Thanks for the food."

"Can't have you starving. I don't want to suffer that fate."

"Do you only feel my pain? Or do you feel other things too?"

"Can't tell." He plucked a grape out of the salad and popped it into his mouth. She decided not to comment. He brought it, after all. "You haven't felt anything other than agony since you got here. It's only been a matter of degrees." She shot him a glare. He smiled. "What, am I wrong?"

"Last night—before you showed up—was all right."

"Ah, yes. How was the pier? I'm sure you all had a great deal of fun mocking me behind my back."

"Honestly, you didn't really come up."

The way his face fell made her laugh. There was nothing more insulting to an egotist than not being the focus of attention. She grinned at him. "The only time you came up was Jack making sure you weren't doing anything inappropriate."

"Ah, yes. I saw you two talking together. I saw how close he was sitting to you. I'm shocked you didn't go to his train car last night instead." He grimaced. "I was surprised to find you walking back on your own."

The jealousy there was thick and hard to miss. She sat back in her chair to watch him. "Is that why you attacked me? You were afraid I'd pick him over you?"

"No."

She didn't believe him, but she opted not to fight with him about it. "Two things. One, I'm not going to screw him. Second, he didn't offer."

"He's going to. Someone will. Someone always does. Circus families are notoriously, eh...inbred."

"You're saying people get around. That explains Ludwig and Trent." Cora shrugged. "More power to them. I'm not a prude. It's just not my style."

"Ludwig has a difficult time saying no to physical affection. It's one of the few things left that he can feel at all." He paused and clearly debated saying something. With a shrug, began speaking again. "I do not know what else I'll feel from you. Last night, I knew you were in the arms of someone, but I think that was because it was, in fact, *me,* and had nothing to do with my stolen seity." He shot her a small, satisfied smile. He was gloating.

"I...it was a dream. Your shadow showed up in my dream, but he...he looked like you did before that happened." She gestured at his face with her fork. "His eyes were normal, and he was wearing all black."

He looked at her quizzically and sat back in his chair. "Huh. And he could speak?"

"Yeah."

"What did he say? I'm dying to know. Especially if it got

you to spread your—" He stopped when she shot him a vicious look, and he coughed. "What happened between you two?"

"You said he's your subconscious, right?"

"More or less. That's a simplification. Don't stall." He plucked another grape off her plate.

"He was desperate for attention. His emotions were all over the map. He tackled me like a linebacker and rambled on and on about how nobody talks to him, and he can't touch anything. He kissed me. That's all that happened."

"He tackled you, and got a kiss?" Simon huffed. "I nearly got my eyes clawed out. That's not fair. But perhaps it was the dream state that was the difference?" He watched her with a curious expression. "Have you let anyone touch you since Duncan?"

She shot him a fiery glare and didn't answer him.

"That would be a 'no,' then." He smirked. "Am I wrong?"

"I'm going to stab you with my fork."

"That is most definitely a 'no.' Don't they say talking about trauma helps in the healing process?"

"You know what helps me in the healing process? *Stabbing you with this fork.*"

He cackled and stole another grape from her plate, clearly not taking her threat seriously. He was right on both counts. No, she hadn't let anyone touch her. And no, she wasn't actually going to stab him.

Yet.

She watched him for a moment. He was such an odd creature. But his fast expressions and ever-present smile were starting to...grow on her. Like mold. She had plenty of reasons not to want him around. She looked for another. "I take it you're on the list of sleeping around?"

"No." Simon wrinkled his nose. "I dislike them too much to ever dirty myself with any of them."

"Damn. Ruining my mental image of you 'getting stuffed like a Thanksgiving turkey' by Ludwig."

He blanched comically and made a noise as if he were going to throw up. "I would rather sit on a fence post. I think it'd be a better lover."

She snickered. "I don't know. Trent is pretty particular, and he came back a whole bunch of times. So, what, your puppets are anatomically correct, then? Making yourself fucked-up versions of blow-up dolls?"

"You've got a vile mind, Cora. I like it. I'm sorry to disappoint, however. Making myself a doll to have relations with is a level of depravity I think might even outweigh my own." He gagged again. "Why the sudden interest in my sex life? Want to change our mutual recent runs of celibacy?"

She held out her fork in his direction.

He leaned back in his chair with another laugh. "I had to try."

"Are you trying to sleep with me because I have a piece of you and it feeds your clear narcissistic streak, or because you can't stand the idea that one of them might touch something that you feel you own?"

"Perhaps I'm merely attracted to you, or I find you enticing."

She raised an eyebrow at him and waited.

"It's both." He pushed his glasses up his nose with the press of a ring finger.

"Both things I said, or both things you said?" Talking with him was like playing tennis. It was a game and a competition.

"I'll let you decide." He stole another grape.

She rolled her eyes and went back to eating. He had won that point. "I think I know what part of your seity I stole."

"Oh?" He tilted closer eagerly.

"Yeah. The part of you that liked to masturbate in the mirror. That's why you're interested in me." She grinned at him. He had served her the perfect setup.

His expression went to one of surprise, then amusement, and he sat back, howling in laughter. "Well played, Cora dear. Well played, indeed." He watched her from behind those two-tone sunglasses, his head tilted to the side, as if seeing her for the first time. It made her cheeks go warm, and she didn't know why. "I like this version of you that isn't so afraid all the time. You're feisty."

"Uh-huh. Then stop terrorizing me."

"Never." He paused. "Today, I thought perhaps you would like to start training for your new role as Contortionist."

"No, thanks."

"What're you going to do instead? It's not like you have anywhere else to be." He gestured around her boxcar. "Unless you want to stay cooped up in here all day."

"Mr. Harrow wrote me a note, and I want to reply. And besides that, I—"

"He *what?*"

At his loud exclamation, she paused. Oh. Right. That was a big deal. She probably shouldn't have told him that. *The Faire talks to Harrow, and Harrow talks to Ringmaster. That's all.* She murmured her answer, trying to play it off like it was no big deal. "I went to his door last night and asked to talk to him, and he wrote me a note instead."

"Where? Where is it?" Simon was acting like the room was on fire. She reached into her coat pocket on the wall and pulled it out, handing it to him. It was a little more crumpled than it had been when she got it.

Simon snatched it from her hands and quickly read it. He stood from the table and began to pace. He read it, re-read it, and kept re-reading it. He turned it over in his hands. "This...I don't think you understand. This is...dangerous. This is incredibly dangerous."

"Dangerous?"

"He doesn't speak to anyone. Ever. Only to Ringmaster. He's *never* written a note to anyone! Why you? Why now?"

"I don't...know?"

"I wasn't asking you." He shoved the note into his coat. "You cannot tell anyone of this. No one else. Especially not that overstuffed gopher in a top hat. Come with me." He headed for the door. "Now."

"I—"

He glared down at her. "I'll make you."

With a groan, she picked up the garlic bread and followed him out of the train car. It seemed like this was going to be her new life. Following Simon around like an idiot.

Great.

HE GLANCED over his shoulder and saw her following him. Good. He was pleased for two reasons. One, he hadn't traumatized her badly enough last night that she wanted nothing to do with him. Two, she was willing to come along of her own volition.

He was also angry. *How dare Mr. Harrow speak to her, and not to me?*

He was also worried. *What does this mean?*

He was also excited. *How can I use this to my advantage?*

The pile of emotions tangled with the fact that he still *very* much wanted her, the events of the previous night only giving him a new barricade to dismantle. He was a veritable crock pot of warring priorities.

But they all centered around *her.* And that annoyed him, somewhere in the back of his mind. He had better things to be doing. *Do I, though? Do I* really *have anything better to do?* The answer was, sadly...no. He could be in his tent, working on a new act, but he had been doing that for a hundred and thirty-five years since coming to the Faire. It was boring. She wasn't.

But he did not like not being in control. Cora dictated the speed of their dance, even as she was the one trudging behind him, eating her garlic bread. He was a generally domineering creature, demanding people do what he wished of them, so he couldn't blame his lack of control over Cora entirely on his need to bark orders at her and drag her around the park at his whim.

He'd probably be doing it anyway.

But she had received a letter from Mr. Harrow. It was frustrating! It was maddening. He was seething with jealousy. He needed to find a way to work this to his advantage. Cora could either be his final undoing...or his greatest gift. She was a weapon.

A beautiful, tiny, mouthy little weapon.

And what a mouth she had on her. He grinned again at her snide shot at him, about what part of his seity she had taken. *I've never masturbated in the mirror. That I know of. Madness is funny sometimes, so I suppose I can't say for certain she's wrong.* He snickered loudly. She shot him a curious look and, seeing that he wasn't going to explain the random outburst, shrugged and shook her head. *Get used to it, cupcake.*

She was a weapon. He just needed to figure out how to use it properly. Perhaps he could finally rewrite the Faire to his own desires...or perhaps he would end up blowing off his own hands in the process.

Either way.

It'd be good for a laugh.

9

CORA TRAILED BEHIND SIMON, not even sure where he was taking her. She had to half-jog to keep up with his stride. Stupid tall bastard with his stupid long legs.

Finally, she realized they were headed for his own train car with the fifteen on the door. He cleared the steps in one jump and opened the door, flying inside. With a sigh, she went in after him. She didn't like the idea of going inside his "room," but there wasn't much to be done about it when he could tug her after him.

The car looked like hers, only somehow older. She had expected the place to look like a hoarder lived there. Pieces of string, dolls, or paint. It was shockingly...tidy. The surfaces were clear, except for the kitchenette table covered in dozens of pieces of paper. They were larger and thicker sheets than typical desk paper. And they weren't covered with letters—but drawings.

Simon was digging through drawers in his bedroom area, pulling things out and trying to find something. She stepped up to the kitchenette table and began leafing through the sketches.

She knew he was a painter. She was still impressed at how good an artist he was. He was incredible. And there were drawings of every kind in the pile. Charcoal or pencil sketches of buildings, of people, of the rides in the park. Of some of the other Family members she'd met. She recognized Donna and Rick, even if they were upside-down in a trapeze.

It was close to the top of one pile that she paused. It was a sketch of herself.

He'd drawn her.

No one had ever done that before.

She picked up the piece of paper and found herself fascinated by it.

The paper was ripped from her hands. He put it back on the table, face-down. "Don't get a big head. I draw everyone."

He thrust a folder in her hands. She took it and, opening it, found a small collection of notes. Each one looked like it was written on absolutely ancient paper, stained and brittle. She was almost afraid to pick them up, as she could already see flakes of them in the crease of the folder. She put them down on the table and began to carefully lift them.

They were letters. All from Mr. Harrow. And all addressed to Ringmaster. Not a single one was addressed to anyone else. "Where did you get these?"

"I stole them. Ringmaster keeps them in his boxcar in a safe." Simon grinned. "I know the combination. Fat old fuck hasn't thought to ever double-check it, or maybe he thinks they just magically disappear on their own."

"Why take them?"

"Why not?" He sniffed dismissively. "I have every right to have them. And there might be a clue hidden in them somewhere. But I never found anything. And he has never written to anyone else except Ringmaster. Not until you." He was scrutinizing her like she was somehow the secret. "Why you?"

"I don't know."

"I'm still not asking you."

"Great. Enjoy the note." She turned to leave. "I'm going to go write one back. I'll tell you if he replies."

He jumped around the table to block her exit. She had to rear up to keep from smashing into him. Again. She found herself bumping into him a lot. He looked down at her intensely, his brow furrowed. "What are you going to say to him? I should be the one to write it."

"What? No. Why?" She tried to move around him, but he stepped back in front of her. "Simon."

"Because you'll just ruin this chance. If I write it, this could be useful! If you do it, you'll just muck it up."

She wanted to set him on fire. She wished she still had that fork. She'd honestly stab him with it. "You're an asshole."

Seeing her expression, he seemed to try to dig himself out of his hole, but it was too late. "Well. I mean. Fine. But we should write it together, at the very least."

Rolling her eyes, she shoved him out of the way, went to the door, and opened it. "We aren't doing anything together, Simon. You just keep showing up."

"But—"

She didn't let him reply. She shut the door behind her and headed back to her own train car. The last thing she wanted to do was encourage the egotistical jackass.

He clearly encouraged himself enough as it was.

Storming back to her train car, she pulled up short. Simon was sitting at her kitchenette table, hunched over a piece of paper with a pencil. "What the f—"

"You were right about the door being a suggestion and not a rule."

She looked behind her, then back to Simon, then back to the door. "How did you..."

"Shortcut. You used the path. I cut between the rows." He smiled. "I cannot fly, sadly."

"Please go away."

"Shush, I'm focusing."

She rubbed both hands over her face and tried not to scream at him. She shut the door quietly. "I'm not letting you write this note for me."

"What would you say? Whine about how you have a life to return to? That he made a mistake? Please. Don't be so banal." He waved his hand dismissively. "This is an opportunity we cannot waste."

"We?"

"If he returns you to the world, I get my missing piece back. So, yes." He glanced at her over the top rim of his sunglasses. "We." He scratched out a line and tapped the tip of his pencil on the paper. He grunted.

"What?" She sat back down, at least happy that she could finish her lunch now.

"I don't know what to write."

She snickered and sat with her back against the wall. "You're seriously an epic asshole."

"You keep saying that. I fail to see how I'm wrong in wishing to write this letter for you. I'm more versed in the Faire. I know what might be useful to say."

"Then say it."

It was his turn to glare at her for a change. "Quiet, you."

She picked up her plate of salad from the tray and began poking at it with her fork again. "The fact is, Simon, I *do* have a life to return to. Mr. Harrow has made a mistake."

"Why?"

"Excuse me?"

"What about your life is worth returning to?" Simon put his pencil down and folded his arms on the table.

"I—" She paused. "What are you asking me?"

"What makes your life so special that you need to go back to it? No one remembers you. If you had some dying family member in the hospital, no one cares anymore that you're not there to tend to them, because you do not exist. So, why would he make an exception for you when he's never made one before? Why does that world suffer because it no longer has you in it? Are you an artist?"

"No."

"Did you work for charity?"

"No."

"Or some sort of scientific field, perhaps?"

She stared at him flatly and felt like he had shot her in the chest again. She looked back down at her salad and murmured her answer. "I worked at a bank."

"Oh, yes, society has clearly been dealt a terrible and crushing blow. How will the checks be cashed now?" He threw up his hands in frustration.

"Stop it."

"Think of all the bills gone uncounted. Think of all the breakthroughs in change sorting we have denied humanity by—"

"Stop it!" She slammed her plate down onto the table. "I wasn't anybody. I wasn't anyone important! I wasn't a poet, or a painter, or anything! I used to take photographs for a living, but when I couldn't do that anymore because of my disease, I wound up sitting at a bank counter. But that doesn't mean I can roll over and just let this happen to me. I want to go *home*."

He stared at her silently for a long time. His voice was quieter and smoother when he talked again. "I am not trying to imply you are worthless. What I am trying to say to you, my dear Cora, is that your home might not be worth returning to. That this one is better."

"Why, because *you're* here?" She snorted.

He grinned. "In part." He picked up his pencil. "Regardless, approaching this argument from such an expected and trite direction will land you precisely nowhere. If you want to demand your freedom from the Faire, we need to come up with a better reason."

"I don't belong here. There has to be someone better suited to be here than me."

"Most certainly."

She picked up her fork and glowered.

"You seem to like to do this. You get angry when I agree with something you've said. Why is that?"

"Because you're insulting me."

"You insulted yourself. I was only agreeing with you. Why's that my fault?"

"I—" She snarled. He was right. Again. She slammed her fork down and got up from the table to get herself a glass of water.

"Why are you a mistake, then?"

"I'm not a performer. I've never been on stage once in my life."

"No one came here as a performer, except perhaps Magician. Everyone else learned it. And you will too. Why else?"

"I...I don't want to be here."

"Very few people came here willingly. Try again."

"Why are you doing this to me?" He was standing there and popping every balloon she had, just as she finished puffing each one up. She felt small again. She felt powerless. She hated it.

"I want to know how to approach this problem. Consider me your lawyer. I need to know how to spin this to the judge. And right now, I've got nothing to work with."

"My life is not nothing."

"Then tell me why it had value."

She turned to lob her glass at his head and found him smiling at her. Something about his expression was daring her to do it. Suddenly, she didn't want to give him the satisfaction. "I'd ask you to try to be nicer to me, but I'm pretty certain this is about as nice as you're capable of being."

"Correct."

Someone pounded on the door. "Simon, are you in there?" It was Ringmaster.

"Go away. I'm having sex," Simon shouted back.

"No, he is not!" Cora scrambled for the door and threw it open. The tall Turk looked befuddled at best.

"Why does everyone always want to ruin my fun?" The Puppeteer threw his hands up in frustration.

Ringmaster shook his head and clearly decided to skip over the whole thing. "You're late for your matinee, Simon."

"Oh. Hah. Yes. It's Saturday, isn't it?" Simon stood and strolled out of the train car, in absolutely no rush at all. "Very well. I'll be back when I'm finished, Cora dear. Do not write that letter before I get back."

Once Simon was gone, Ringmaster turned his attention to her. "Letter?"

"I want to slip something under Mr. Harrow's door. Since he won't talk to me in person." It wasn't a lie. It wasn't the whole story—that Mr. Harrow had started it—but she no longer had any proof. Simon had stolen the letter.

Simon's warning played in her head about not telling Turk anything about Mr. Harrow's note.

She knew Simon couldn't be trusted. But she knew she didn't trust anybody else yet, either.

Ringmaster nodded. "I don't know if it'll do you any good, Ms. Cora, but I wish you all the best of luck. And whatever Simon thinks he's going to get out of this—I don't think you should let him help you."

"I don't plan on it. He seems to do whatever the hell he wants. At least he'll be distracted for the next hour." She chuckled.

"Very true." Ringmaster went to leave but stopped as he thought of something. He turned back around. "Will you join us for dinner tonight at the cafeteria? I think everyone would like to meet you officially."

"When I'm not standing out in the rain like an idiot?"

He chuckled. "Exactly."

"Sure. Why not." *Maybe I'll be home by then. Or, more likely, I'll have nothing better to do.*

"Great. I'll see you then."

And with that, she was alone again. She shut the door and sat down at the kitchenette and took the pencil Simon had been using. He had brought a few sheets of paper. Pulling out a new page, she started at the top.

She made it as far as "*Dear Mr. Harrow*" before she stopped. Simon's words echoed through her mind. Damn him. Damn him to hell.

I'm already in hell.

She folded her arms on the table and put her head down on them. He was right. There was nothing in the world that made her special. Every time she tried to come up with an argument, it fell apart.

Everybody at Harrow Faire had a story, she was sure.

Everybody had a reason they shouldn't have been taken. Even Simon, the super-creep, had lost his fiancée. She tried to picture him as a normal man, and it was a comical image. She wanted to imagine him a sappy nerd. A little bit like his shadow had been. Wild and unpredictable. And dorky.

Why should *she* be spared when no one else had been? She pushed up from the table and headed out of the train car. She needed some fresh air to clear her head. She would wander the park for a little bit before coming back and writing the note before Simon returned to do it for her. She didn't know what she was going to write, but she sure as hell wasn't going to let him do it.

Halfway through her walk, she got a lemonade from a stand, thanked the nice semi-person who was working the counter—*it's so weird they're not real*—and then found a place to sit where she could watch people wander around the park but be away from the main path. It was on the edge of a small grassy section and under the shade of a tree.

Someone tapped her shoulder. Looking up, she jumped. "Oh, sh—" She put her hand to her chest. "Oh, fuck, you startled me." It wasn't every day she found a skull staring back at her. It was the Clown with his face that looked painted, but that Simon claimed was permanent.

He traced a finger down his cheek under his eye and frowned. He was apologizing.

"It's all right. You haven't scared me any worse than anybody else has in the past two days."

He smiled and clapped his hands excitedly.

She suddenly suspected that he was either putting on a great act, or that he was mute. "Would you like to join me?"

He nodded quickly. She scooted over and patted the ground next to her. He sat down eagerly, crossing his legs, and smiled out at the park. He was an average-height guy, and skinny. It was hard to tell how old he was. It was also hard to tell if the scraggly hair on his head that was a ghastly shade of green was real or a wig.

"It's nice to meet you. I'm Cora." She held out her hand to him. He shook it comedically fast. She laughed. "You're Clown, correct?"

He nodded excitedly again. He tapped his chest, then made a heart with his fingers, then pointed at her, and then pointed at the Faire itself.

"You love that I'm here?"

He clapped, his toothy-painted smile splitting wide to reveal his actual teeth. He seemed very excited that she caught on to his charades. She had always loved playing the game as a kid. Namely, because she always won. Her dad said she should have taken up a job as an interpreter if she had failed in photography, because she was good at reading body language.

"Thank you. I'm not so thrilled about it, myself."

He frowned. He rested his head on her shoulder. It was so utterly harmless a gesture that she allowed it. Even with the freaky-painted face, he wasn't nearly as creepy as Simon, and she usually didn't like clowns. She didn't hate them. They didn't scare her, she just never found them interesting or frightening in either direction.

"I'll be okay. I guess it took Simon being a complete douche to get me to realize I'm not the only one here who lost their whole life. If I don't think I'm special enough to be here, then I'm not special enough to be the only one allowed to leave."

He lifted his head from her shoulder and shook his head. He pointed at her and then cradled his hands together like he had something very precious inside of them.

"I'm not valuable."

He shook his head, as if arguing with her. He pointed to the gate and crossed his fingers into an X, and then pointed deeper into the Faire towards the staff-only area and gave her two bright thumbs up.

She struggled with that one for a moment before she finally put it together. "I'm not special to the outside world, but I am here?"

He nodded frantically then hugged her with both arms. She laughed and hugged him back. "Thank you, Clown. Thank you. I don't know that I believe you, but I appreciate the sentiment."

He squeezed her harder for a moment before letting go. He sat there next to her, smiling happily, and propped his head on her shoulder again.

She liked him. She didn't know why. She didn't know if she should. But she did. There was something peaceful about him. Something that she didn't expect at first glance. "Mr. Harrow wrote me a note last night."

Clown looked up, surprised, and put a hand over his mouth. He motioned for her to keep going with his other hand, like he was watching a movie.

She chuckled. "I asked to be set free. He said no."

Clown's face fell, and he let out a loud raspberry.

She smiled. At least he didn't seem to be panicked that Mr. Harrow had talked to her. She didn't trust Simon. She didn't trust Turk. But Clown seemed...harmless. Nice. She trusted him, and she wasn't quite sure why. "I've been debating what to write back to him but...I can't think of anything. I don't have a leg to stand on for an argument. But I don't know how to just roll over and accept that this is my fate now. I feel like I should be burning the place down. Or screaming at Mr. Harrow's door until I lose my voice."

He reached for her hand, and she let him take it. He was

clearly trying to comfort her. She appreciated it. "But it won't do any good, will it?"

He made a pop with his lips. She'd take that for a "no."

How stupid was it that coming from him, her being trapped here felt more final? That for some reason the weirdo with the permanent face paint carried the gavel. *Or the scythe.* She remembered Maggie, the Soothsayer's cards.

Everything began to click into place. The reading had been accurate. She had just been too stupid to see it at the time. Everything always made sense in hindsight. The Contortionist card. The Puppeteer. And...Clown. Death. Maggie had warned her that everything was going to come to an end. That it was her choice whether or not to accept it.

Her heart deflated. "I'm never going home, am I?"

He pointed his other hand toward the staff area again.

"I know, I know...this is my home now. I just don't want it to be."

He squeezed her hand again for a second.

"Doesn't mean I have to like it. Am I really going to have to put up with Simon for the rest of eternity?"

Clown raised one butt cheek and let out a loud fake fart. That cracked her up.

"Oh, I see how it is. Even the mime is making fun of me now."

Clown shot to his feet and almost tripped over himself.

Looking up, Simon was leaning up against the trunk of the tree with that ever-present sadistic smile. "Hello, Cora. Hello, Clown."

Clown stuck his tongue out at Simon. He continued to make a series of bizarre and insulting faces at the Puppeteer like he was an eight-year-old. Cora tried not to laugh for a few seconds before she finally gave in.

"Don't take his side." Simon reached down for her hand. "Come, Cora. Let's go. We have work to do."

"I like his side. Fart noises and all. At least he makes me laugh."

Clown now had his back turned to them, bent over at the waist, and was slapping his ass cheeks with his hands. That sent Cora into stitches.

"You're encouraging him, you realize," Simon complained.

"Good!" Cora hadn't laughed that hard since she had arrived. And god damn, it felt cathartic.

Simon stepped over her and gestured. Clown made a loud *gack* noise as he was turned end-over-end. Suddenly, he was in the grass on his back, gripping his throat tightly. She watched as something thin and invisible dug into his neck, drawing blood. Simon's strings.

"Stop it!" Cora shot to her feet and yanked on Simon's arm. "Leave him alone."

"It won't be the first time I've torn his limbs off." His face was a mask of anger. He sneered down at the Clown. "Won't be the last. Mock me now, you cretin."

"He was just trying to cheer me up. Leave him alone!" She yanked on Simon's arm again.

With a heavy sigh, Simon dropped his hands. Clown scrambled back up and ran away without even another glance at them. Annoyance and frustration left him like the flick of a light switch, and he turned to her with that same sadistic, overly pleased smile. "I could think of another way to cheer you up. Give me a kiss, Cora dear."

"No."

"Suit yourself. Come, we have a letter to write."

"I changed my mind."

He blinked. "You...what?"

"I'm not going to write him a letter. Not yet."

"Why not?" He looked so disappointed it was almost funny. Almost.

She'd have laughed if her heart wasn't broken. She took a step away from him. "Because you were right, as much as I loathe to admit it. I have nothing to say that he'd pay any attention to. Until I can think of something good, I'll save my chance. I might only get the one shot at it." She turned away from him and hopped off the little lifted area. She had every intention of leaving him behind. "That, and I don't want to have to spend any more time with you than I need to."

"At least you admitted I was right." He was beside her. It seemed getting rid of him wasn't going to ever be as easy as just walking away. "What are you going to do with your afternoon, then? Mope around the park, cuddling with Clown?"

"I don't know."

"Why not train for your first performance?"

"I'm not ever going to perform."

"I think you underestimate how boring it can get here. I suppose you could pester Bertha for some of her books. But all she tends to read is *romance*." He stuck out his tongue. "Not much to do to pass the time except drink, screw, and perform on stage. At least let's see what you're capable of. Let's find out how far our new Contortionist can bend, huh?"

"And why would I ever let you help me?"

"Because, dear, I'm not going to leave you alone. You're my responsibility, and as I said, I plan to keep you *very* close. Do you think I'll let anyone else train you? Please." He scoffed.

"I hate you. You realize that, right?"

"Everyone hates me. That's nothing new." He slung his arm around her shoulder and tugged her into his side. "Come, now. A few hours of work. And then you can wander off to dinner with the others and ramble about how much of a fiend and a terrible lout I am."

"Please stop touching me." She pushed out of his grasp. He let her go and shrugged as if to say it was her loss.

"Sit in your train car and count as the seconds tick by, or explore what your newfound abilities have gifted you. What'll it be?"

She had to admit she *was* curious. More than a little bit, if she were honest. "Whatever. Fine. Just this once."

"Fantastic! I win again, as usual." He smiled up at the sky. If he were a bird, his feathers would be puffed up. He looked so damn proud of himself.

She shoved him, and he staggered away for a step before coming back, still grinning in triumph. "Fine. But you don't have to always look so fucking smug about it."

"I suppose, then, that when we finally fuck, I'll have to be careful to not look smug about that, too." He lowered his head to her like he was going to try to steal a kiss.

She hit him upside the head. Hard.

"Ow!" Simon rubbed where she'd made contact. "What was that for?" he whined.

"Why not?" She whacked him in the arm. "Do I need a reason?"

"Yes! Why're you abusing me?" He swatted at her hands.

She shoved him again. "It's fun."

He jumped away from her, pouting comically. "Everyone is so mean to me."

She laughed. He was so terrifying. She had seen what he could do to Clown. She knew his strings were dangerous and were capable of far more damage than what he had ever done to her, yanking her along beside him. But he was also witty. And there was an odd charm to his manic wildness and his quick expressions. He could rocket between looking like a harmless cherub to the literal devil with the flick of a switch.

She remembered his kiss. Something coiled inside her, far more treacherous than he was. She smacked him in the arm again.

"Ow! Now you should just feel bad."

No. She didn't feel bad. Not in the slightest.

And she couldn't find the strength to be concerned about that.

10

WALKING into Simon's tent gave Cora the chills. The red and black stripes that seemed made for him made her feel like she was sticking her head into the maw of a monster. She couldn't decide if he was harmless or dangerous.

He's both. Which is impossible. But here he is, and that's the problem.

Or maybe it was the way Simon's shadow was arced up on the wall over her, looming with an altogether far-too-pleased and far-too-twisted smile on his face. The shadow creeped her out. Even with what had happened in her dream, he made her skin crawl. She took a step away from him, even if she was fairly certain he couldn't touch her. Not here, at any rate.

She looked up at the shadow. "Hi."

He waved at her, his smile widening at her greeting. She remembered how lonely and desperate he seemed in her dream. "Next time you feel like invading my dreams, hands off, okay?"

The shadow's expression fell, wilting like a cartoon

plant. It almost looked like he was going to cry. If shadows could cry.

"Don't look at me like that." She felt like she had just kicked a puppy. "You can't just break into people's dreams and start manhandling them. It's not right."

The shadow just kept looking at her tearfully.

She sighed and looked up at the roof of the tent. "You can visit me in my dreams. But we'll play checkers or something." When she looked back at the shadow, he was cheerfully clapping his hands, cackling in silent happiness.

"Why are you nice to him?"

She jumped at the sound of Simon's voice. He was standing right behind her, inches away from her shoulder, his head tilted close to hers. She took a step away to put some distance between them. "He's just lonely."

"So...if I came crying at your feet, begging for the gift of your touch, whimpering like a dog, you'd say yes?" He smiled thinly. "I think I might be able to manage that."

"Knock it off, Simon." She went farther into the tent. Really, just because she couldn't stand the way he was looking at her. It did things to her that she didn't want. Things she didn't want to deal with. Things she didn't want to admit were real.

"I never thought I'd be jealous of my own fractured psyche, but here we are. Oh, how the world seeks to debase me at every turn. Ah, well." He headed past her toward the stage, humming and whistling to himself. "Don't worry, I sent all my dolls away. I know how they trouble you, and I don't want you to feel any more nervous around me than you need to."

"Right. Sure. Thanks." She stopped halfway down the aisle, remembering the last time she was here in his tent.

She shuddered. *They're all monsters in their own right. They just hide it better. So, what does that make me?* "Simon?"

"Yes, cupcake?" He turned to look at her with that effortless smile.

"Am I going to turn into a monster?" She rubbed her hand up her arm, feeling awkward in asking the question.

"Hum?" He tilted his head curiously. "What do mean?"

"Like you. Or...there was a guy with goat's eyes. Like Clown. Or like those conjoined twins I saw. Am I going to—am I going to change?" She moved a few steps forward again and stopped. Mostly to avoid the shadow that was still lurking near her on the wall, watching her with its weird spiral eyes and it-would-be-goofy-if-it-weren't-so-pointy smile. "I don't mean to call you a monster. But you kind of are."

"Oh, my darling." He sat down on the edge of the stage, dangling his long legs off the front. He didn't look upset in the slightest. "You have already changed. That's why I brought you here. To show you the gift you have been given by the Faire. And yes, it's hardly as spectacular or as dangerous as mine, but it certainly has its benefits." He grinned wickedly. "I can think of a few."

If she'd had something to throw at him, she would have lobbed it at his head. "I'd tell you to go fuck yourself again, but as I have part of your 'seity,' I suppose that's exactly what you're trying to do. Knock it off."

He sighed dramatically and lay back on the stage, sprawling his arms out wide. He collapsed there like he had been shot. "My hopes and dreams are dashed. Dashed."

"I know you don't like me, Simon. You're putting up with me because you're trying to find a way to eat me. Maybe you're lonely. Maybe you're bored. Maybe you're just a horny douchebag, I don't know. But it's very clear the only reason you're keeping me near is because you don't want anybody touching what you think is 'yours.'" She didn't know where she worked up the nerve to rant at him, but now that she'd started, she found she wasn't going to stop until she said what she thought. "I don't belong to you. Not now, not ever. Especially when the only reason you want me is because you want yourself."

He lay there silently for a long moment. Finally, when she was beginning to wonder if he had passed out or died, he spoke. "You're right."

She winced. She had back-handedly insulted herself, saying there was no other reason he could possibly want her. But he was only agreeing with what she said. She couldn't very well hold that against him.

"Or at least, you would be if this were any normal situation, on any normal day. But it isn't. I enjoy talking with you, cupcake. If I didn't, I wouldn't wish to do it so frequently." He scratched at his chest over his heart. "I dislike this situation greatly, and it troubles me that I don't hate you."

"You're upset that you don't despise me?"

"Very."

"You're a piece of work, Simon Waite."

He snickered. "Write that on my tombstone." He sat back up, his legs still dangling over the edge. "Come here, Cora dear."

"No."

He rolled his eyes and gestured. She felt the strings snap around her. Her limbs moved like they were out of her control once more, and she walked up to him, glaring a hole through him the entire time.

He brought her to stand between his knees, her thighs

touching the lip of the stage. It was intimate. It was personal. Her face bloomed in warmth, and she couldn't tell if it was out of embarrassment, rage, or if she was...excited to be so close to him again. She blamed it on the first two. "Simon, cut this shit out."

"No. I need you to listen to me and to focus, and I can't have you running off or trying to hit me with something." He rested one of his hands on her hip and the other against her jawline, his thumb on her cheek. His fingers were just touching the hair behind her ear. She fought back a shiver.

"Simon, let me go. Now."

"Not until you hear me. *Really* hear me." He leaned forward, his face now only a few inches from hers. For a moment, she thought he might kiss her again. Something twisted in her stomach. Something traitorous and wrong.

He watched her for a moment, his eyes barely visible through the two-toned sunglasses. "Everything I've done since Mr. Harrow chose you to join us has been to help you."

"Bullshit."

"I convinced you to come out of the rain, didn't I? I put a bullet in your heart, but I did it to make you accept your new reality. I insisted on writing that letter for you, so that you might realize you had nothing to say. You're here, now, in this tent with me, so I can show you how your body is no longer the one you came with when you first stepped through those doors. You aren't human anymore. And perhaps when I use my strings to bend you into wonderful and bizarre ways, you might understand." He smiled. "I'm helping you because I *want* to."

"You're only trying to help yourself."

"Then I'd leave you to the affairs of others. You'd find them far less jarring than you find me."

"Fine. But you're helping me in the worst ways possible."

"Have we met?" His smile split into a grin. His hand lingered at her cheek. He stroked his thumb over her cheek slowly, back and forth. Her face was still too warm. "I think I might like you a little, Cora. I certainly want you. But I did not expect to enjoy you."

"Liar."

He huffed a laugh. "Maybe."

She tried desperately to change the subject. "Were you always like this?"

"Afraid you might lose your mind like me? Become a madwoman like the Great and Terrible Simon? Yes. I was always a little...eh...fractured. The Faire only finished the job. We are chosen for the roles we take because we are close to the aspect we represent. The role of the Puppeteer is to represent sin, temptation, wickedness, and fear. I am both the chains of bondage and the joy of breaking them. I was a bit of a hedonist before I came here. And on the verge of being a lunatic."

"And what am I supposed to be?"

"The Contortionist is..." He chuckled. "As far away from me as one can get, perhaps. New beginnings, creativity, and spontaneity. Bravery. Hope."

"I'm not brave. All I've done is panic since I got here."

"Is that so?" He was still stroking her cheek. She didn't know when she stopped being afraid of his touch. All it left behind now was warmth, and a strange electricity that crackled through her. He hummed thoughtfully. "I am not so sure. You came here to save your friend, knowing it would be your own demise. You have stood up to me at every opportunity. I think you are not as weak as you have come to believe."

He moved to kiss her, and she stalled for time. "Do you miss your family?"

He pulled his head back, surprised at her question. "Hm?" He thought about it for a moment. "No. Nor do I miss the man I was. I enjoy what I've become. That is another thing you should come to accept. That all of us here *like* what we are."

The scent of an antique store and old-style cologne wafted over her again. His touch was warm against her cheek, and the fingers of the hand on her hip were toying with her shirt. It was all too much. She wanted to slap him.

And part of her wanted to kiss him. Or wish he'd do it for her.

No! No, no, no, no! You're lonely, you're scared, and he'd be handsome if he weren't a murdering, lying, manipulative monster. "I shouldn't be here. You're trouble."

"That I am. That I very much am. But I think you like a bit of trouble, don't you, Cora Glass?" He traced his hand up to her hair, combing his fingers through it. "And that will never change. Not even you could manage that, impressive as you are."

Was that a compliment? He was probably just making fun of her again. He took a strand of her hair and twirled it through his fingers, wrapping it around them before letting it go.

Her words were little more than a whisper. "Let go of me, Simon." Now she wanted him to release his strings for two reasons. Indignancy was the first. The second was that if he went any farther, she wasn't sure if she'd tell him to stop.

And that terrified her.

"Do you still want to practice? I'd love to see what you can do. I'm sure you must be curious."

She was, even if she probably shouldn't be. Everyone kept calling her "the Contortionist" and she couldn't imagine being anything of the sort. She was always bendy, thanks to her disease, and she had no problem sitting in a split. But that didn't make her a contortionist.

"Please?" He smiled sweetly at her again. "I think it would help settling things in your mind to realize that you are no longer human. You are no longer the Cora you were two days ago—you're something more."

"Fine..." He could force the matter if he wanted to. She supposed she should be happy he wasn't just yanking her around constantly. "No strings."

"But—"

"No. No strings."

He sighed, disappointed. "You're no fun. Fine. We'll do this the boring way." He gestured, and she felt the tight, mostly invisible wires around her let go. She took a step away from him and out of his hands.

Simon stood and went backstage. He came back with what looked like a shipping blanket, or a cotton drop cloth. He folded it up and put it on the wood like a pad. He motioned for her to come closer.

She noticed that his shadow was cast high up onto the wall, and it was clapping excitedly. Silently, at least. *At least that damn thing can't talk in the waking world.* "Shut up, you fucking Peter Pan reject," she said to it.

Its expression fell, and then it cackled silently. When it stopped laughing, it was smiling at her with the ends of its mouth curled around like the Grinch.

"Yelling at him doesn't do much good." Simon motioned her over again. "It's best to just ignore him. That's what I do."

"Why is your shadow all messed up? You said it's your subconscious, but...why is it like that?"

"I'm not sure. He just showed up one day. Annoying, but effective at scaring people. Come, now, Cora. Focus. We don't have all day."

Finally peeling her eyes off the eerie and ghastly thing, she walked up to the pad and stood on it. "Now what?"

"We'll start with a back bend." He knelt on the ground next to her. "Shift a leg a little bit behind you, balance your weight on it, and bend back as far as you can."

"Why're you kneeling?"

"To spot you. To catch you if you fall. Can't have you cracking your head on the stage. You'll just yell at me some more."

"No, I wouldn't."

"Yes, you would."

Yeah, she would.

He put a hand on the back of her thigh, and she jolted in surprise. He grinned at her reaction but had the decency not to say anything about it. "Go on. Try."

With a long-suffering sigh, she did as he instructed. She put her right leg back a little and bent backward. She waited for the pain. The searing agony. But there wasn't any. She hesitated in disbelief.

"Keep going," he urged. "You are not the broken creature you were. I promise you."

"I'm going to fall." She wanted to find a reason—any reason—to stop. This wasn't normal. *This wasn't natural.* And it meant she also wasn't either of those things anymore.

"I have you." He spread his fingers where he was touching her on the back of her thigh. "Don't be scared."

"I'm not." *I'm terrified.*

She swallowed thickly. But a large part of her, the louder

part of her, wanted to know what was at the end of the dark tunnel in front of her. It was like she was walking into the skull-faced "Dark Path" at the entry gate all over again. This time, she had already gone past the point of no return.

She kept bending backward, her arms now up over her head, carefully shifting her weight in her hips forward to keep from toppling over.

"Good, yes, that's it...more."

More? She was already almost bent in half! "I—"

"Does it hurt?"

"N—no—"

"Then keep going."

She turned her head to him, now looking at him upside down. He was watching her earnestly. There wasn't, for a change, an ounce of sadism in him. She wasn't quite sure what his expression was. Eager, maybe? Excited about something? She decided she didn't want to flip over that rock and see what was crawling around underneath.

Her abs and her quads in her legs felt tight. Tight, but not sore. Like this was just a normal stretch. She kept going.

Her shoulders touched the back of her legs. Her palms reached the fabric pad. "Oh—oh, God. Ooohh, this isn't okay!"

Simon let out a slow breath. "You're all right, Cora. Are you in any pain?"

"No..."

"Then keep going."

"Keep going? Where the fuck else am I supposed to go?" She glared at him. Well, as best she could while entirely upside down.

"Reach your arm between your legs. Pull your head through your knees."

"Fuck you!"

"Don't tempt me right now, Cora."

Something about his words were dark. Thick. He meant it. She shivered and tried not to imagine how she must look to him right now. But it wasn't disgust that curled in her stomach like snakes. "I can't do it."

"You can't, or you won't? Trust me."

"I don't think I'm ever going to trust you."

"Well, fine. Be that way." He chuckled. His hand stayed on her thigh, giving her a sense of balance. His fingers pressed into her just a little. "But try anyway."

"I'm going to fall over."

"No, you won't."

Arguing with him was pointless. She let out a small, wavering breath and reached an arm *through her legs the wrong way around.* She let out a wail. "This is so wrong!"

"Not from my perspective."

"Shut up!"

He cackled. "Now, you're going to have to shift your weight off your hand again. Move your hips forward." He moved his hand to the front of her thigh.

She'd yell at him for feeling her up, but if he wasn't there, she'd likely eat the stage in the worst possible way. She did as he instructed, shifting her weight farther out to balance carefully on her feet again. Threading her arm through her legs, she...just...kept going.

Her shoulder was now between her thighs. She looked —well—up. It was only when her head was between her legs, looking at the world right-side-up, that she felt like she couldn't go any farther. Mostly because her bones existed. It seemed like her muscles and tendons were perfectly fine with doing something impossible.

Simon was silent. That wasn't like him. When she

turned her head, he was watching her with a strained expression.

"You okay?"

"I'm fine." He looked away, rubbed a hand over his face, and cleared his throat. "You are far more talented than Hernandez ever was. But talent is not skill, and you need practice before you can join my act."

"I'm not going to be in your act."

"We'll argue about this another time." He pressed his fingers again into her thigh. "Now, do the same thing as you did to get here, only in reverse."

She was more than happy to be done feeling like a human pretzel. Even if it didn't hurt, and it felt kind of good to stretch muscles she didn't even know she had, there was something about the way Simon's voice had changed that was making her feel strange. It wasn't that he was making her uncomfortable. It was just *wrong.*

When her hands touched the ground again, she shifted her feet to try to change her balance.

"Stop that."

"Huh?" She turned her head to look at him. He was glaring off somewhere else.

"Not you." He glowered at whoever he was yelling at. "Stop that at once. She'll get mad, and I'll end up being clocked with a frying pan again, and it'll be *your* fault!"

Turning her head the other way to see what he was yelling at, she expected one of his dolls had crept into the tent. She didn't know if what she saw was better or worse than that.

His shadow was next to hers where it was cast on the stage wall. His shadow had a wide, overly excited, lascivious grin on its face. But that wasn't all it was doing.

It was bad enough to have his shadow petting hers the

other day. It was bad enough to have his shadow trying to cuddle hers. What it was doing now was far worse than that. She didn't watch long enough to get the details, but she knew it was touching her own shadow in all the wrong ways.

She squeaked. "Holy fuck!" She tried to stand up but did so way too quickly and in the wrong direction and toppled over.

Right onto Simon.

He caught her in his arms, and they wound up sprawled on the stage. He laughed. "Well, hello, cupcake."

"Get—get off—let me go!" She shoved against him and scrambled away. He let her go without a fuss, lifting his hands in a sign of surrender.

"I didn't do anything."

"You—your shadow—"

"I told you, he's harmless. Annoying, but harmless."

"But he—it—you—"

"She, they, the, what else are we forgetting?" He stood and brushed himself off. Offering her a hand up, she shook her head and got up on her own. He shrugged it off. "He's an irritation. And he gets me into trouble." He glared at the shadow on the wall, who was only laughing silently, its eyes squinted in little upside-down U's. It was a cartoon. A creepy, terrifying, unsettling cartoon.

She watched as the shadow's head turned into that of a cartoon wolf and howled up at an invisible moon.

Now she could add "horny" to the list.

"I'm leaving." She hopped off the stage. "You and your shadow can go screw each other. Get it out of your systems."

"Now, that's a mental image. Can't say I've ever considered trying. I suppose that would be the culmination of all my narcissistic fantasies, wouldn't it?"

She rolled her eyes. It was a funny retort. She wouldn't give him the benefit of admitting it.

Simon sat on the edge of the stage, smiling like everything had gone exactly to plan. "I'll see you at dinner. Perhaps we can practice again tomorrow, hm?"

She flipped him off over her shoulder as she left the tent to the tune of his sharp laughter.

11

SIMON WATCHED Cora leave the tent and was glad she didn't notice how he had stuffed his hand into his pocket when he got up from the stage. Or, more specifically, *why* he had stuck his hand into his pocket. He grunted in dismay as he let go of the offending part of his body.

And he glared at the other offending part of him, the irritating shadow on the wall. "You nearly ruined everything." He pointed a finger and snarled at his shadow, who was trying to look innocent. Too bad nothing about him, especially not that disembodied part of his psyche, could ever pretend to be anything of the sort. "You can't just randomly molest her. You know she's...sensitive about that kind of thing, for one. And two, it's simply bad manners. We can be a lot of things, you and I, but *manners* are key!"

His shadow frowned then glared at him accusatorially.

As if all this was *his* fault.

"What did you expect? How was I meant to react, seeing her like that? I have a body. I can't help it. You have no such excuse." He stormed away from the reflection of himself and into the workshop at the back of his tent. Slumping down onto the stool in front of his bench, he pulled his sunglasses off and tossed them aside. He barely noticed wearing them anymore, but it was nice to see normally from time to time, not through the tinted lenses. He rubbed his hands over his face.

Cora. She was so right about him. Yes, he had only started following her because of his stolen seity. About needing to protect her from the others getting too close. And that was still true. But he deeply enjoyed sparring with her, even if her insults were crude. Clever, but crude. She was a fiery thing.

But watching her...

He had wanted her before. He had hoped it would be a quick itch to scratch. One brought on by the fact that she had a part of him beating inside her body. He was drawn to her because she was him, even just a little. It was narcissism in its purest form; she was right about that.

When he'd started pursuing her, he hoped he could just get a quick rut and then he'd be able to focus again. That it was a one-time, forbidden-fruit kind of ordeal. Once he had her, he'd get bored, and he could stop focusing on her.

Like he always did.

If she'd just let me have her, just the once, I could stop thinking about her.

She claimed not to trust him. But that wasn't quite true, was it? She pressed into his hand as she bent into that impossible position. She trusted him not to let her fall. And when she had fallen, he had caught her. It had felt so good to have her in his arms.

Brief as it was.

Struggling as she was.

His body had betrayed him the moment she began to twist backward. Watching the lines of her body move in ways that were both sensual and bizarre had triggered a desperate need inside him. One he couldn't remember ever feeling before.

It wasn't like a circus was short on women willing to do strange things with their bodies. He had watched Amanda perform in her lyra and on the silks. He had watched her act a thousand times as she twirled around in ways that were ostensibly beautiful. Even Donna, as she flipped through the air, had an undeniable grace.

But never, not once, did anything affect him like this.

Like her.

Like Cora.

He rubbed his fingers over his eyes and pinched the bridge of his nose, silently ordering that offensive part of him to sit down and shut up. But the image of her, twisted up in front of him, *trusting him even just a little,* wouldn't let him go.

"Father? Where have you been?"

He snarled at the doll that came toward him. His frustration turned to fury. He reached his hand out and snapped his wrist to the side. The offending creation shattered and toppled to the ground in pieces, shredded in an instant by the threads that answered his command.

He could tear this place apart at the seams if he wanted to. The whole circus existed in peace because he allowed it!

Who was she to do this to him? No one!

She was dangerous. Worse than he was. Because if she controlled him—any part of him—what did that make her? *If I am a god in this place and I kneel at her feet, what is she?*

The other dolls shrank back into the shadows. He had been neglecting them. Ignoring them. He had been too busy with his newest distraction. She should have been his from the start! She should have been like the others, a doll—obedient, compliant, supple.

Instead, he was the one compelled.

He was the one on strings.

He had to have her. Just *once.* Just once, he had to convince her to let him taste her. Then his obsession would end. He knew it. One sampling would shatter the fantasy in his mind. He would know she was just another *normal* girl, like all the rest, boring and trite.

Like every other time he had ever had an infatuation. It always burst like a dream with the first light of dawn. She would be the same.

She just had to be *difficult,* didn't she?

Why was his life so hard all the time?

He thumped his head on the table and snarled in frustration. If he didn't know the pain would be remarkably outstanding, he'd ball up his fist and pummel the part of him that had seemingly taken over his rational mind.

Perhaps it was the way her cheeks grew pink when he touched her. When he had her so close to him. The fear in her eyes had wavered as he ran his hand through her hair. It was so soft, those long, dark, curling waves. They tangled so wonderfully around his fingers. She smelled so good. She felt so warm. He wanted her there against him in the darkness, wanted to be between her legs. His imagination ran wild, picturing her around him. He wanted to twist her into those strange and erotic shapes at his whim.

Oh, how sinful it would be to watch her face grow flush and hear her whimper his name in the shadows of his tent. How he wanted to feel her in his hands again, trusting him, when she trusted no one else.

He howled and thumped his head harder against the table. "Stop it, stop it, stop it, stop it, *stop it!*" Pounding his knuckles into both of his temples, the pain lancing through his head successfully drove those images away. He sat up and pulled in a sharp breath through his nose. He needed fresh air. And a cold shower. Yes. That'd fix the problem. Maybe a jump in the lake.

Or a stiff drink.

His shadow was on the wall next to him, a knowing and satisfied smile on his face. Like a sated cat who had just eaten and was basking in a sunbeam. Growling, he picked up a pot of ink and hurled it at the apparition. He knew it wouldn't do any good. But it gave him some kind of satisfaction as the jar shattered against the wall and sent the black substance oozing down the surface. He liked breaking things.

His shadow soundlessly laughed at him.

Like everyone was going to laugh at him.

I'm acting like a lovesick child.

I need to fix this before it gets worse.

CORA HEADED BACK to her train car. She wanted to shower, change, and take a moment to breathe. Simon's creepy and perverted shadow was the least of what was bothering her. She crossed in front of Mr. Harrow's train car on her path and stopped to look up at the door. She couldn't tell if the lights were on or off in the afternoon sun.

She didn't know what to say to him. But she still felt the need to try. Shaking her head, she focused on the task at hand. She kicked a few pebbles in the pathway as she wandered along. Realizing that her shoulders were up by her ears, she forced herself to try to relax.

There was no way she should have been able to bend

that way. Simon had wanted to show her she wasn't human anymore, and it worked. Stepping into her train car, she shut the door behind herself and opened a few of the windows to let the breeze in. She kicked off her shoes and looked down at her feet.

Out of curiosity, she bent forward. And kept going. And kept going until her shoulders were on her legs. She wove through until her arms were on the other side of her legs. It should have been fun—or funny—but she felt defeated. Straightening back up, she stretched her arms behind her back. Farther than they should have been able to go. Nothing hurt. Nothing was sore.

Heading to the train car's bathroom, she stripped off her clothes and ran the shower. She climbed in once it was hot and went about the familiar and simple action of cleaning herself. She hadn't broken a sweat. But she still felt wrong.

Simon should make her skin crawl. She should be disgusted by him. He was a fiend, he was dangerous, and he had tried to kill her. And he had shot her. And he had manipulated her. And chances were, he still was.

And when he touched her, he made something twist in her stomach like snakes. He took her breath away. There was something captivating and alluring about him, and when he had her in his arms, she had wanted to feel him pull her closer.

That, combined with her newfound...weird superpower, she just needed a break. Flipping off the shower when she was done, she dried off. Wrapping the towel around herself, she rustled through her clothing. What she really wanted to wear was a pair of Converse, some jeans, and a tank top.

And that was exactly what she found.

They weren't hers—she didn't recognize them from her

closet—but they were definitely the same kind of things she used to own.

The Faire provided whatever she wanted; wasn't that what people said? *Except my freedom. Everything except that.*

I'm an animal in a cage, and it's making my enclosure as natural as possible to keep me happy. Now she felt bad for all the tigers and lions she had always been so excited to see in the local zoo.

It really was a zoo, wasn't it? They were the animals, drawing in the patrons to tap on the glass and pay their fee of a bit of their souls to see the freaks. She dressed, brushed her hair, and checked the clock. It was getting close to dinner, and she figured the others probably ate in shifts.

She didn't want to go. But she was hungry. And being alone with her thoughts was dangerous. Especially because Simon was likely to jump out at her at any point. He obviously didn't respect doors or privacy.

Pulling on a light spring coat, she instinctually reached for her phone. It was weird not to have it, after being so dependent on it for so long. She wanted to call Trent or Emily. She wanted to text Lisa and see how her kids were doing. She wanted to call her mom. Or to check Facebook, or Twitter, or whatever.

But that world was gone to her now. Her lack of a phone was just the symptom of the truth; there was no going back.

Not unless she could convince Mr. Harrow to let her go. But how?

Her thoughts swirled around that problem as she made her way to the tent that served as the cafeteria. She stepped in shyly. She didn't know what to expect. She saw a small pack of people sitting at a long family-style table, laughing and chatting with each other. She recognized Aaron and Bertha the Bearded Woman, but none of the others.

Abort. Abort!

She turned around to flee.

"Cora!"

Damn it!

"C'mon over."

She turned to see Aaron waving at her. Sheepishly, her hands tucked into her pockets, she gave up trying to hide. It was too late. The table had a smattering of people sitting at it, each of them looking like a caricature. A skinny man with a ridiculous curly handlebar mustache. A dark-skinned man with short dark hair and an award-winning smile. And a man with slicked-back blond hair and mismatched eyes. One was blue, and the other was brown.

"Uh. Hi," she greeted them shyly as she approached.

"Sit!" Aaron scooted over and patted the bench next to him. She obeyed, not knowing what else to do. Everyone was staring at her. She wanted to hide under the bench. Now that she knew how bendy she was, she kind of wanted to fold herself into some small dark crevice and stay there.

"Let me introduce you to some more of the Family. You already know Bertha," Aaron said as he pointed to the bearded woman, who smiled at the introduction.

"Good to see you again, Cora." Bertha's smile grew a little sad. "I wish it wasn't like this."

"Me too," Cora mumbled but smiled back at her.

Aaron continued with his introduction. "This is Pierre." He motioned to the little guy with the curly mustache. "This is Bruce." The man with the beaming smile waved casually in greeting. "And this is Louis." The blond man with the mismatched eyes smiled and nodded in greeting.

The little man with the silly mustache smiled. "Hello, Cora my dear. Welcome to our Faire." His French accent was so thick that, coupled with his mustache and his name, it made her snicker. Pierre pursed his lips. "What is funny?"

Bruce laughed loudly and whacked Pierre on the back. "You are, Frog. You're a breathing cliché."

"I am not." Pierre folded his arms over his chest in disgust.

"Yeah, you kinda are." Aaron laughed. He looked back to Cora. "Anyway. Pierre is our juggler, Louis is our Magician, and Bruce is our firebreather, sword-swallower, nail-into-the-head kind of man."

Cora looked at Bruce and wrinkled her nose. "You can put a nail into your head?"

"Anybody can. It fits. It just feels weird the first few times." Bruce smiled and fished his straw out of his drink. "Wanna see?"

"No!" Everyone shouted at once.

"Losers." Bruce stuck his straw back into his glass of ice and what looked like cola. "All of you."

"Be a dear, Brucey," Bertha started. She reached a heavily tattooed arm over to pat him on the back. "Get Cora some pasta and a drink, would you?"

"Sure, sure. Anything for the new gal." Bruce pushed up from the bench and headed toward the back of the tent where there was a buffet table set up with food. It did smell good, whatever it was. She hoped they had more of the garlic bread she had scored for lunch.

"How're you settling in?" Pierre asked.

Cora smiled and looked off toward the rest of the park. The man's accent was still ludicrous, but the humor of it was starting to be less overwhelming. "It's all a bit much to handle. Every second I feel like I'm on the brink of a nervous breakdown. Like, any second I'm about to burst into hysterical tears."

"You're handling it great, then." Bertha chuckled. "I spent four days in my train car. Wouldn't come out. Threw things at anybody who came near. I didn't used to be like this, y'know." She tugged on her beard. "But we all get dealt a different shit hand in this scenario, don't we?"

"I suppose."

"I heard your friends were here yesterday," Louis said to her. She looked over at him and found him smiling at her mildly. Like he truly understood. "I lost my younger brother in the same way. I watched him forget all that we had done together...and turn around like I was a lunatic on the street. I'm sorry you had to go through that."

"Thanks. I..." She paused. "It hurts. But it'd be selfish to think I'm the only one here who's suffered that loss. Thanks again."

"Anytime you want to talk, we're here for you." Louis sipped his drink. It looked like his was a glass of wine. "We're Family, after all."

"I'm still not sure how to feel about that," Cora replied.

"You'll get used to it, sweetie." Bertha twirled some pasta around her fork. "We all do. You'll grow to like it. I heard Simon has taken a shine to you. That bastard takes a shine to nobody. My condolences."

"He's part of the reason I think I'm going to snap at any point," Cora admitted darkly. "I think he feels like he owns me because he was forced to make me like this. He won't... he doesn't leave me alone."

Being alone right now is worse. But maybe it doesn't have to be him. Maybe these people would keep me company.

The memory of Simon's voice, low and husky, dripping like wax, as he urged her to keep going when she was on his stage. The feeling of his hand on her thigh, squeezing just a little bit. She shivered despite herself.

Aaron, mistaking her shudder for horror, and not her horror at what it really meant, rubbed his hand up and down her back. "Poor gal. Life here is hard enough to accept without his stupid grin hovering over you at every turn. You ever need somewhere to hide, you come to my boxcar, eh? Number eighteen."

"Oh, Aaron, let the paint dry on her door before you start trying to get into her pants." Bertha wagged her fork at the Barker accusatorially.

"I am not trying to get in her pants!"

"You are too." Pierre rolled his eyes.

"I mean, I wouldn't say no." Aaron smiled at Cora. "What do you think?"

Cora stammered. "I—no, I mean, I'm flattered, but no—"

"You want Jackie instead?" Aaron lifted his drink and took a huge glug out of it. It was an old-school glass Coke bottle. "He's a nice boy. Sweet and gentle. Or we could go all at once."

"Whoa, what?" Cora scooched away from him. "What the hell is wrong with you?"

Bertha laughed. "Don't worry about it. Aaron is just the resident slut. He puts Ludwig to shame. He likes to rope Jackie-boy into his debauchery. Well. He puts Ludwig to shame in the quantity department. Not in the size department."

"Hey!" Aaron tossed a piece of his roll at Bertha. "I've never had a single complaint. Not once."

Cora laughed despite herself. "I'm flattered, I guess, but no. I'm good, thanks." She shook her head. Simon wasn't kidding about the Family being inbred. "I'm not much into, um...that kind of thing."

"Shame. You'll get there." He smiled, seemingly perfectly unharmed by her rejection. "Immortality is boring, and there's only so many of us. You can dally with the guests if you prefer to keep things simple."

Cora picked at the edge of the table where a bit of a splinter was sticking out of it. Everything here looked well-loved and old. "Nothing about this place is simple."

"Wise words, sweetie." Bertha popped a meatball into her mouth and talked as she chewed. "Wise words."

Bruce came back with a plate of spaghetti and meatballs, and—yay for small favors—more garlic bread. "I didn't know what you like to drink. I guessed root beer."

Cora smiled at him. "Root beer is great, thank you."

He set the tray down for her, and she happily dug into the food. It was good. It made her think of home. Spaghetti with meat sauce was her lazy, go-to dinner for one. Then, when she inevitably made too much, she could stick the other half in the fridge as leftovers. Leftovers that she inevitably ignored and threw away, but hey, she made the attempt.

"So...I gotta ask," Bruce started. She looked up at him curiously. "Have you tried yet?"

"Tried what yet?"

He waved at her then looked away sheepishly. "Doing your thing. Your contortion thing."

Cora laughed. He looked so shy about it. She wondered why. Nobody else seemed to be reluctant to ask her weird questions. But Aaron's knowing grin told her there might be something else going on.

"Want to help her practice, Bruce? See what shapes she can make for you? Moving in on my territory already?" Aaron slung an arm around Cora's shoulders. "Everybody's eager to get the first taste, huh? Well, hate to disappoint you, firebug, but I've called dibs."

"Get your hand off her, Barker. Before I tear it off at the joint."

The voice washed over them like a cold wind on a summer day. Aaron immediately ripped his hand away from her shoulder. Cora shivered and looked up at the very annoyed face of one very perturbed Puppeteer. Simon was glaring a hole into Aaron like he was on the brink of making good on his threat.

Aaron shifted away from her on the bench. "Just playing around, old boy."

"She does not like to be touched without permission." Simon smiled sadistically. "And you'll respect her wishes."

"And you won't talk for me, Simon." She glared up at him. "You don't own me, and I'm not your property."

"You aren't anyone's property, Cora dear. Least of all his." Simon still didn't take his glare off Aaron. "That's only the point I'm making. You aren't a deli meat product waiting for the next number to be called."

"No, I'm not, and I don't need you making that point *for* me, jack-hole." This whole thing was giving her a headache. She put her hand over her eyes. "Aaron, thank you, but I'm going to pass. And politely request you stop making jokes to that effect. Bruce, yes, I have tried, and it's weird and I'm not comfortable with it yet. And Simon, stop being an utter douchebag and either sit down or leave me alone. I hate you looming over me. As for you three." She looked up at Bertha, Louis, and Pierre. "You're fine."

Bertha laughed. "Oh, I like you, sweetie. I like you a lot. You're going to do great."

Simon sat down on the bench next to her obediently and was sulking in a dark cloud of whatever myriad emotions he was obviously feeling.

The Bearded Woman was clearly unafraid of the

Puppeteer, even if the others were. "Did she really clock you in the face with a skillet?"

"She did." Simon reached over and stole Cora's root beer, pulling the straw aside, and drank nearly a quarter of it. She debated stabbing him with her fork again. "She hits hard. Watch yourself, Aaron."

"Why are you here, Puppeteer? You never come to the cafeteria for dinner." Aaron eyed the other man narrowly from the other side of her. She really wanted to get out from between them but couldn't see a graceful way to do it.

"Making sure you weren't trying to talk her into some disgusting orgy. Which is exactly what it seems I interrupted, so I was correct. She's overwhelmed and needs time to adjust to her life without you trying to sniff her underwear."

"That's disgusting." She glared at Simon. "And the person who's been flirting with me the most—and badly, I might add—is you. I'd tell you to keep your mouth shut, but it's clear that's not possible."

Everyone else at the table looked stunned.

"My dear old boy," Aaron began with a teasing grin. It seemed he had no sense of self-preservation. "Do you have an interest in someone after all these years?"

"I will rip that terrible mustache off your face and feed it to you, Barker," Simon hissed through clenched teeth. "Mind your words."

"Oh-ho-ho, I think he does!" Aaron slapped the table with both his palms. "Simon's got a crush!"

The next few seconds were mayhem. The bench tipped over, sending her crashing to the ground. She whacked her head hard on the packed dirt, and she lost a few precious seconds. There was a smashing sound. Shouts. A scream. Something wet splashing on the dirt next to her. When she came around, Bruce and Louis were kneeling next to her. Bruce was keeping himself between her and whatever was creating all the noise. When she turned her head and blinked a few times, she realized that the source of the wet slap...was an arm.

Aaron's arm.

Torn off at the socket. She knew by what. Strings.

Aaron was on the ground, stretched prone, and Simon was standing over him. The air in the cafeteria was a wild, crisscrossing mess of silvery, spiderwebbing strings. No one could get near them.

Aaron was screaming.

Simon was laughing. That loud, maniacal laughter that gave her chills.

Cora was left to watch as the string around his neck tightened until he gagged, then blood gushed from the wound. The string cinched tighter and tighter until his head just...popped off. The wire cinched so tight that his head had no other choice. It rolled away from his body.

Nobody else seemed terribly concerned. That was the worst part. Bruce and Louis were helping her up to her feet, but Pierre and Bertha were still...eating their lunch like nothing had happened.

Simon brushed his hands off, straightening his clothes. He turned to face her and smiled. "Now, then. Where were we?"

Cora screamed and ran.

12

CORA SLAMMED the door to her boxcar shut and pressed her back against it. She was shaking. She slid down onto the ground and stayed there, her hands pressed against the floor, trying to slow her racing heart.

She had just watched Simon rip a man into tiny pieces.

And nobody seemed to really care.

She didn't know which was worse! Putting her head into her hands, she let out a low groan. *I don't belong here. This is a huge mistake. I'm going to turn into them—either being ripped apart by Simon, or worse, I'll become a monster like he is.*

It all just redoubled her need to get out of this stupid place. The Faire was going to either corrupt her or consume her. She couldn't let either of those things happen. But there was only one way out. Mr. Harrow.

When she felt like she could breathe without throwing up, she sat down at the kitchenette table and reached for the pencil and the letter she had started writing. She stared at it for the longest time before she finally knew what she needed to say.

"Dear Mr. Harrow,

I know you don't make exceptions. But—"

She broke off as there was a knock on her door. "Please go away," she called to whoever it was.

"Cupcake, open up."

She cringed at Simon's voice. "No. Especially not for you!"

"Why not?"

"I just watched you kill a man!"

Simon scoffed. "He'll be fine in a few hours."

"That—that doesn't make any part of this better. Go away, Simon."

"I'm incredibly stubborn, you know."

"Then have fun sitting out there all fucking night. I'm not letting you in." But she couldn't focus on her letter anymore. She stood from the table and threw open the door. Simon was standing there, smiling like he always was. "Go. Away."

"Mmm—nope." He stepped into the doorway. She blocked his path. He chuckled. "Oh, cupcake...you know better than that. After what you just saw? You know I can make you."

"I just watched you tear a man to pieces for no reason. I'm not letting you inside."

"No reason? I was trying to protect you." He rested his arm against the jamb, leaning down close to her. "And this is how you thank me?"

"I don't need your protection." She tilted back. Damn him for correctly calling her bluff. "Why're you here?"

"I have something I want to say to you." He stepped up to her, and she had to retreat to keep from him pressing against her. He took another step until he was inside, and he carefully took the door from her and shut it behind him.

"Say it and leave." She felt powerless. It was clear he

could snag her with his strings at any point. He could tear her to pieces like he had done to Aaron. She wished she had the frying pan all of a sudden.

Simon paced toward her slowly, and she retreated with each of his advancing steps. She backed into the kitchenette table and squeaked, startled. He chuckled at her reaction and placed his arms on either side of her, caging her in against the chairs.

"I—"

"Shh..." He moved closer to her. She felt his breath wash against her cheek. She turned her head away and felt his lips graze her ear. She was shivering. But it wasn't the same kind of panic she had felt when he woken her up in bed. She was afraid, yes.

But it wasn't all fear.

The smell of his old-fashioned cologne hit her. Tangy and crisp. She gripped the edge of the table tightly in both hands. "Simon..." She hated how she sounded—small and afraid. She squeezed her eyes shut.

She felt his forehead rest against her. "I'm proud of you, cupcake. Standing up to me like that...If they see you unafraid to face me down, no one will mess with you. I'm not upset. Dress me down all you want in public, because someday soon you'll let me dress you down in private." He placed a kiss against her cheek, just by her ear. Slow and sensual.

Her stomach dropped like she had fallen off a cliff. Her knees felt weak. If she hadn't been holding on to the table, she would have likely collapsed to the ground.

When he pulled his lips away from her, it felt like her face was on fire. He tilted her head to his with a gentle press of fingers on her cheek. He gave her every chance to turn away. His lips ghosted over hers, and she held her breath.

Then...he kissed her. Carefully at first, tentative, exploring. He broke away and waited for her to fight him. When she didn't—when she couldn't do anything at all except feel trapped like a fly in a web—he closed the embrace again, harder than before. Her stomach hit the bottom of the cliff and started to tumble down the rest of the incline into whatever pit was swallowing it whole as he stepped into her, pressing her against the table.

She had never been swept off her feet before. She didn't know the meaning of the phrase. It was just over-romantic dribble. But she understood it now. Especially as he picked her up like she weighed nothing and sat her on the edge of the table, stepping between her knees to deepen the kiss. When she tried to pull back, he caught her face in his hands, cradling them in his palms, not letting her escape so easily.

He just killed a man. He just ripped him to pieces and laughed.

Oh, God.

Why am I holding on to him?

Sure enough, her hands were wound into his crimson overcoat, gripping him tightly. And it wasn't to push him away. When he finally broke the kiss, her heart was racing and thumping loudly in her ears. She felt overheated. He pulled away from her just enough to study her. He stroked her cheek and chuckled at what must be an obvious blush on her face.

She looked away from him shyly. She couldn't take his gaze. It saw through her, and it was too knowing—too proud of what he'd done. Of what they'd done. "I can't."

He let out a thoughtful hum. "Too fast?"

She nodded weakly. "And it's wrong."

"Wrong. Sure." He let his hands drift down to rest idly

on her thighs. "I think that's the least wrong thing I've done all day, cupcake."

"You're not going to force me, are you?"

"Never. Never, cupcake." He rested his forehead against her temple again. "Let me make one thing perfectly clear, though, Cora dear...nobody touches you but me. You can tell me no as many times as you want, every time I ask between now and when the sun burns out. But there's a part of me there inside you. And if they defile you, they defile *me,* and we can't have that."

He lifted a hand to her cheek and turned her head toward him. He hovered his lips over hers, barely an inch away. She held her breath, feeling like she was held on the edge of a knife, wondering if he was going to close the gap and kiss her again. If he did, she knew she wouldn't have the will to tell him to stop.

And she did want him to stop.

She also wanted him to keep going.

He grinned, as though victory was already his. And maybe it was. He backed away from her suddenly, and his absence was just as abrupt as his arrival.

It was like a spell had been shattered. She shook herself free of it and glared at him. "I don't belong to you. If I want to go off and fuck every single person in this god-forsaken Faire, it's my right."

He tilted his head to the side slightly. "Oh, really?"

"I don't belong to you. Not now, not ever."

"We'll see about that. Ta-ta for now, darling. Get some rest. I'll see you tomorrow, promptly at two for another practice session." He opened the door, flashed her one last sadistic smile, and shut the door behind him.

She sank into a chair and put her head in her hands again.

I need to get out of here. This place is going to drive me insane. That man is going to do it singlehandedly.

Swiveling back to the piece of paper, she picked up the pencil and began her letter for a third time.

"Dear Mr. Harrow,

I know you don't make exceptions. But I have to insist that I don't belong here. Perhaps you believe I do, but I can't allow myself to become a monster like the creatures you've collected. I can't be like them.

I will do anything to be set free. Name your price. Tell me what I need to do, and I'll do it. But I can't stay here.

Thank you, Mr. Harrow. I hope you know how serious my request truly is.

Best,

-Cora"

It was insipid. She knew it was childish. But she had to try. She folded the note in half and stood from the table, heading to the door. She opened it and peered around to make sure Simon wasn't waiting in the shadows or lurking in a bush somewhere.

Seeing that the coast was clear, she went to Mr. Harrow's boxcar. In the fading sunlight, she could see the lights were lit behind the curtains that obscured any possible view into the room.

Nervously, she approached the door and knocked on it. "Mr. Harrow? I'm sorry to bother you. But...I...I need your help, please." She slipped the note underneath the door. She waited for a minute, but she didn't even know if he was inside, let alone if he was going to answer.

She took a step away from the door and moved to leave when she heard a rustle from behind her. Turning, she saw a note had been slipped back under to her. It wasn't the white paper she had used—it was old, yellowy paper like the kind he had used before.

He'd answered!

Snatching up the paper, she unfolded it and read it quickly. She expected it to be a simple "no." What she got instead made her heart drop.

"Dearest Cora,

I understand your concerns. I will free you of this place, but it will cost the lives of all the rest in my employ. I will be forced to start over.

You have until tomorrow night at midnight to decide. Neither this offer, nor any other, will be extended again.

All my best,

-M. L. Harrow"

She had claimed that she would do anything to be released from the Faire. She thought she was willing to pay any price. Now she knew what the price would be. Mr. Harrow would let her go...

But everyone else in the so-called Family would have to die.

Simon paced in his boxcar. He was always amazed he hadn't trod a groove in the middle of the car with all his constant travels back and forth. His shadow was up on the wall, smiling contentedly.

"I know you like her, but I can't have this—this constant need. I can't handle this." He sighed and tugged on his hair with both hands. The feeling of her against his lips had almost broken his resolve. He'd almost dropped to his knees at her feet and begged her to let him have her. Just a little bit. Just a tiny taste.

But that would be the end to all dignity, wouldn't it?

There'd be no coming back.

When she'd told him off in front of the others, he had expected to be angry. Instead, he found it only redoubled the burning he felt. He felt somewhat bad for staking his claim on her in public in such a fashion, but he had very much enjoyed tearing Aaron's limbs off.

He always enjoyed tearing Aaron's limbs off.

Going to his liquor cabinet, he pulled out a bottle of gin and poured himself a triple. It was going to be a long night. Sinking down onto his bed, he shut his eyes and immediately regretted it. All he saw was her, sitting on that table, her knees against his hips, trembling in nervous anticipation.

She said she couldn't. She asked him politely to relent. It wasn't anger. It wasn't disgust. It was fear of the act itself—not fear of him—that made her hesitate.

She hadn't struck him.

Simon had certainly tasted her fear—the thing that had stabbed at his heart like a knife when he had startled her out of her sleep. He knew what she was like in a moment of utter terror. And what he had seen from her was...not that. It was not anger either that made her cheeks turn pink when he had kissed her.

And oh, what a kiss it had been. He couldn't remember anything like it.

He placed his fingers to his own lips and remembered how she'd felt. So soft. So warm. She tasted sweet. *Like a cupcake.* Perhaps he had been wrong to deny himself the company of a woman for so long. Maybe if he hadn't, she wouldn't be so frustrating.

He took a drink. When he opened his eyes, his shadow was on the wall across from him. That stupid, obnoxious smile on his face. The shadow jerked its head toward the door. Telling him that they were so close, so *close,* and so he should go and seal the deal.

"No, you idiot. That's not how this works. I can't just barge in there and hump her. You see how well that went last time I tried."

His shadow frowned.

"I have to play this slowly. We have all the time in the world, don't we? I can wait a little before I have her. You saw how she shivered at my touch. She'll give in." He drank his gin again. "It's just not going to be tonight."

His shadow snapped its fingers silently.

"And you're going to stay out of her dreams. You're going to leave her alone. I'm not going to have you screwing this up for me." He waggled a finger at his shadow, who pointed a long talon at himself as if to say, *"Who, me?"*

"I dislike you immensely."

The shadow stuck out his tongue at him.

Simon downed the rest of his gin in one go, coughed at the burn, and lay down on his bed fully, sprawling his limbs out. He was tempted to relieve himself of his need, but that felt utterly debasing. He didn't want to give Cora that kind of power over him. She'd already taken so much from him.

He'd gone to her boxcar with the intent to take something back. In his mind, he'd hoped the night would end with her naked and him finally curing himself of his recent obsession. While that certainly hadn't happened, he didn't leave emptyhanded, either. The look on her face...fear and desire. That was the trophy buck he had shot and killed.

Tomorrow, he would wait in his tent and see if she came to him for another hour of training. He was eager—very eager—to see the level of her ability. She was certainly gifted but lacked the discipline and skill that came with practice. And he would be happy to teach her some discipline.

He snickered at the mental image and stopped himself short of letting his hand wander to his own body.

Soon, it'll be you touching me, Cora. Very soon.

CORA SAT ON HER BED, reading and re-reading the note in her hands, as if she expected it to change each time. She could be free. She could go home! It was what she wanted. But in order to do it...everybody else was going to die.

Good. They're a bunch of dangerous, soul-sucking maniacs. They have no right to exist. They're a bunch of parasites feeding off humanity.

But on the other hand, most of them had been incredibly nice to her. Everyone except Simon had greeted her like a friend and family. They had welcomed her into their fold with open arms. Sure, they were a little too flirty, maybe, but that had really just been Aaron. And she was pretty sure he would take no for an answer.

Her angry tirade at Simon had been true. He was the worst one of the bunch, by far. He had threatened to mutilate her and turn her into one of those dolls. He would have gotten away with it if it hadn't been for Ringmaster showing up.

It was so clear that the big Turk and Amanda were in love. She saw how Donna and Rick smiled at each other. They all seemed happy, for the most part. Content in their lives.

But at what cost? They're eating people!

She was told the cost when she went through that skull-faced gate. She just chose to write it off as bullshit, like she did everything else that had happened to her. It was just a bunch of mumbo jumbo.

It took my favorite color away from me and fed it to Simon.

But she wouldn't care if she hadn't been told. She wouldn't have even noticed it was gone. It was like the most harmless kind of vampire. Just picking off little pieces of people's personalities to keep itself alive.

It's still a vampire, though. It's still a monster. It deserves to die. They all do.

But it wasn't the Faire she was going to destroy. The monster would live on. It was just going to be all the people she had met and all the ones she hadn't. She thought of Clown, the goof who had made her laugh and given her comfort when she was sad. Jack, who seemed so concerned for her. Even Aaron had tried to look out for her.

Amanda and Donna seemed like such nice people.

They're all past their expiration dates. They all deserve to die. I can go home! I can really go back to my life!

She saw a hole in the bargain. Mr. Harrow had never said if she could return to her life. He just said she'd be free. What if she took the deal, ran out of the park, and still nobody knew her? She'd have no life, no history, and nothing to go back to?

She re-read the note again and felt a cold sense of dread

roll down her back. She'd read enough Poe and watched enough horror movies to know that every little Catch-22 was what finally got you in the end.

It's better to be nobody with no life than to be here like this.

But was it?

Was it really?

She lay down on her side on the bed, hugging her pillow to herself. She had a little over twenty-four hours to decide. She didn't need to figure it out now. It all came down to one thing—whose life was worth more? Hers or theirs?

She didn't know.

It took her a long time to fall asleep as her thoughts whirled and crashed around each other. Finally, unable to hold on to consciousness anymore, a dreamless nothing came for her. She was glad for it.

Dreamless except for one thing, maybe.

The feeling of lips against hers.

13

Cora was dreaming. Again. Or having a vision. Again. She wasn't quite sure which one it was, mostly because she hadn't made up her mind on what these moments actually were. But either way, she had accepted the fact that when she found herself sitting in a place she didn't recognize, she probably wasn't going to be alone.

But coming into awareness with the feeling of lips against hers made her jolt. She jerked her head back from whoever was kissing her and smacked her head on the wall. *"Ow!"*

"Oh! I'm so sorry—" Hands flew to the back of her head, cradling it, as if trying to stop the pain by just touching her. "Sorry, sorry, sorry..."

"Simon." She pushed at the man in front of her. "It's fine, just get off me." He was wearing all black, a perfectly tailored Victorian suit, if morbidly colored, and his eyes were cyan. It wasn't Simon. Or rather, it wasn't the Simon from the waking world. She probably should have guessed from his repeated sorrys. After all, Simon had told her she would only get the one. "Oh. Hi." She jabbed him in the chest with her finger. "I told you to stop doing that."

"I know." He frowned and sank down onto his knees at her feet. "I'm sorry. I couldn't help it. You're just...you're just..." He paused. "You." He smiled up at her dreamily.

She was sitting on an old-fashioned sofa, the upholstery sporting loud flowers and stripes. She was in the same room she had been in once before. There were paintings everywhere. Some on easels, some propped up on the walls, some scattered all over the floor. There was no pool of blood, at least. And Shadow wasn't busy stabbing a piece of wood into his leg.

He was just kneeling at her feet, his hands on her knees, looking up at her like she was the whole world. Like she was everything that had ever existed. She cringed. How the hell was she supposed to be mad at someone who looked up at her like a puppy looked at his owner? If he'd had a tail, he'd probably be wagging it.

"It's all right. Just stop sneaking up on me with that, okay?" She narrowed her eyes at him. "And stop humping my shadow."

"But...it's not like you can feel it." He blinked. "Not like I can feel it either."

"Then why do it?"

"Why not?" He smiled and laid his head on her lap, his cheek close to her knees, and shuffled close to her. "It's fun."

In the running game of "which version of Simon is more of a nutjob," it was currently about tied. At least this one seemed utterly harmless. Handsy, fine. Overly affectionate, fine. But he wasn't shooting her or dragging her around on strings.

She wasn't sure why she did it. Impulse, maybe. She reached out and stroked her hand over his curly dark hair.

He shuddered and wrapped his arms around her calves to hug himself tighter to her legs.

The poor creature. Alone with nobody to talk to. Nobody to see, or touch...he was a ghost. No wonder he was insane. She frowned and continued to stroke his hair. Her heart broke for him, even if she wasn't sure what to make of him. "I don't know what to call you."

"My name is Simon. You know that."

"I know, but..."

He responded to her without picking his head up. If anything, he snuggled closer. "We're not different people."

"I know. It just feels weird to call you Simon."

"Why?" That finally made him pick his head up, and those startlingly sky-blue eyes were full of honest curiosity. This version of the man wore his emotions on his sleeve. *Maybe that's all he is—emotions.* He got up from the ground to sit on the sofa next to her. "Do you like him better than me? Is that why?"

"I thought you just said you were the same person."

"We are." He smiled.

"But you just said 'him.' That makes no sense."

"But it does." He shrugged. "It makes perfect sense. Oh!" He snatched her hand and dragged her off the sofa. The abrupt movement made her yelp as he pulled her behind him, and she struggled to stay on her feet as they left the room and into another adjacent space. This new one was decorated like a traditional Victorian parlor. He tugged her over to a chair in front of a small table and deposited her into it, shoving down on her shoulders until she gave in.

He sat across from her, and excitedly gestured to the table in front of them. It was a checkerboard, ready to go with red and black pieces.

She shut her eyes and sighed. "Simon."

"Hmmm? What? You said you wanted to play checkers. Here we are! Playing checkers. I'd rather kiss you over every inch of your body until you let me do more things to you, but—this'll be fine. I suppose."

She shot him a look, but there was only happy innocence in his eyes. She didn't know how it was possible to say things like that with such upbeat harmlessness, but there was proof to the contrary sitting across from her. With that hopeful smile on his face.

What was she supposed to do? "All right. We can play."

He clapped his hands together once in excitement and shifted in his chair, clearly so eager he could barely contain himself. He reached out to move a piece, then stopped. "Oh. You go first."

"I haven't played checkers in a long time." She moved one of her pieces forward. "You're going to win."

"Oh, I probably will. But the fun is in the game." He moved one of his pieces.

"I don't know what I'm doing." She moved another of hers and chuckled.

"We could just go lie outside in the grass instead if you want." He smiled wryly, that first hint of deviousness showing through the veneer of overeager happiness. The first small hint that this man and Simon really *were* the same man. Just different pieces of the same fractured whole. "Or I could come up with something more fun to do."

"No, it's fine." She watched him move his own piece, and she answered with one of hers. They sat in silence for a moment as they moved pieces around, until she had to make the first kill. But she could see it would leave her open to losing more pieces than she'd gain. She sighed. "Damn it."

He chuckled and reached over to place his hand on top of hers. "It's just a game."

"I know, but I hate losing." She jumped his piece, and he answered it by taking two of hers.

"Losing two pieces isn't the whole game. It isn't over until it's over." He didn't let go of her hand, and instead interlaced their fingers, letting his thumb travel a lazy path back and forth along the side of her hand.

It should bother her. She should yank her hand away and tell him—and the other Simon—to stop touching her. The problem was that it felt good. It was nice. It was exciting. She just looked at their hands where they were intertwined and forgot entirely that it was her move.

I could be free of the Faire. But that means killing everyone. That means him, too.

"Cora?"

"Hm?" She looked up at him. "Oh! Sorry." She looked down at the board and, chewing her lip for a moment, made another move.

"What was wrong?"

"What do you mean?"

"You looked so sad for a minute there. What was it?" He shifted closer to the table, his thumb never ceasing its slow trace along her finger. He made his move.

"If you could choose to die, would you?" She hopped two of his pieces and set them aside.

"Like..." He quickly claimed that one piece of hers in return. "Really die?"

"You wouldn't be trapped anymore, stuck in a world you can't interact with. Wouldn't death be better than what you're going through?"

He sat back, letting go of her hand, and looked out the window at the grassy lawn. There were rows of hedges, carefully maintained and cut into strange shapes. Simon, whoever he had been, clearly came from money. "I miss being really alive. I miss being able to touch things...feel things. I miss being talked to. I miss being heard. But that doesn't mean I want to die." He furrowed his brow when he looked back at her. "Are you going to kill me, Cora?"

"No—I—" *I was thinking about it.* "It was just a theoretical question. I'm sorry." And she did feel sorry. Sorry for even considering it. But could she really choose to stay in the Faire? Could she really pick a bunch of murderous undead psychopaths over her own freedom? Especially Simon, or any part of him?

He smiled dreamily. "Do you know...you're the first person to talk to me, even when I'm just a shadow? Nobody else ever has. They all ignore me, or scream at me. Nobody even tells me to go away. They all just yell at the other half of me."

She reached down and made another move, hopping a piece over one of his and taking it. That time, he couldn't recapture her piece for a change. "I'm sorry people are so mean to you."

"It's all right. I don't think they realize that I'm real. They think I'm a trick. They don't like me—him—us—whatever." He seemed to struggle to get it sorted in his own head, so she didn't feel too bad for being confused. "So they don't pay close enough attention. But you don't seem to hate us. Do you?"

Did she?

She should.

She really, *really* fucking should. With everything that Simon had done to her—terrorizing her, shooting her, harassing her, trying to turn her into a bizarro doll-monster to slowly eat off of her? She should.

But...

"I don't trust you. Him. Whatever. He tried to turn me into one of those dolls against my will. Forget the rest of it. That alone is enough that I should hate you both."

"I know." He sank into his chair, looking down at the table, sadness overtaking his features like a cloud passing over the sun. "I was screaming at him to stop, but he didn't listen. He never does. I don't think he hears me anymore. That's why we're in two pieces. He didn't want to hear me."

"So, you're his conscience, then?" She smirked at the idea.

"No, no. Maybe?" He looked up at her thoughtfully. "No. I'm just the part of him that hurt too much. The part of him that cared about things." He scratched at his chest over his heart. Just like the waking version of him. "When we first came here, we cried, and screamed, and pulled out our hair, and then I had to go away, because otherwise we'd never stop. But now you make him feel those painful things again. When you hurt, he hurts. And it scares him because he thinks it'll make him break again." He sniffed. "I probably shouldn't be telling you these things. But—what's the phrase? Screw it."

Oh. That explained so much. "Is this the place you grew up?" She looked around the room again curiously. She didn't know much about Simon. She knew he was a hundred and sixty-six years old, that he had lost his fiancée, he was vaguely British, and he had liked to paint. She knew nothing else.

"Mmhm. Welcome to Waite Manor." He shrugged, looking bored by the subject. "Why?"

"Will you show it to me?" She stood from the table and held her hand out to him. "Let's go for a walk."

He beamed. His face lit up like she had just accepted his

marriage proposal. He jumped out of the chair so fast he knocked it over backward. It clattered loudly to the ground, completely forgotten, as he snatched her hand and eagerly took her out of the room.

He took her from room to room, pointing out the family members in the paintings. "The Waite family is old blood. Very rich. Very...proper." He waved his hand elegantly. "I was supposed to be the beautiful eldest-born son of one of the most powerful families in England. I was to sit in the House of Lords, or...something." Simon squinted a little, as if struggling to remember. "Was it that? Or was it that I was meant to join the Navy?" He shrugged. "Doesn't matter! Well, I had a talent for painting. So, that was good enough. As long as it was a respectable trade in high society, all was well in Mum's eyes. Father was a bit disappointed, as you can imagine, but when I was accepted by the Royal College, he warmed up."

"You were going to go to the Royal College of Art?"

"Mmhm. I was already quite well-known, even at my age. I could have been another Monet. But...the Faire took me instead." He frowned. "It took everything. My life, my love, my future, my family. Gone. We traveled here because I wanted to paint the White Mountains, and Suzanna had always wanted to see America. We stopped at the Faire on the way. I never got to paint the mountains. And I never got to leave."

She squeezed his hand. He looked like a painting himself, almost. So tragic, so beautiful, and so drastic with his pale skin, dark hair and clothes, and bright blue eyes. She hugged his arm to her and pressed a kiss to his forearm over the fabric. "I'm sorry, Simon."

"You're an artist, too, aren't you?"

"I'm a photographer."

"That's art." He smiled down at her, his eyes twinkling a little at her kiss. He wore his emotions brazenly on the outside, and he looked so touched by her simple gesture of affection, it broke her heart. "I would love to see more of your work someday. Maybe you can take my picture."

"I'm sure my camera is broken, and I don't have a printer."

"The Faire provides whatever we need to be happy. Pretty soon I'm sure you'll have a fish tank too." He chuckled. "Soothsayer has a cat. Pretty little fluffball. But she's scared of me." He frowned again. "Everyone's scared of me."

"I'm not. Not anymore. You just need to stop startling me." She paused. "And humping me."

He whined. "Can't I just pick one to stop doing? One, I can manage. But *both?* Why do you have to be so mean?"

She laughed, and he laughed along with her. He took her outside to the gardens, strolling along the hedges with her. There was a gravel path that ran to a large gurgling fountain. "Your home was beautiful."

"It was. I never really thought so at the time. But things don't look exciting when they've always been there. When you grew up with them. But now, I guess it does look rather grand next to a train car in a field." He sat on the edge of the fountain and tugged her over to sit next to him. He turned to her, and before she could do a damned thing, his hand was tangled in the hair at the base of her neck, and he had pulled her head in close to his.

She froze, just as his lips ghosted over hers. "Simon..."

"Ssh." He smiled against her. "I want to thank you. This has been the nicest moment I've had in...a hundred and thirty-five years. Maybe later we can finish our game. You were about to start winning."

He kissed her. Slow and passionate. She tangled her hands into his clothing.

She should hate him.

She should want to drown him in the fountain.

But she kissed him back.

14

Cora woke up from a fitful sleep. She couldn't stay still. It was like all the nights she had spent tossing and turning from her chronic pain. But this time, it wasn't the ache in her limbs that woke her up. It wasn't even the shadowy version of Simon's kiss that woke her up.

It was turmoil.

Simon's shadow hadn't gone any farther than a simple kiss. Her dream had faded away a few moments after he had broken away. He had wished her sweet dreams, and it had just turned to black.

She got up from the tangle of sheets and went outside. The early spring night was cold, and her breath turned to fog in the air. It felt awesome. She knew she was in her pajamas, just a long t-shirt and cotton pants, but she didn't much care if anybody saw.

They were *Family* now, right?

A faint glow in the corner of her eye caught her attention. It was a single ember of something, glowing brighter and then diminishing. Looking over, she saw Jack sitting on the steps of his boxcar, which was numbered twelve. He wasn't too far away from her. The numbering scheme didn't make any sense. The boxcars seemed to just be scattered around randomly.

He lifted his cigarette in salute. She smiled and waved.

"Can't sleep?"

He didn't have to talk loudly to be heard. The night was silent. Just the stars and the moon overhead. All the lights of the carnival were off, save for the giant observation tower in the center of the park that always seemed to be on.

"Apparently not." She folded her arms over her knees. "You?"

"Nah."

"Why not?" She'd make a crack about how he always seemed like such a happy guy, but she knew from experience that the happiest looking person could have a deep river of sadness in them. Hiding depression was a skill that was practiced and sharpened like a knife. Some people were damn good at it.

"Too many thoughts. You?"

"Same."

"Do you smoke?"

"No, but thanks."

"It ain't tobacco, if that changes anything."

Cora smiled faintly. "I used to use medical weed, but it was for pain. Guess I don't need it anymore."

"I don't think that's why most people smoke weed." Jack chuckled. "Sure as hell not why I'm sitting here smoking it."

She laughed quietly along with him. "That's fair."

"Come on over, Cora."

She debated it for a long moment, and then figured *what the hell.* She stood from the stairs and headed over to him and sat on the step beneath his. He scooched over for her as she did. He offered her the joint.

She took it, turned it over thoughtfully, and with a shrug, handed it back. "I'm okay." It certainly wasn't the first time she'd smoked. The need was a little different now, but who was she to judge? What was the difference between this and booze? That was the argument she always told to her mom when she'd fussed about Cora using it for pain relief, anyway. "But thanks."

"Anytime. You all right?"

"I honestly don't know." She folded her arms across her knees and rested her head on them. "This sucks."

"Bruce told me about what happened to Aaron in the cafeteria. Told me about what Simon did. How you dressed him down, and Aaron the Idiot got a little too bold." Jack sighed. "He's a moron sometimes."

"Sometimes?"

"Good point." Jack chuckled and took a puff of the joint. He exhaled after a moment. "So, Simon's got a thing for you, huh?"

"Don't worry, it's just straight and unadulterated narcissism. I have a piece of him. I think he's desperate to know what it's like to fuck himself and not be gay about it." She grinned as Jack laughed. He was easy to talk to, and she appreciated that.

"Look, about what I'm sure Aaron said to you, don't let it get to your head. Yeah, yeah, we all trade bunks around here. But nobody's gonna pressure you into anything. He just doesn't know when to shut his mouth. It's his gift and his curse." Jack flicked some ash over the side of the stairs.

"No kidding."

They sat in silence for a minute, with him occasionally puffing on the joint. It was a companionable kind of silence. It felt normal. Natural. *Friendly.* Jack finally spoke up. "Simon ever hurts you, you come to me, okay?"

"I will. I think I'm safe. As safe as I can be from him, anyway. He's...I honestly think he's trying to be nice to me. I just don't think he knows how."

"Because he wants to get close to you for his own ends."

"Oh, I know he's a self-serving piece of shit, don't worry about it. I don't trust his long ass as far as I can throw it."

Jack chuckled. "I just hate to see him prey on someone like you."

"I'm not helpless."

"I know. I'm not saying that you are. I'm just saying..." He sighed. "You bashed his face up with a frying pan, I know you don't need my help. I guess I'm just talking myself into a hole."

She nudged his leg with her elbow. "I know, Jack. I'm not mad about it. Thank you. You're a good person."

"I hope we can be friends, Cora. I think I'd like that a lot."

She paused, and something cinched tight around her heart. "Me too." She didn't want to know the answer. She didn't. But she had to ask. "Are you happy here, Jack?"

"Hum?"

"In the Faire. Are you happy?"

"I suppose. I have my Family. I have friends. I have good laughs, good stories...I like watching the performances. I like to know I had a hand in making it all happen. Without me, nobody could get up to the skies to dazzle the crowd. Nobody applauds my work, but it's important. That's enough for me."

"Would you end it all, if you could?"

He looked down at her, his brow furrowed. "Like, what, commit suicide?"

"Yeah."

"I could if I wanted to. Simon and Hernandez proved

that. I don't know. It's complicated. There's so much more to experience, even stuck in this little bubble like we are. Every time we come back from the Inversion, I see new and exciting things. I get to see how the world has progressed. Cars. Phones. People. Fashion. Y'all women wear a lot less than you used to, and I'm used to dealing with girls strutting around half naked." He snickered. "But I like it."

She laughed with him and rested her head on his knee. He stroked her hair. It wasn't sexual, it was just...comforting. And she was grateful for it beyond words. "You're already a good friend, Jack. Thank you."

"Anytime."

She yawned and grunted at the end of it. "Damn it. I'm always tired outside of bed, but the moment I get in bed, I'm wide awake. Stupid brain, make up your mind."

"Why do you think I'm smoking weed?" He chuckled and sat back, taking his hand off her hair. "Go get some sleep, Cora."

"We never talked about what was keeping you awake."

"Never talked about it with you either, to be fair." He shrugged a shoulder. "Next time."

She smiled faintly. "Next time." *If there is one.* She stood from the stairs, waved to him lightly, and went back to her own boxcar. She hesitated, glancing over to number fifteen. Simon's car. The lights were off. She didn't know why that was a disappointment to her.

Why she almost wanted to go knock on his door and talk to him. Tell him what she learned about him in the dream with his shadow. And ask him more questions. And—

She cut her thoughts off there. No. *Shut up, stupid brain.*

She abandoned the idea for the shelter of "her" boxcar. She shut the door behind her and crawled back under the covers. This time, she had no dreams to bother her. Not even the memory of a kiss.

———

MORNING CAME, and Cora was starving. She showered, dressed, even put on a little makeup she found in the bathroom—she actually looked halfway decent for once—and headed out to the cafeteria for breakfast. She could smell the food cooking from her room, and it was too tempting to pass up.

The tables were all straightened out, the blood was cleaned up, and it was as if a man hadn't been brutally torn to pieces and beheaded right there the night prior.

There were a smattering of people eating, some by themselves, some together. She passed the man and woman who were joined at the hip and shoulder. They had two arms, two heads, and three legs. They both smiled at her as she passed. "Good morning, Cora," they said in unison.

She smiled shyly. "Hello, good morning." She tried not to stare. She succeeded, but only because she forced herself. It wasn't like she was judging them—it was just...well, she'd never seen conjoined twins before. Although the man and the woman looked nothing alike, which struck her as odd. Conjoined twins were always identical, weren't they?

More Faire voodoo, she guessed.

She piled up some food onto her plate at the buffet line. Scrambled eggs, sausage, a waffle, and a large mug of coffee. It wasn't a bad way to start the morning, even if she did have a looming cloud over her head.

You can be free, but they all have to die.

She had the note in her pocket. Not that she really needed it, but she was afraid to leave it in her boxcar. She didn't trust Simon or anyone else not to rifle through her things while she was gone.

And for some reason, every time she opened it, she expected the writing to have changed. It never did, but it didn't stop her from suspecting it might. She sat down at a table by herself. She didn't recognize anyone there that morning, and she didn't really feel like launching into a long conversation with someone she didn't know.

Her peace and quiet lasted for about twenty minutes. It was enough time for her to put away most of her breakfast. She was nursing her cup of coffee when someone sat in the spot next to her and leaned into her. "Fancy meeting you here."

She recoiled from Simon. "I thought we were meeting this afternoon?"

"Oh, we are. But I came to get my cup of tea and saw you all alone, and thought to myself, *Simon, you old dog, you can't let her be lonely, can you? Not when you can fix it.* So here I am. Fixing things." He grinned. "And you admit you're coming to my tent today? Good. I wondered if you might back out."

She swore at herself internally for having admitted it without intending to. She hadn't decided she was going to go. But she also hadn't decided *not* to go. She was curious about what she could do, for what little time it might last. And she was caught between the urge to slap the stupid look off his face and one that found herself stupidly curious to learn more about him. She wondered if she could do both.

He killed a man. "How's Aaron?"

"Sulking at the front gate, waiting for his shift to start. He's perfectly fine. Grumpy, but perfectly fine." Simon picked up one of her remaining sausages with her fork and began munching on it. She'd yell at him, but it was a buffet, and she wasn't really planning on finishing. She had plenty of reasons to actually be mad at him without having to invent more.

"How many times have you done that to people?"

"What, ripped them apart?"

"Yeah."

"Family, or guests?"

She cringed.

He chuckled. "Calm down. I don't murder mortals. We're not allowed to. No, cupcake. I eat people gradually, remember?" He took another very slow bite of the sausage, making a show of it. "Waste not, want not."

"Were you really going to force me into being one of your dolls?" Maybe he was just trying to scare her. Maybe she could find something redeeming about him.

"Mmhm."

Nope. She sighed.

"Don't blame me! You're...hm. Like a fine wine. Once I got a taste, I had to have the rest of the bottle. It would have been a great time." He smiled. "There are worse things in this world than being my doll."

"You're not making this better at all." He placed his arm around her waist and tugged her into him. She growled. "No, Simon."

"Oh, lighten up. I'm not trying to make a move." He nudged her hand with his then jerked his head in the direction of the entrance of the tent. "I'm making a point."

Looking up, she saw Jack standing there. His shoulders were tense, and his jaw twitched. Simon smiled sweetly and waved. "Good morning, Jackie-boy."

Jack walked slowly up to the table where they were sitting and stopped. "Cora?"

"I'm fine. It's fine." She shoved Simon until he was forced

to scoot away from her. "I was just leaving." She got up and headed for the tent, taking her coffee with her. She was not going to waste a good mug of caffeine.

"I'll see you later in my tent, cupcake. For our *training* session." Simon was clearly goading Jack with every word. They dripped with self-satisfaction, as though Simon were a cat preening himself on the other side of the glass from a dog who couldn't get through no matter how hard he barked and snarled.

"Simon, leave her alone."

"She's coming to me! Oh, please don't tell me this is the beginning of some terrible love triangle. How utterly *boring.* Jackie, this isn't a triangle. It's an exclamation point. And you're the dot."

"I just have the good sense to know when to leave a lady alone." Jack's words were stretched thin. She knew he was going to throw a fist.

Cora sighed, hung her head, and headed back to Jack. She put her hand on his arm. "It's not worth it. It's all right. I'll beat him senseless if I need to. I have no shortage of cast iron in my boxcar."

Jack's shoulders finally lowered from up by his ears. "Fine. But I swear to God, Simon, if you—"

"What God?" Simon laughed and stood from the bench, his long limbs and dark outfit cutting sharp silhouettes against the morning sun. "Swear to your God all you want. He's long since forgotten us. I'll see you later, cupcake." He winked at her from behind his mismatched sunglasses and strolled from the tent, whistling contentedly.

"He's such an asshole," she muttered.

"You've got that right." Jack turned to her. "What's this about him training you?"

"I—" She paused. "He said he could help me learn what I could do. I don't know. I guess I'm curious."

"But him? Why him? Amanda could teach you."

Cora paused. She swore in her head a few times. She shrugged. "I don't know."

"You shouldn't go anywhere near him. He's bad news. He's going to manipulate you. Any time he makes friends with someone, they just wind up as one of his dolls. I don't want to see that happen to you."

"It won't." *I might destroy all of you before he even gets close.* "I promise I'll be careful with him."

"You're a big girl. You can make your own choices. But I think you're making a mistake by letting him anywhere near you." Jack shook his head and tucked his hands into his pockets. "He'll get in your head."

I think he's already there. "He doesn't really give me much of a choice. He's always at my door. Or around every corner. He backs off when I tell him to." *Or when I hit him in the face with cookware. Or try to claw his eyes out.* "It'll be all right."

"All right, Cor." He shortened her name. It was cute. Trent used to call her that. It was a bittersweet reminder. Jack patted her shoulder. "I'll see you later, then."

"Have a good one, Jack." She waved goodbye and headed back to her boxcar. Her mind swirled around Simon. She didn't quite know how she felt about him. It was a mess. Somewhere, in some deep and sick part of her, she was starting to accept that she was incredibly attracted to him.

On a surface level, he was beautiful. Sharp cheekbones, unruly dark hair, and he was all angled lines and smooth surfaces. His smile was as dangerous as it was wicked. He'd be one hell of an adventure in bed; she knew that much.

And holy shit, he knew how to kiss.

She crammed those thoughts back into the sewer they

crawled out of. He was a sicko. A killer, and a manipulative bastard. Not once had she allowed anyone near her since Duncan, and she wasn't going to let another abusive piece of shit into her life. That was a mistake she wouldn't make twice.

He stopped at the first sign that something wasn't right. He could have tied me down from the very first moment. He said even he has higher standards than Duncan. Something about that made her chuckle. That the serial-killing psychopath thought himself a better person than her ex.

There was something twistedly alluring and seductive about Simon. Something that pulled her toward him, and it wasn't his strings. She blamed the part of him that she'd been forced to take. Something in her called to him because it *was* him. For the same reason he was drawn to her.

She wondered if this shit happened to any other of the "sponsor and recipient" pairs. Although, from the sounds of things, everybody just went around porking everybody else anyway. *I really should just kill everyone and get the fuck out of here.*

The memory of Simon's kiss in her boxcar made her shudder. If he had tried anything else, she didn't know as she would have had the heart to stop him. *I'm going to end him before it can get worse. Or I might not.*

I just have to make up my mind.

In sixteen hours.

Fuck.

15

SIMON RAN his finger over the piece of paper and read the words for the third time.

He sighed in disappointment.

"Oh, cupcake," he muttered to himself. "I told you I was making a point when I put my arm around you in the tent, sweet Cora. You thought I meant I was showing off to Jack. No, darling, my point was that you can't ever hide anything from me."

It had been easy enough to lift the note from her pocket when he had slung his arm around her. She was so innocent, so quick to write off his sudden nearness as his desire. It was a logical excuse. She hadn't felt him pick the note from her coat and palm it into his sleeve.

What a dangerous, wonderful, *disastrous* little minx the world had decided to drop on his lap. She seemed so harmless on the surface. Cheeky and feisty, sure. But he hadn't expected her to be the biggest threat to his life since he had come to the Faire. A shame. She was so beautiful. So tempting.

Let's be honest, old boy, she never was going to let you touch her. A violent cretin like you? She knows who you are. She knows what you're capable of. Why would she ever let you take her to bed? You're delusional. Suckered in by a few stolen kisses. This is for the best.

Best to get rid of her before she kills us all.

I'll lose a piece of myself in the process...but better that than losing everything.

He stuffed the paper into his pocket and made his way to his tent. He had a lot of work to do. He wasn't sure what would happen to him when he ripped out her seity and put it in the unfinished doll he'd made for her.

It might kill him. Part of her had come from him, after all. What would happen when he tore out his own seity from another person? It had never been done before. Not that he knew of, at any rate.

Or it might restore that missing portion, and all would be right with the world.

It was a fifty-fifty shot. It was a risk he hadn't been willing to take until now. And...no small part of him was beginning to enjoy having Cora around. He preferred her as flesh and blood. She was more *fun* that way than as one of his dolls. He looked forward to their verbal sparring matches and the chance to sneak another kiss each time they met.

But Mr. Harrow had upped the value of the pot to a winner-take-all scenario, and that had changed. As he strolled into the shadows of his work room, his own shadow was glowering angrily at him. Or along with him. He wasn't quite certain which it was, and he honestly didn't care.

He hadn't destroyed the doll he had been making for Cora. Why would he? He knew he might need it someday. But he hadn't expected it so soon, so he had tucked it away as a project for another time. Now he laid out the doll on his bench and picked up his jars of paint and sandpaper.

He could put her in the doll as it was, but why not make a few improvements while he was at it? It gave him time to think.

Time to sulk.

Simon was *mad.*

What on Earth did Harrow want with her? Why offer her such a deal when he'd never given anyone else such a choice? He grimaced in disgust. How many days had he spent pounding away at that door, begging for freedom, begging for his life to be given back to him? And he had a fiancée, and skill, and a purpose! He was going to attend the Royal College of Art and mean something to the world. They had come to New England to celebrate, and then everything had gone wrong.

Who was she?

Just a girl.

Just some sad, foolish, local girl.

He took out his sanding block and began to work. Cora had to be stopped. More importantly, she had to be punished for her betrayal. And he would do it the only way he knew how. She would become his doll like she was meant to be.

He was going to damage himself in the process. It rubbed him the wrong way to admit defeat, but he would bid farewell to that missing shard of his personality in exchange for making sure she would never threaten his life again.

Better to lose a part than the whole.

Better to gamble on winning than commit to losing.

Perhaps, when she became his pet, he would consume that part of himself back in the process. Perhaps he'd find it hidden within the layers of her seity over the next few years like an Easter egg hidden in the grass.

He glanced up over the rim of his glasses at his shadow that was glaring and gesturing wildly at him. It was clear his shadow was angry at him now. Not at Cora. "What?"

The shadow glowered and made angry, sharp claws at him, threatening him.

Simon laughed at the foolish attempt. "You're protective of her? She was going to kill us all."

The shadow shook his head rapidly.

"How do you know that?" He had become quite accustomed to arguing with himself over the years. Quite accustomed and quite skilled.

His shadow reached up his claw and placed it over his heart.

"Poppycock." Simon looked back down at his work and continued to sand the top layer of the wood to prepare it for paint. He could finish it, but that meant he had a lot of work to do in only a few hours. He could see the movement out of the corner of his eye as his shadow vehemently tried to get his attention. He didn't look up.

Why wouldn't she kill us all? That's what I would do. That's what I would do in a heartbeat. I never would have taken the day to enjoy the sights and eat the food. I would have marched right back to Mr. Harrow and taken the deal.

He picked up the wooden hand and continued to sand at the joints. He'd need to oil the brass sections to get them working again in perfect condition. He hadn't minded putting her into a half-finished doll. But now, it was an insult to how beautiful she was. *She has stolen part of me, but she is not me.*

Perhaps she is going to choose to stay...

He laughed at the idiocy of the thought. No. She would

never do anything of the sort. She would come into his web once more, step willingly into his trap, and he would enjoy a few hours of time with his dear Cora before he destroyed her, and a piece of himself, in the process.

It was disappointing.

But that was life, wasn't it?

Disappointing.

CORA DECIDED to go on a walk for lunch. Now that she knew that eating a bunch of bullshit fairground food wasn't going to make her fat or sick, she had no problem going and getting a giant funnel cake and whipped cream. She was in a bad mood and, damn it all, she deserved it.

After that, in desperate need of something to combat the overwhelming sugar overload, she grabbed a large lemonade and once more wandered through the park, slurping it through the straw. She didn't care about the noise she made. Honestly, the sweet substance probably didn't help her sugar overload. But it felt like it did.

Neither helped her mood, however.

The two sides of her decision weighed heavily in her mind. Over and over again, she ran through the pros and cons of each.

Killing everyone, pros—saves the world from a bunch of murderous freaks and monsters, and she could go free. No more Simon.

Killing everyone, cons—the Faire would just start over from scratch, so she'd only be stalling it for time. Everybody she'd met, with one notably large exception, had been nothing but sweet and kind to her. They all seemed like...as much as they could be, good people. Chances were, she'd be homeless, lifeless, and friendless when she got out. Mr. Harrow had said she would be *free,* not that she'd get her life back. She assumed details really mattered in moments like this. She'd probably have EDS again, and her chronic pain would come back.

Another con?

No more Simon.

She swore at herself and chewed on the straw of her lemonade. She somehow hated him and didn't hate him, both at the same time. She was afraid of him, but she was drawn to him. It was stupid.

She was ready to kill everyone just to spare herself the debacle that he was causing in her mind.

She thought about what would happen if she was freed with no trace of her former life. What would she do? Go to the police? No. They wouldn't believe her. And with no ID and no record of her existence, she'd just get shipped off to the hospital. She'd tell them she had lost her memory. Severe amnesia. She'd end up in a mental ward, and they'd take care of her. Sort of.

Trapped in a mental ward. That sounded *great.* Didn't sound much different than where she was now.

Who was to say she wasn't already in one, anyway, and this was all just some elaborate fantasy? That she was stuck in her own psychosis, strapped to a bed somewhere, laughing like an idiot. Sounded a lot more likely than a supernatural man-eating murder-circus.

Either way, her life as she had known it was over. She just had to pick which version of fucked up she preferred.

The first one was where she was alone in a white-padded room with orderlies while doctors tried to hunt down her history. They'd fail. She'd probably grow old and die in the system. Friendless, hopeless, and lifeless.

Or the second one where she was here, at this circus—a semi-immortal, soul-sucking circus performer. Surrounded by people who were killers and madmen, demons and monsters, but who...cared. She remembered Jack last night, sitting on the stairs with her, trying his best to comfort her. Or Clown and his successful attempts at cheering her up.

They could be friends. Or Family. Or more.

Even Simon wanted to help her. He was probably just inspired by a purely selfish drive, and he was doing it in all the worst possible ways, but he was *trying.*

"Cora!" Someone called her name. A woman.

She looked around but didn't see them.

"Up here, silly."

She looked up and blinked. "Oh. Hi, Amanda. Hi, Ludwig." The Aerialist was standing on Ludwig's shoulders, balancing easily with a foot on either side of his head. They were standing on a small stage, surrounded by people who were happily watching the show.

Lost in thought, Cora hadn't noticed them. She scanned the crowd hopefully, looking for Trent, but found no one she knew. Not like they'd know her even if they were there. Her hope was dashed as quickly as it came as she remembered.

"Come on up." Amanda waved her over.

"What?"

"You must have great balance now! I'll show you how. Ludwig here is a big sweetheart, aren't you?" She crouched to pat Ludwig on the head. He smiled faintly. His broad features held the expression for a moment before it faded.

She remembered what everyone had told her about the Strongman. That he didn't have much of himself left. That unexpectedly broke her heart. The poor man. Cora looked back up to Amanda. "Something tells me you make this look a lot easier than it is."

"Oh, definitely. But I haven't had a doubles partner in so long. Donna doesn't like to do this kind of thing." Amanda waved her over. Ludwig lifted a hand up toward his shoulder, palm up, and Amanda shifted so she had one foot on his shoulder and the other in his palm. He got down on one knee and held out his other hand toward Cora.

"This is insane." But she still went up to the stage, put her lemonade down on the lip, and hopped up. She smiled shyly at the crowd. "I work here, I guess. But I'm new," she felt the need to explain to them.

The crowd gave her a small round of applause, and their smiles were encouraging. She had expected laughter. But they really did seem to want to cheer her on. With a small shake of her head, she cautiously approached Ludwig and Amanda. She didn't know what to expect.

"Foot goes on my thigh," he explained and patted his leg, right by the crook of his hip. "Step up with your left foot. Amanda will take your hand, and you put your right leg on my shoulder. Turn so you face forward, like me. Then, step up. Yes?" He had an accent now that she heard him talk a bit more. He sounded a little German, and his words were stilted like English was his second language.

"I…I think so." She did as she was told. Amanda reached for her hand.

"Other hand sweetie, or you'll be facing the wrong way, as cute as that'd be."

She laughed and switched her hands. She felt like she was stepping on a rock. "I'm not going to hurt you?"

"You weigh nothing." Ludwig smiled at her gently.

"We play this game with Rick, and he weighs easily twice what you do," Amanda explained. "Ludwig can base Turk."

"Look, what Ludwig and Ringmaster do in their spare

time is private, and I don't really need to know the details." She put her foot on Ludwig's shoulder as she was told to but hesitated in stepping up. She had every bit of confidence that she was going to slide right off him and land in a heap on the wood stage.

Amanda laughed hard. "No, no. It's not like that. It's a circus term. The base and the flyer. Right now, we're the ones flying, and he's the one basing. Get it?"

"I guess?"

"I think I have the hard job, and he thinks he has the hard job." Amanda smiled and loudly whispered. "He's right, but don't let him know it."

"Up, little Cora," Ludwig interrupted with a smile. "You are safe."

"Debatable."

"Ready…hup!" Amanda tugged on her hand.

"What?" Cora stared at her blankly.

"Hup is the magical circus word for 'do something.'" The Aerialist smiled. "It's interchangeable. We use it all the time. Now, when I say 'hup,' jump up onto Ludwig's shoulder with both feet. It'll be fine. You won't hurt him."

"I'm more worried about breaking my face on the stage. Shouldn't there be mats put down or something?"

"We bounce back, don't we?" Amanda shrugged. "And people love the sense of danger. Okay. Ready?"

"I guess." Cora chewed her lip.

"Put your other hand on my head if you must," Ludwig coached.

"This seems really stupid." Cora chuckled at the ridiculousness of it all. She'd never climbed a man before.

"Ready…hup!" Amanda tugged her hand.

Cora hopped her left foot up onto Ludwig with the momentum of the pull. Pretty soon she was…standing on his goddamn shoulders. She squeaked and stuck her other hand out for balance. But he was like standing on a wood log. There was plenty of room, even if it was rounded.

She wavered but didn't fall. "Oooh, fuck."

The crowd laughed at her obscenity, but many applauded her little moment of progress.

"Great!" Amanda was beaming. "Now, turn to face the crowd, and put your left foot into Ludwig's left hand. Like I'm doing on this side."

Cora turned slowly, carefully, convinced she was going to fall off at any moment. She kept her right foot on the thick part of Ludwig's trapezius—*thicker,* she corrected herself. They were all thick parts. Ludwig held his left hand up to her, palm up, fingers closest to his shoulder, just like he was doing on the other side for Amanda.

Holding tightly to Amanda's hand, she stepped carefully into Ludwig's palm. Her foot fit there easily. She laughed nervously. She felt honestly...pretty secure where she was.

"Okay, now I stand up." Ludwig began to shift.

"Oh, fuck!" Cora squeaked loudly and flailed her arm for balance. The crowd laughed. Not at her, not really, but with her. It didn't feel cruel. Honestly, she'd be laughing, too, in their situation. Amanda was smiling and chuckling, but she looked as though she couldn't be happier or prouder.

Suddenly, she was a good three and a half feet higher than before. Ludwig was standing. The jostle made her incredibly nervous, and she swung her left arm around to try to keep her balance. But in the end, she didn't topple from the six-foot-and-change height of his shoulder.

"See? Not so bad! Now, straighten up. Smile for the crowd, sweetie. You're a performer."

"Nope. Still a victim." Cora did as she was told, though, straightening her back and trying to mimic Amanda's pose.

The crowd laughed at her comment again, but as she matched Amanda's pose, they cheered loudly. Her antics had drawn more people over. She felt her face go hot as she blushed.

"You're just the sweetest thing, Cora. Look how much they love you. You're great!" Amanda was beaming on her behalf.

"Only because I'm the comic relief."

"Hey, nothing wrong with a clown act. Ever." Amanda chuckled.

After the applause was over, Ludwig went back down to one knee.

"How do I get down?" Cora asked curiously.

"A lot easier than up," Amanda chuckled. "Just hop off the front. Ready? One, two...hup!"

Together, they jumped from Ludwig's shoulders and landed on the deck in front of him. He stood behind them. To the applause of the crowd, Amanda and Ludwig took a bow.

A heavy hand on Cora's back forced her into a bow as Ludwig pushed her into bending over. She laughed. "Sorry."

When the crowd finished and they were standing, she watched as the patrons wandered away. Ludwig patted her on the shoulder. "You did very well."

"I had no clue what I was doing." Cora chewed her lip again nervously. It was a bad habit. "But thanks."

He smiled. "No one does when they start." And with that, the big man wandered away without another word. The more she watched him, the more she realized that he was...vacant. Like something was missing.

Once again, it broke her heart.

"He was the kindest of us." Amanda sighed. "You should

have seen him in his prime. I called him the laughing lion. I don't think it'll be long now."

"Long...before what?"

"He fades away." The Aerialist shook her head sadly. "It's a quiet way to go. He'll go to sleep some night and just not wake up. He'll always be a part of us and a part of this place." Her expression perked back up as she clearly forced herself to think about something happier. "You did great! I can't wait to get you up on a trapeze with me. I bet I could base you, no problem. And being so bendy, you'll be fantastic up there."

"Everybody wants me as part of an act. I'm just sitting here trying not to set myself on fire in desperation." Cora shook her head.

"No, that's Bruce's routine. He'll be jealous if you steal it. And we all just want you to feel like you belong. You're Family now." And with that, the Aerialist threw her arms around Cora in a giant hug.

She hugged the woman back, not sure what else to do. "Thanks, Amanda. That helps."

"Anytime, sweetie. Anytime. I have to go get ready for my matinee. Bye, now!" Amanda walked away then, leaving Cora alone on the little wooden stage. She shook her head and scooped up her lemonade.

That had been a little fun.

Just a little.

Horrifying, but fun.

She looked at the clock. It was almost two. Speaking of horrifying.

She passed Simon's tent and paused to look at the painted façade proudly announcing "The Puppeteer" and the theatrical depictions of dolls on strings. She'd never seen one of his shows. She hadn't really had the stomach to, after knowing that she was almost a permanent part of it. It was hard to watch some poor creatures dance around on the stage knowing they were broken human beings.

She shivered.

But it didn't stop her from going inside.

16

As Cora headed into the tent, she was surprised to find it empty. She had expected Simon to be waiting for her. She turned around a few times, inspecting the shadows, wondering if he was going to come leaping out of nowhere at her.

Despite how eerie it felt, with its black and bright red stripes, there weren't any faces smiling at her from the darkness. She took a moment to really look at it for the first time without being menaced by the Puppeteer.

There were quite a few wooden benches. Two rows of ten. It meant that he had a decent audience size. It wasn't the huge big top in the center of the circus, but it was respectable. *I wonder if I would get my own tent. If I stay. If I don't decide to kill everyone.*

She sat down on one of the benches.

And began to realize she...couldn't do it.

How could she kill everyone?

That wasn't like her. Even if they were undead. Even if they did eat bits of people.

She wasn't a murderer.

She pictured Jack's face and imagined looking him in the eyes and saying that her sad, empty life was worth more than his. She imagined saying that to Amanda, Donna, Rick, Aaron, Clown, and all the rest. Everyone who had only been nicer to her than most people in her life had ever been.

She even pictured saying it to Simon. To his shadow. *I'm worth more than you all combined.* It wasn't true, no matter how much she wished it were.

I bet Mr. Harrow knew I couldn't take his deal so that was the only reason he offered it all. He knew I wouldn't be able to destroy everyone. I bet if I tried to take him up on it, he'd take it back.

She imagined looking at Simon and telling him that her fish mattered more than he did. She tried not to laugh at how he'd react to that. Maybe that part was right—maybe her fish were better than him.

But if that were true, why was she sitting here in his tent, nervous but excited to be near him again? The memory of his hand on her leg as he helped her balance into that bizarre and impossible position lingered longer than it should have. She had let him kiss her. She had wanted him not to stop.

She shouldn't be attracted to him. At all. Ever. That made her self-destructive and too stupid to live. She let out a beleaguered sigh. Something caught her attention—the barest bit of movement out of the corner of her eye. She looked up and shrieked in surprise.

A ghastly and cartoonish shadow was on the wall next to her, looming over her. He was frantically pointing toward the exit, flailing his arms around. "What's wrong?" What the hell was he trying to tell her?

The shadow kept wildly pointing at the exit.

"You want me to leave?" She blinked as the shadow nodded vehemently. "But why?"

"I'm back here, Cora dear," Simon called from somewhere in the back of the tent, distracting her. "I have a little work to finish before we begin, if you don't mind."

Shaking off the shadow's weirdness, she smiled at him. "We can go for a walk later, okay?" The shadow silently wailed and sunk to the floor in a heap. Silly creature. She smiled at his melodrama. "Don't pout. It's fine."

She stood from the bench and went to the stage and climbed the little set of stairs that led up to it. Heading toward the back, she saw stacks of flat-painted scenery and drops of various fantasy lands and foreign places.

It was a puppet show, after all. He probably told crazy stories. *No pun intended.* She kept her eyes peeled for any of the freaky creations of his, but there were none to be seen. A flap of a curtain by the back was pulled up, and she could see light streaming from inside. She peered in curiously.

This was what she had expected his boxcar to look like. Doll parts and paint jars, brushes and woodworking tools everywhere. Simon was standing with his back to her, wearing nothing but a thin white short-sleeved shirt, black pants, and an apron. He had black suspenders. She wanted to snap them. She resisted the urge. His glasses were on the table next to him. There was sawdust covering the floor. He had a paintbrush in his hand, and he was carefully detailing the features of a wooden hand. The rest of the doll was under a sheet.

"Hi," she greeted him shyly.

Simon glanced over his shoulder at her and smiled. It was an oddly gentle and happy smile. "Lovely to see you. I'm glad you came. A little surprised but pleased nonetheless." He looked back down at his work. He moved his hand gracefully, and she watched in fascination as he skillfully painted on the doll's fingernails. "Have a seat." He gestured toward a stool with his elbow.

She sat down and watched him. "Adding to your collection?" She asked with dread. She couldn't imagine some poor person coming in here and choosing to turn into a doll, like she had been considering. But people did weird things when they were desperate.

"I might be. It depends. Nothing's ever set in stone until it happens. Even then, sometimes there's always a way back."

"What do you mean by that?"

"Nothing. Just being cryptic." He smiled again. She could see him in profile, and he was utterly focused on the work he was doing. He probably wasn't even paying much attention to what he was saying.

Holy hell, he was beautiful. She tilted her head a little bit. She wondered if she could cut her hand on those cheekbones of his if she hit him the wrong way. Attraction surged in her again, and she desperately tried to stamp it out like a wildfire threatening to catch.

Instead, she turned her attention to her surroundings again. Sketches and landscape paintings were stuck all over the walls. She recognized some as smaller versions of the backdrops she saw out on stage. They must have been preliminary sketches. "Your artwork is beautiful, Simon."

"Flattery."

"No, I mean it. It's all gorgeous. You're an amazing artist."

He paused. His brush hovered over the surface of the doll. He turned to look at her, and for once he looked...she didn't know what he looked like. His unnatural eyes—black for white, white for black, and the rest a shade of devilish red—had an uncommon warmth to them. He smiled, and it was a tender one. "Thank you." He looked back to his work. The moment had passed. "No one has complimented my art in...oh, long time. Since before I came here."

"I'm sorry. Your shadow told me last night about the Royal College of Art."

"Hm. He's been flapping his gums, has he? Sounds like me. Desperate for a little affection, and off he pops with all the dirt." He grunted. "I hope that was the most embarrassing thing he said."

"Yeah. Don't worry." *Except for the part where he explained a little bit more of what he is.* But it felt bad to rub that in.

"He didn't do anything untoward, did he?"

"He stole another kiss or two. That's all." She chuckled at the jealousy in his voice. "We played checkers, and he showed me the home you grew up in."

"If you let him touch you before me, Ms. Cora, I'm going to be very cross with you." He glanced over at her with a playful smile. "But that bit of history is true. I was to be an artist." He dipped his brush in the paint and went back to deftly adding color to the fingernails. "Now I paint scenery and dolls and consume the seity of the living to survive." He chuckled. "Life is terrible sometimes, isn't it?"

"I...guess. Yeah."

"And still, I don't think I'd give it up. I like it here. I like being as I am. Given the option, I wouldn't choose the grave over this. There is beauty to be seen in all things. That's what artists like us are supposed to recognize, isn't it?"

Shit. It felt like a nail had just been driven into her chest. Cora looked up at the wall, seeing movement, and nearly toppled from the stool as she saw his shadow there, frantically gesturing at her. It was making angry, terrifying faces trying to...do...something. Or say something. "What's wrong with your shadow today?"

"He gets into moods. Ignore him."

"Kind of hard to do when I think he's trying to chase me off."

Simon straightened his back and turned to glower at his shadow. *"Enough."* The vicious anger in his voice sent a chill down Cora's spine. It even seemed to frighten his shadow, who shrank low to the ground and tried to make himself seem as small as possible. He was just an inky black blob with a pair of eyes.

The Puppeteer's expression switched back to his usual cynical and manic smile. "Like a dog, sometimes. I swear." He turned back to the doll hand and, picking it up, turned it over. "She's getting there. She still needs some work. But I'll need to let this stage dry before I do more." He put the hand back down on the table carefully and took his work apron off.

It was the first time she had seen him not in a full suit, except for that first dream they shared. She realized he wasn't skinny at all. He was muscular—but like a swimmer, not a pro-wrestler like Ludwig. He was all long lines, and she could just make out the V of his abs and—oh, she was staring. She looked away, feeling her cheeks grow warm.

No. No. No. Look at his eyes! He's a goddamn demon. Remember what he's done. Remember what he tried to do.

His hand on her cheek startled her. He could move silently for someone so tall. He was standing over her, studying her with a strange expression. His fingers were resting lightly on her cheek.

She might as well have been frozen in stone, so little she felt like she could move and break the moment. Whatever it was. She didn't even dare speak.

He ran his thumb along her cheek slowly. "Say what you like about my egotism...that I am only pursuing you because of my breathtaking narcissism. But you truly are beautiful, do you know that, Cora?"

Her cheeks must have burst into flame. She wanted to reach out and put her palm against his chest. She wanted to know what he felt like. She wanted to grab him by those silly suspenders and drag him down to her. Damn her to hell, she wanted to *touch* him.

Answering her silent plea, he tilted down to her, shrinking the distance between them. Pressing his palm to the table beside her, cradling her head in his other hand, he inched his face closer. When he spoke, his voice was thick with need. "Do you know how badly I want to kiss you again...?" He chuckled, low and sultry.

Please, yes.

Please, no.

"May I?"

Damn him. He was going to make her ask. Every other time, he had just done it. But now...he wanted her to outright agree to it. It was outwardly gentlemanly, but secretly devious.

She couldn't answer him. After a pause, he let out a thoughtful hum and tilted his head up to place a gentle kiss against her forehead. Not nearly as sensual as what she wished he would have done. He straightened, and once more his sudden absence was just as jarring as his sudden arrival. He strolled out of the room and onto the stage.

And she was sad he was gone.

"Don't dawdle, cupcake. We have work to do, don't we?" He was whistling to himself as he strutted out. It left her sitting there on the stool, her heart thumping in her ears, her breath short. "Chop, chop!" he called from the stage.

With a grunt, she smacked her cheeks with her palms and tried to shake off whatever it was he had just done to her. She followed him out to the stage. "What's on the docket today, coach?"

He had plucked up his button-down shirt from somewhere and was slowly doing up the buttons on the black silk fabric. "Have you ever performed a handstand before?"

"No."

"That will be a decent place to start, then." He fetched a drop cloth and folded it as a pad and dropped it down on the ground for her. He gestured for her to take her spot on it.

Cora walked up nervously but took her position as instructed. He tucked his shirt into his pants, and she tried not to stare. He was just getting dressed. But she still felt shaken up—and was still tempted to reach out and undo the work he'd just done.

"Shoes and socks off. It'll be easier that way." Simon gestured at her Converse.

She unlaced her shoes and did as she was told. She tossed them and her socks aside. She tucked her shirt into her pants. The last thing she wanted to do was flash Simon. "Why?"

"You'll be able to control your balance better when you can use your toes. Now. Palms to the ground, and then I want you to kick up one leg at a time."

"I'll fall over."

"I'm going to hold your ankles." He smiled as if she were an idiot.

"My arms'll give out, and I'll bash my face on the floor."

"That is exactly what I'm proving to you won't happen. Eventually, you can practice against a wall until you're steady enough to kick up and balance on your own. If you do slip, tuck your head and roll onto your back."

With a sigh, she bent down and put her palms on the ground. She felt stupid.

"Now, kick up."

"Easier said than done."

"Most things are."

She hesitated, did a false start twice, and shook her head. "I can't."

"You can. You're just afraid. Fine. Then just lift your leg up to me. You're flexible enough."

It was still so odd to think she could do anything close to that. After a pause, she lifted her right leg up, and kept going, until it was straight with her torso, and over her head. His hand caught her ankle.

"Good girl. There you are. Now the other one."

"I—"

Something snatched her other ankle. Something thin and tight. One of his strings! He pulled her ankle up to match the other one. She squeaked in shock and went rigid. Which was apparently what she was supposed to do, as the floor did not rush up to meet her face. The string released her ankle.

"Engage your shoulders, you silly thing." He poked her between her shoulder blades, and she squeaked again. "Right there. Push your shoulders apart and press away, like you're shrugging."

She did as he said, and she felt more stable. "I hate it when you're right."

"That explains why you dislike me so much."

"I dislike you because you're an asshole, Simon."

He chuckled. "One begets the other, doesn't it?"

"No. You can be right all the time and not be a douche about it."

"I'll have to take that under advisement." He knelt at her side, and she tried not to get too distracted by his nearness. "Now. I would like you to bend your knees. You're going to bend one forward and the other back to keep your balance."

"I...uh..."

"I won't let you fall." His hand touched her lower back, placing his palm there, and she almost fell over from that alone. It wasn't because he had startled her or knocked her off balance. He chuckled at her jolt. "Go on. Try."

"I..."

"Please. For me."

She didn't know if that made it better or worse. But the way he said it...it felt sincere. She did as he asked and carefully moved her left leg behind her and her right leg in front of her. Keeping her legs bent made it easier to balance; he was right about that.

She wavered a few times. But each time she did, Simon placed his hand on her stomach to steady her, opposite the one on her lower back.

God. Damn.

His touch was warm. Firm, and sure.

No. No. No. No. Focus!

When she regained her balance, he dropped the hand from her stomach. "That's it, cupcake. That's it. Keep going. You're doing wonderfully."

"Is your shadow molesting me again?"

"For once, no."

"For once? I thought it was just the once!"

He chuckled. "Like I said. Ignore him."

"If he's your subconscious, does that mean subconsciously *you* want to molest me?"

"I consciously want to molest you, darling. I thought I had made that quite obvious. But you've also made it painfully clear how unrequited it is. Metaphorically and literally."

It's more requited than I'm ever gonna admit.

"Whatever," was her clever retort.

"I'll take your stunning lack of creativity as a symptom of the fact that you're upside-down and quite focused."

"I'd flip you off if I could."

"Someday, I'm sure you'll manage from this position. But we'll master two-handed handstands before we master single-handed, single-birded handstands."

She laughed despite herself. Damn him and his wit. After what felt like ages, she was in a bent-legged split. Upside down. "Holy shit."

"See? It's almost like you're capable of what I said you were. It's almost like I was right. Again."

"Remember the douche thing?"

"Yes, yes."

"How do I get the hell out of this now?"

"Same way you got in, but in reverse. How did you think?"

"I don't know. That's why I asked."

He patted her lower back. "You're a silly thing."

She was really glad she had tucked her shirt into her pants. Really glad. Otherwise, his hand would be on her bare skin. She straightened her legs, nearly toppling over a few times, but every time Simon kept her upright. When she was back to vertical, she put her feet down one at a time and then knelt. She shook out her wrists. She was a little tired, but not sore.

His hand was in her hair, then. Combing through it. "Well done, Cora dear. Well done."

Turning to look at him, she was reminded of how close he was. Only a few inches away, kneeling beside her. She could smell his antique cologne, mixed with the scent of old things and the sawdust he had just made in his workshop.

If she sat up and tilted just a little closer, she could kiss him. She knew he wouldn't stop her. The only thing in her way was herself. And her resolve was fading. Would it stop there? Or would she let him take her back to his boxcar? Or hers? Or even more scandalous, here on his stage?

Don't start something you're not able to finish. It's mean to lead him on. And she wasn't ready to follow through. Not now, maybe not ever.

But he was gorgeous. And he was so *tempting.* Like a sinful cookie in a glass jar. Even with his bizarre, terrifyingly colored eyes. His devilish smile scared her, but it was also a large reason she was so damn attracted to him.

His hand settled at the base of her neck, still tangled in her hair. He inched his face closer to hers, daring her, tempting her, and silently asking her. "Go on," he whispered. "You want to."

I do. I really, really do. But I also don't know if I can stop it from getting out of hand this time. She put her hand on his chest to slow him down. "I'm sorry," she whispered. "I can't. It's not you. I just...I'm not ready."

"We've kissed before. Or is your resolve to refuse me beginning to weaken, Cora dear?" He hummed at her silence, as if he heard her silent thoughts as clear as day. "I understand." He moved his head to her ear and whispered, "Don't want to lay a man you're about to kill, hm?"

Cora tried to yank back from him, but his hand in her hair tightened into a fist. She pushed against his chest, but she might as well have been shoving against a wall. He was inhumanly strong. When she tried to rip away from him, her hair be damned, he gestured his hand, and suddenly she couldn't move. "Simon!"

He had her in his strings. The ever-present trap that he could snap shut around her without warning. He stood, leaving her on her knees, and he grinned sadistically. He towered over her, cutting a frightening silhouette against the stripes of the tent.

"Simon, let me go!"

"No. I was an idiot to trust you. I should have known you were as backstabbing as I am." He sneered. "You do have a piece of me, after all. I told you I was making a point at breakfast. What do you think I meant?"

"You were just showing off to Jack. What's this about, please, Simon—"

He plucked a folded piece of yellowed and water-stained paper out of his pocket.

Her heart sank into the abyss.

It was the note from Mr. Harrow.

"I've watched every single move you've made since you came here. Do you think I didn't see this? Did you think I wasn't going to snatch it from you the moment I had my chance?"

His arm around me at breakfast. He stole it! "It's not what you think, Simon, please—"

"Not what I think?" He snarled. With a flick of his wrist, she was yanked up to her feet. He caught her throat with his hand and squeezed. He didn't need his hand to choke her—she'd seen that when he killed Aaron. But it seemed he wanted the more personal touch. He held the note up to her face. "You plotted to kill us all!"

She coughed against the pressure on her throat. "No, please, listen to me—"

"Never again." He crumpled the note in his fist and chucked it over his shoulder. "I didn't want to lose the piece of myself that was stolen away. I had foolishly entertained the notion that you and I might be...allies." He trailed his gaze down her body and then back up. "Now I see you're just as treacherous as I am. So, I must sadly say goodbye to the part of me that lives within you."

"Wh—what're you going to do?"

He grinned. Wolfish and cruel. "I'm going to finish the doll in my workshop while you sit here and wait." He let go of her throat to cradle her head in his palm. "You truly are so beautiful. It seemed only fitting to finish your doll before I took you."

He gestured, and she slid backward along the stage. Before she could react, she was lashed to a post that held up one portion of the tent. Her wrists were bound tightly behind her back.

She screamed.

Simon followed her, tutting and shaking his head in disappointment. "You'll alert everyone with all that noise. I can't have them butting in. Can't have them meddling. Can't have them knowing how you betrayed them all, can we?" Pulling a piece of silk out of his pocket, he gagged her with it, tying it securely behind her head. "What would they think, knowing our sweet Cora had plotted to kill us? No. Better they be spared my pain."

She screamed again, muffled and useless. She shook her head, pleading with him, kicking at the post and yanking on her wrists. But his threads were unbreakable.

He caught her head in both his palms and turned her to look at him. "Such a shame. But you'll be such a wonderful addition to my collection. Now...stay put." He left her then, heading toward his workshop. "I'll be back in just a little while."

She screamed. It did no good. Tears rushed down her cheeks as she continued to struggle.

She stopped as she saw a shadow on the wall. One that was looking at her in pure heartbreak. Its twisted features were...disappointed. In her, or at her fate, she didn't know. She sank to the ground, sliding down the post, and stuck her legs out in front of her. Escape was hopeless.

Escape had always been hopeless.

Bowing her head, she let herself weep.

And waited to die.

17

SIMON HEARD her screams give way to loud sobs, and then heard those die off as she surrendered to her fate. Panic was so hard to maintain, after all. He looked down at the face of the puppet he was painting. It was as beautiful as she was. He would destroy her, but he would keep a little piece of her around to remind him of what he almost had.

They would have their dreams. But it wouldn't be the same.

She had wanted to kiss him. But she knew she wouldn't be able to resist the temptation to take it further. He shuddered at the thought. If he had moved closer and cradled her in his arms, he might have been able to have her. It would have been nice, just once, before he took her body away.

Cora had apologized for not being able to follow through, as if it were her fault. It wasn't. He grimaced in disgust at what had happened to her. Her cruel mistreatment at the hands of "Duncan" had left her damaged and scared. And yet she apologized! The poor broken thing.

If she hadn't betrayed him, it would have taken careful

work on his part to earn her trust. He looked forward to the challenge. Well, to earn her trust between the sheets, anyway. No one in their right mind—or un-right one—would ever fully trust him.

For once, it hadn't been his treachery that had led him here. It had been hers. And it...hurt him. He scratched his chest over his heart. He hated this kind of pain more than anything else. It had nearly driven his mind into oblivion. He had successfully removed it from his life. And now she had brought it back to him.

He looked down at the painted face of his doll and saw only her staring back at him. "I thought I might...I thought you might..." He didn't even know what he was saying. *What was I hoping for? What did I think this might be?*

A passing lust. A desire to eat the cupcake that is just a little out of my reach.

But there was something else, wasn't there? A child's foolish desires haunted him. They were memories of his youth. Of holding a girl's hand and laughing with her. Kissing her. Holding her. Of being held in return.

But it was time to say goodbye. Goodbye to her, and goodbye to those desires.

It was time to rip her to shreds. To bid farewell to the part of him within her. He picked up his screwdriver and hovered it over the linkages that would start to connect the pieces of the doll back together.

The idea of her turning that wooden head up to face him and utter the word *"Father"* made him drop his screwdriver to the tabletop. He put his head in his hands. He had wanted that only a few days ago! He had wanted to bottle her and sip her like the fine wine that she was. But now the idea churned something in his stomach.

The image of the doll standing under her power and

looking to him with those mirrored and painted gray eyes was revolting to him.

He knew his shadow was thrashing around on the wall beside him. He could sense it, even without seeing it. He was skilled at tuning the shadow out, but the damn thing was still a nuisance. He didn't need another reminder that this all felt wrong.

It wasn't just disappointing.

It hurt.

He scratched at his chest under his shirt, stinging his skin as he scraped it with his fingernails. The physical pain was a relief.

He looked up and glared at his shadow who was making threatening faces at him. "Stop."

The shadow froze in mid-gesture.

Pushing up from the stool, he went back out onto the stage to where he had left Cora, sitting, tied to the post. Gray eyes turned up to him. Full of tears, and sadness, and hurt.

But no fear.

She knew she was going to die.

Why did that hurt him even worse? He knelt at her side. When he put his fingers to her cheek, she didn't flinch away from him. She only looked up at him with those big, beautiful stormy skies as though begging him. But for what?

Mercy?

Or forgiveness?

Neither were things he had paid anyone in a very, very long time. There were a lot of things about this situation that were memories dredged up from his past.

She muttered something against the gag.

He tilted his head at her. Not because he was curious about what she said. No, it was because the sight of her like this—tied to a post, gagged, tears staining her cheeks—did terrible and wonderful things to him.

Dear Libido, you pick the worst possible times. Love, Simon.

Those eyes would never change color again, would they? They would never go from stormy to bright, and shine like polished marble. They'd never look at him again in laughter, in anger, in...want. That was what he had seen from her in his workshop. That was what he had seen from her after training.

She was fighting it, she was resisting it. She knew better than to give in—but she *wanted* him.

He couldn't remember the last time anyone did. Not really. Oh, from time to time, a curious girl would wander into his tent with the desire to explore what he was capable of. But it was few and far between. And it was never with Cora's level of understanding.

As a doll, she'd be empty of those things. She'd serve him, but it would be meaningless. The idea made him feel... alone. Empty. He scratched at his heart. Damn her! Damn this stupid pain!

But he couldn't trust her not to rush to Mr. Harrow and kill them all. It was precisely what he would do in her shoes.

Hope, the terrible barking beast, reared its head at him.

She's not me.

I would kill everyone for my freedom. But I'm a monster.

Maybe she's not.

CORA WATCHED SIMON WARILY. At any moment, she expected him to rip out her heart, or do whatever it was he did to make his dolls. She was going to...to live out the rest of her existence like that.

Suddenly, being part of the Family didn't seem so bad in comparison.

He was watching her studiously, something dark and hungry in his eyes. She'd call it lust, but she didn't dare to let her mind go in that direction. Tied to the post, gagged, at his mercy, she knew he could do whatever he wanted to her. All she could do was hope he wasn't the monster he claimed not to be. She was helpless.

Muttering against the gag, she shook her head at him, trying to plead with him as best as she could to listen to her.

Simon sat down on the ground next to her, his back to the post, his arm resting on hers. "I understand wanting to kill me. I understand entirely why you wouldn't value my life. I had hoped I had impressed upon you some kind of geniality, but I can see why I was wrong. I find myself insulted that you would cast me away, but I'm not surprised in the end. But I'm shocked about the others. I am shocked you would kill them all so readily."

"I'm sorry," she muffled into the gag. Not like the words came out. But she tried. *"I wasn't going to do it."*

"Cora..." He put his hand to his chest and scratched at something over his heart. He had been doing that the whole time. "I don't think you understand. I don't *feel.* Not like Ludwig because I can't, but because I choose not to." He gestured his shadow who was sitting there watching Simon talk with an uncommonly interested and unexaggerated expression.

I do understand. She watched him. His brow was furrowed. He was still not wearing his glasses, and his bizarre eyes bothered her less and less the more she saw them. She was slowly adjusting to them, she supposed. Something was flickering in those black-red-white orbs. Something like agony. She knew he could feel hers, and she had a lot of it to share right now—but something else was cutting into him.

"I hurt, Cora. I read the note, and I realized what you were going to do, and I felt *betrayed.*" He stared down at his lap, as if he were trying to make sense of the whole thing. "The only reason a person feels betrayal is if they put stock in something in the first place. Now, I should tear you apart and place you inside my doll. I should make you one of my pretty toys like I did with Hernandez and so many others. But...I don't want to. Because the idea *hurts* me." He clenched his fists. "For that reason alone, I should do it. I should rid myself of the complications you bring. I should destroy you to protect myself. But then I think about you never—" He paused, sighed heavily, and dropped his palms into his lap. "I think about you like that, and I can't do it, Cora. I can't."

Stunned, she didn't know what she would say even if she could speak. She watched him and felt something in her own heart crack for him. He had turned himself off to the world. Some part of her understood why someone might resort to that, given what had happened. She nudged him with her shoulder. "Mmmf."

"Hm?" He looked at her and chuckled. "Ah. Right. Yes." He reached over and pulled the gag out of her mouth, slipping it around her throat instead. "I forgot."

"Simon...I wasn't going to do it."

He blinked. "What?"

"You never let me explain. You never let me say anything at all." She glared at him then sighed, looking away. She couldn't stay mad. She understood. "I decided not to take the offer. I was thinking it over all day, and...I just can't. I thought about going up to Jack, or to Amanda, or to Clown, and saying 'my life is more important than yours.' I realized

I couldn't do it. And if I can't do it to their faces, I'm not going to do it in secret. I'm not a coward. I know I look like one, but I'm not."

"I never took you for a coward, Cora." Simon sat back against the post and rested his head on it. "What about me? Could you kill me? If that note said, 'I'll let you free, but Simon dies,' what would you do?"

"I…" She decided not to lie to him. "I don't know. You're a monster, Simon. And this is the second time you've come within a few seconds of killing me." She paused. She looked over at the Shadow on the wall, who was watching her with wide, hopeful eyes and a mournful frown. He was being honest with her. He was dancing around a subject that he seemed not to understand himself. That he liked her for her —even a little. "No. I don't think I could. And if I can't kill you, then I can't kill them. And you freaking shot me."

"Oh, get over the bullet wound already, will you? You saw what I did to Aaron, and he isn't even holding a grudge!" He threw his hands up in frustration.

"He's used to it. I'm not."

"You will be, if you keep this up." He eyed her narrowly. "What should I do with you, Cora?"

"Let me go, for one." She yanked on the restraints, but his thin strings were taut and sharp. They bit into her skin, and she stopped trying.

"And run the risk that you change your mind? Please." He snorted. "I'm not an idiot. You're going nowhere until after midnight, sweetheart. I meant my question in a more philosophical, permanent sense."

She glared at him. "You can't keep me here."

"Oh, I can. I plan to." He answered her glare with a grin.

"This is my choice to make. Not yours." She half-heartedly kicked his foot.

"You just said you weren't going to kill us now." He eyed her suspiciously. "Are you lying to me?"

"No, but you still can't take it away from me." Now she was pouting. She hated feeling powerless. And he could do whatever he wanted to her.

"Oh, yes, I can." He laughed. "This is a stupid argument. I'm holding a cookie and a punch in the face, and I'm giving you the cookie, and you're mad because you didn't get to choose."

"Yes."

"Women."

"Douche-canoe."

He laughed. She joined him. It was a sad kind of laughter for her, one that commented more on her ridiculous situation than not. She shut her eyes and rested her head back against the post. "I wasn't going to do it."

"I believe you. I'm still not letting you go to change your mind. Self-preservation, dear."

She understood, sadly enough.

They sat together like that in silence for a long time. Minutes, maybe. Just quietly contemplating. "Simon?"

"Yes, cupcake?"

"I'm sorry I hurt your feelings." She stared down at her lap. "I didn't mean to make you feel like I had betrayed you."

He was silent for a long time. He kissed the top of her head, holding the gesture for a long time. When he broke away, he tilted his forehead to rest his head on hers. "Apology accepted."

She let her eyes drift shut and the sensation of him up against her shove her worries and her concerns away. He shouldn't be comforting, but he was. "I don't hate you. I should. But I don't. And I hate that I don't."

He chuckled. "That's a good start." He turned her head

to look at him. He was so very close to her. She could feel his breath wash against her as he studied her with those monstrous eyes. "But what else do you feel, Cora? Since we're being honest with each other." His gaze wandered to her lips. "I have bared my truth to you...now it's your turn. Do you want me, Cora?"

Her heart lodged in her throat. She watched him, wide-eyed. *Oh, Lord, I do. I really...really do.* "I—"

"Puppeteer!" someone bellowed from the entrance of the tent and saved her having to answer. She looked up to see the large frame of the Ringmaster as he entered. Turk took one look at them on the stage, and her tied to the post, and his expression darkened.

"What in the name of the prophet are you doing to her *now,* Simon?"

"I see you got my note." The Puppeteer grinned and popped up to his feet gracefully. He picked up the balled-up message from Mr. Harrow on the stage and tossed it to Turk as he approached.

The big man caught it and looked at the Puppeteer curiously, then looked to her. "Are you all right, Cora?"

"All things considered," she muttered. She winced, knowing what was about to happen and dreading it.

Ringmaster smiled faintly. He uncrumpled the letter, and she watched his expression darken. "What is this, Simon?"

"Someone has been passing notes in class. It's the second one she's received from our reclusive Mr. Harrow. You're not the only one he speaks to anymore." Simon folded his arms across his chest. "Now you see why I'm holding her here."

Turk looked up at her, and she felt the palpable disappointment that he was casting her way. He was much more wounded than Simon was, and that said something. "Cora..."

"I wasn't going to do it! I swear." She felt terrible. Honestly terrible.

"That's a relief, at least." Ringmaster sighed heavily and tucked the note into his coat. "Keep her here until after midnight, Simon, then let her go."

"But—" She started to argue. "This isn't my fault!"

"We can't take the risk. I'm sorry." Turk scratched his chin. "I have a Family to worry about. I have to keep them in mind, too. We say nothing to the others. I don't want her to be an outcast. It's bad enough that they know she chooses to spend time with you. I don't want them to have a reason to turn their backs on her so quickly."

Simon rolled his eyes at the insult. "Oh, yes, of course."

Honestly, she understood. She got it. She was the newcomer, and Turk didn't trust her. She'd do the same thing in his position, she supposed. "What time is it?" she asked. She honestly had no idea.

Turk fished his pocket watch out of his vest and glanced at it. "Three."

They were going to leave her tied to the post for *nine hours.* Great. Fantastic. She groaned loudly and thumped her head against the post. "Can't you just lock me in my boxcar or something?"

"No. I don't want to have to drag you through the park on my strings," Simon strolled back over to her and propped his elbow on the post over her head, grinning as he loomed over her. "People would get suspicious. And we can't have that, now, can we?"

"I'll come up with some excuse as to where you are tonight." Ringmaster began leaving, then stopped. He turned to cast a hard glance at her. "If you try to communicate with Mr. Harrow again, for any reason, you will be punished. Simon can tell you about the five years he spent in the tower."

Simon blanched. For effect, or because it really had been that awful, she didn't know. She pulled her feet up closer to herself, instinctually making herself smaller. "I—I won't. I'm sorry, I didn't mean for any of this to happen. I didn't *do* anything. I was just trying to go home."

"It's all right, Cora. Just so long as this stops here. What's the phrase Bruce is always using? No harm, no foul." And with that, Ringmaster walked away.

Simon sat back down next to her, grinning at her like the Cheshire Cat. "Nine hours with you at my mercy. Whatever will we do to pass the time, sweetheart?"

Cora groaned.

18

Her nose itched.

This was stupid.

Cora hadn't even done anything wrong! Nobody had told her not to talk to Mr. Harrow. They said it wouldn't work. Now they were mad that she actually got a note back from him. Never mind the fact that she decided *not* to kill everyone. *I did kind of think about it for a while, though.*

Now she was sulking. Straight-up, unapologetically, sulking. And her nose itched.

Simon had gotten up about an hour ago. Or maybe it was two hours, she had no clue. He left her there, tied to one of the poles of the tent that sat just off-stage, as he practiced in front of her.

He was "working on one of his new stories," he had said. At first, she was annoyed at the idea of having to watch him dangle little dolls off his fingers and tell fairy tales to an invisible audience.

She should have known better.

When would Simon have ever settled for anything like that?

It wasn't a normal puppet show. Not at all.

She remembered the people who had been streaming out of his tent when she had come with Trent, Emily, Lisa, and her kids. She had been too distracted by the tall and monstrous man from her nightmare walking out of the dream and into reality.

But she now recalled the looks on the faces of his audience as they left. They were all struck with awe. As if they had seen something remarkable, and truly magical. And now she knew what it was.

They weren't normal puppets at all. Able to pull his creations from anywhere and at any angle, his creations were huge, lifelike, and weren't limited to the stage, or his reach. The life-size dolls and fantastical creatures that he brought out to tell his stories were astonishing. At least he promised these were dead. None of them moved without his fingers twitching to pull on their invisible strings.

He made a puppet of a huge dragon dance around on the stage. It must have been fifteen feet long. It wasn't meant to look perfectly real—it was stylized, and the product of a mind that was both insane and maybe a bit ingenious. It was meant to reveal how it hinged together. It was beautiful, if eerie, like the rest of everything Simon designed. Its eye sockets were empty mirrored domes with candles that blazed within them, making them flicker and burn like they were on fire. It was skeletal, with spans of its body covered in mesh or fabric, giving it every ounce of personality, but leaving it translucent and strangely ghastly.

The dragon bounded up to her like a giant cat. She squeaked in surprise as Simon abruptly broke from his script. The dragon's maw opened, revealing rows of sharp—dangerously sharp—pointed metal teeth. They looked like they had been sharpened and filed down to razor tips. She recoiled, wondering if he was going to have one of his toys tear her apart.

And then a large, red tongue rolled out and licked her. It was dry. But it still tickled. It was stuffed like a sofa pillow and covered in leather. She laughed and squealed. "Hey!"

"He likes you. It's not my fault."

The dragon's tongue licked her again, and she thrashed. It tickled! She wailed. "You're doing this!"

"Who says? He's licking you, not me."

"Simon!" She squealed again and kicked. "Knock it off!"

"Pah. You're so upset by affection." The dragon looked meek and contrite, lowering its head and turning away, as if hurt by her rejection.

Why did that break her heart? It was just a stupid puppet. She was such a child sometimes. She shouldn't feel *bad* for a fake dragon, but here she was. "Simon, don't tease me."

"We have another seven hours to kill. What am I going to do for fun if I can't tease you?" But the dragon perked up again, resuming its demeanor as a terrifying beast. She could imagine why he had such a large audience now. His puppets were more like giant animatronics that could walk through the rows of people. They were impossible, but people didn't know that. They must assume there were just gears and servos to blame.

Birds flew through the air, swirling overhead. The dragon snapped at them, disgruntled. She laughed at its antics as it stood up on its hind legs, trying to snatch the birds out of the air, only to just barely miss them. It puffed smoke out of its nose, some kind of powder that Simon could have it release on command.

She knew it wasn't alive, but she would have believed him if he said it was. There was so much personality within his performance that it left her in awe. She shouldn't have written off his shows so quickly. The dragon thumped his tail angrily on the stage and let out a *grow-oou-ooul* sound that could have been wheels rubbing together. It slumped down on the stage and dramatically pouted.

She laughed again, smiling, feeling like a kid watching a movie for the first time. Magic was real. She had just watched a dragon come to life. The Faire was horrible, and it ate people, and it was a monster...but it was beautiful, too.

Like Simon.

Then she realized...he wasn't just practicing. He was putting on a show. For *her.*

Her face went warm at the thought.

"Hey, Simon?"

"Hm?"

"They're beautiful."

He paused, and the motions of the animals around her hung in space. He smiled at her, and she could see once more that her compliment had hit home with him. "Of course they are. I made them." Despite his egotistical response, his expression didn't match his words. And neither did his tone. The creatures sprang back to life.

She watched his show, and when he finished, the creatures all disappeared backstage. "I'd clap, but, y'know." She shrugged uselessly. "Woo, Simon," she sarcastically cheered.

He laughed. He strolled back up to her and sat on the stage near her. She squeaked as he lay back and plopped his head in her lap.

"Excuse me." She shot him a look.

"I'm tired after performing." He looked up at her with a lazy smile. "I do enjoy a mid-afternoon nap."

"You're joking."

"Well, I won't be able to sleep if you keep talking."

"Get your head off my lap, Simon."

"No. I'm comfortable."

She sighed and thumped her head on the pole. He was impossible. She paused. "I never figured you for the cuddly type." She was hoping to insult his manliness. Or his evil dignity, or something.

He smirked. "You never bothered to ask." He laced his fingers over his stomach and shut his eyes. "I'm quite good at snuggling. I'm quite good at everything, to be fair."

Her ploy was defeated. Damn. She went a different route. "Do you miss being human?"

"No. I like being as I am. Who knows how my life as a mortal would have gone? Perhaps I would have failed as an artist. Perhaps Suzanna would have left me or died young. There were no guarantees that it would have been a happy life." He paused thoughtfully then opened his eyes as he looked up at her. "Why did you not choose to be free, Cora? Isn't that what you wanted?"

"It is. The cost was too high. And what I was bargaining for wasn't clear. The letter didn't say I'd have my life back—it just said I'd be free. I've read enough horror stories to know I probably would have gone back to the rest of the world with no life to return to."

He chuckled. "I didn't even catch that. I correct my previous opinions. You're neither dumb nor slow." He shut his eyes again, seemingly quite content to lie there using her thigh as a pillow. "What a nightmare that would be, walking the world as a mortal ghost. You would likely end up in Bedlam."

"It doesn't exist anymore as anything but a museum, but sure, I get your drift."

"It was wise not to make bargains with Mr. Harrow. I

doubt he is an honorable salesman. And I am...happy you made the choice you did."

"I didn't get to choose shit. I'm strapped to a post."

He chuckled and didn't answer her. Silence dragged on for a few moments, and she was honestly curious if he had fallen asleep. When he spoke, she jolted in surprise. "Do you have any hobbies?"

"Huh?"

"I want to know more about you, Ms. Glass. What do you do for fun and leisure?"

"I play guitar."

"Good, that's something."

"I read. I like videogames." A thought occurred to her. "Oh! Hey. My camera. Is it...is it in one piece?"

"Sadly, it broke. I gave it to Mechanic to try to fix it, but he's not sure he has the parts. He's going to do his best." He looked up at her, red eyes scrutinizing her. "But I'm sure we can rustle up some camera equipment. It would be lovely to have a photographic record of our lives."

"The Faire provides, right?" She sighed. "If I just wished *really hard* for a MacBook Pro and a nice Kodak, it'd just pop up in my train car? Along with my fish?"

He chuckled. "It's not quite like that, but yes."

"Which one of the Family members has the giant magically-willed-into-existence dildo collection, that's what I wanna know."

Simon cackled in laughter and slapped his palm on the wood stage. "I like you when you aren't cowering in fear. You're cheeky. And to answer your question, it's probably Aaron."

Cora made a fake and exaggerated gag noise.

"I'm glad he isn't your type."

"No one's my type, Simon."

"Really? Is that true?" He watched her for a moment, a wry smile creeping slowly over his features. "And here I thought I was on the verge of getting you to succumb to me. For shame."

They drifted off into silence for a few more moments. "Simon?"

"Yes?"

"My nose is *incredibly* itchy." She wrinkled it up to try to get it to stop. "I can't take it anymore."

He cackled in laughter. "And here I thought I was going to finally have your admission that you're attracted to me. She evades me once more!" He shook his fist in mock anger then sighed. "I have to torture you somehow, don't I? I thought about tickling your feet, but you might beat me up later." He reached up a finger and carefully scratched her nose. "There. Better?"

"Yeah, thanks." She chuckled. "I...can't you just let me go? I'm not going to do anything stupid. You can stay at my side and yank me back if I go anywhere near Mr. Harrow's train car."

"What if I like having you tied to a post?"

"I'm sure you do, you pervert, but this isn't fair. It's not my fault Mr. Harrow made me that offer. I didn't take him up on it. I'm being punished for no reason."

"This isn't punishment, darling." His expression went thin. "Trust me."

She remembered Ringmaster's words about Simon and the tower. "What...did they do to you?"

"The observation tower." Simon grimaced. "That fat oaf hanged me by my ankles from the center and left me there, upside down, for five years. Five *years*. Take a moment to ponder how many times I died from that before they finally let me down."

"I..." She paused. What the hell was someone supposed to say to that? What was she supposed to reply when she was just told that he had been brutally tortured for five years? "I'm sorry." Now she felt like an idiot. "Did you deserve it?"

"No. Absolutely not."

"What did you do?"

"Hernandez."

"Ah. So, you did deserve it."

Simon's expression turned dark. "He asked me. Begged me. He fell at my feet and wept and said he couldn't go on anymore. But somehow, it's *my* fault when I agreed to give him what he wanted? Why is his sin my cross to bear?"

If the devil were making a plea for his innocence, it would have been that. She looked down at him and tilted her head slightly to the side. "I was close to taking your offer. I might have, if you weren't such a dick about it. I don't blame you for Hernandez."

"Then you're the first. They never stopped to listen to me. They didn't believe me when I told them it was his idea. They think I killed him out of spite."

"Spite over what?"

"I don't even know!" He threw up his hands in frustration. He pulled his glasses from his face and rubbed his hand over his eyes. "I swear, Cora, no one in this park suffers worse than I."

She laughed. "You're awfully melodramatic for someone who has me tied to a post."

"You did this to yourself."

"What should I have done instead, then?"

"Let me write the note to Mr. Harrow like we agreed—"

"We didn't agree to shit, Simon."

He sighed. "Then you should have come to me immediately when you received your reply. You should have pounded on my door, woken me up from my slumber, and told me what you had done. Not hidden it from me."

"I don't answer to you. For the last goddamn time, I don't belong to you."

"I beg to differ." He sat up from the ground and turned so he was sitting facing her, his leg against hers. "I think I've proven exactly how easy it is to pull your strings."

He gestured, and her arm broke free from behind her. She grunted in pain as the stiffness in her shoulders was suddenly jerked around in front of her. She couldn't control her arms. Her hand went to his chest, her fingers splayed out over the silk fabric. "Simon—"

"Isn't this what you wanted to do? I saw you watching me. I saw the look in your eyes." Her other hand came up to rest her palm against his cheek. Warm and smooth under her fingers. But she hadn't put her hand there. "I see you now, frightened and uncertain. You want me, but you're scared..."

"Simon—"

"Tell me I'm wrong. Tell me I'm full of it, and I'll stop. Tell me I didn't see you wondering what it would be like to have me. But that bastard of a man who hurt you left a deep scar on you, didn't he? Have you even tried to be with a single soul since he betrayed you? You haven't, I bet. That night is long since over, and yet it haunts you."

Tears stung her eyes. "Please, wait."

Her arms were under her control again. She pulled her hands away from him and sat back against the post. She was shaking. His words cut her deep. She swiped her arm over her eyes, wiping away the tears before they could fall. "You don't understand."

"I think I do. What he did to you was about power. And

he still has it."

"Wait."

He picked up her hand from her lap and wove his fingers into hers. She watched him, wary and concerned, wondering if he was going to snap her wrist. He bent down and kissed the back of her hand. Slow. Sensual.

She shivered. He placed another kiss against her finger, matching the first. "I can be very gentle, Cora. You might not think so. But I promise you—we can reclaim that part of your soul together. We can kill him and what he did once and for all, if you'll let me. He tore you apart, and I will be the one to put the porcelain pieces back together. Only me, and no one else. I'm so very good at gluing shards of broken things together. Trust me...I've done it to myself plenty of times."

"I can't." Her voice sounded so small, so afraid. She tugged on her hand, but he didn't let her go. He was proving to her that he wasn't going to back down easily. "Please, Simon..."

When she went to slide away from him, he pressed his hand against her shoulder, holding her to the post. He didn't use his strings. It wasn't forceful. It wasn't violent. She could slip away from him, or fight. Something told her that if she did, he'd relent.

But she froze, like a deer in the headlights.

He shifted, straddling her legs, and settled down on top of her until his weight was just barely holding her there. But she might as well have been chained, he was that inescapable. She was left to watch him as he kept her hand trapped in his. His hand on her shoulder left her, drifting down her bare arm. Goosebumps spread in his wake.

He lifted her hand back to his lips and kissed her fingers, one at a time. Slow and gentle. He paused between each touch, his eyes never leaving hers. He was pinning her against the beam far more effectively than he had with his threads, and that was saying something.

He turned her hand over in his and placed a kiss against the sensitive center of her palm. When he ran his tongue along her there, she gasped and shifted underneath him. She needed to move but didn't know what else to do.

Chuckling at her reaction, he drifted his lips to her pulse. He kissed her wrist, once, twice, three times, before he let his tongue drag along her again. "You taste like honey." His voice was dripping with desire. Sharp and dangerous, but sensual and thick at the same time. The danger in his voice scared her.

The rest made her want to beg him not to stop.

He scraped his teeth over her skin, threatening to bite, but not doing it. She was pretty sure he wasn't a vampire, but if he sprouted fangs right in that moment, she wouldn't have been surprised.

Either way, the feeling was too much. She shuddered and pulled her hand away from him. That time, he let her go. "Simon, please...I..."

"I'm done." He planted a hand against the post over her head and leaned in. For a moment, she thought—and almost hoped—he would kiss her. Instead, he trailed his lips to her ear and whispered to her, as if it was a secret only for them. "For now. But you never said no. You never told me to stop."

Without warning, her arms were yanked around behind her back again. She grunted at the pain.

He sat back on his heels, still straddling her legs, and looked like the cat who had eaten the canary whole and felt not a single ounce of regret. "Six hours left to go, Cora dear. What shall we do next?"

19

SIMON WAS HAVING A BLAST.

Not as much fun as he might be having, if Cora had opened up to him and let him spread those pretty legs of hers, but he would take what he could get. He thought he might erupt from the constant tension he felt low in his body. It was beginning to verge on pain. She was keeping him in a state of constant torture. And so, he felt obliged to do the same to her.

He knew he was a rogue for keeping her tied to the post on his stage. He could let her roam around or at least sit there obediently—he was fairly certain she would—but it was just too tempting. She never complained once, although she shifted from time to time to try to ease the strain on her shoulders. Except for that one time her nose itched, she hadn't whimpered about anything.

It was clear that living with her disease had left her with a high tolerance for suffering. He grinned wickedly. He was eager to test out that theory. Patience would be required before she let anything of the sort even come close to happening, however. Bit by bit, he would push her a little farther every time. Already, she let him touch her in ways he knew she would have railed against only a day prior. She was already so much more at ease with him. Her wide-eyed reaction to his kisses against her hand and her wrist had left him like a volcano ready to burst from beneath the surface of the Earth.

But she didn't tell me to stop. She didn't say no. She had begged for mercy, for him not to push her so hard, but she never turned away from him. He was the one who backed down, not wanting to push her too far and threaten his victory on the battlefield.

It wasn't the war, but it was a battle. And he'd take it.

Always leave the audience wanting more. That was the old rule, yes? And he would leave Cora begging for him. Only then would he take her.

Resting with his head on her legs proved to be both comfortable and served the purpose of getting her used to his presence. He knew he was...what did the Soothsayer always call him? "A bit much." He didn't need the old coot to tell him that. He knew he was overwhelming. And he wanted Cora to rely on him, to want to be near him, and not to run from him.

Well, okay, running now and again in good fun was always entertaining. Especially if it ended in a steamy sexual encounter. *Down, boy. Down! Don't make this more uncomfortable for her.*

He had summoned a few of his threads and was creating old cat's cradles tricks with it to amuse them both. Stars, ladders, various geometric shapes. He was quite good at it.

"Oh! Cora. Hold on. I need you to hold that piece of the string for me, that bit right between my thumbs."

"Simon. I'm tied to the fucking post."

He grinned. Oh, right. Yes. He almost forgot. He held his hands up close to her face. "Bite on it."

"You're a lunatic. No."

He whined. "C'mon, Cora! Please? I just need you to hold that for a second so I can slip my thumb into the other loop."

The glare she shot him would have withered plants. Her gray eyes were dark like smoke from a fire. *Gods in hell, I'm going to lose what's rest of my mind if she doesn't let me have her soon.*

He stuck out his lower lip and tried to look as cute and harmless as possible. "Please?"

She squeezed her eyes shut and, with a long-suffering and beleaguered sigh, muttered, "Fine."

He cackled in excitement and moved his hands a little close to her. "Right there, cupcake." He watched as she bit the string in front of her, and he slipped his thumb out of the loop and moved it to another slot over. "Perfect! You can let go now." When she did, he twisted the shape over, flicked his fingers, and yanked it into an elaborate geometrical shape. "Tah-dah!"

"You're such a ham, Simon."

"I'm not sure if I enjoy that nickname. I call you cupcake. At least those are cute, sweet, and delectable treats. Hams are…fat and greasy." He cringed.

She laughed. "No. I mean you're a showoff."

"Oh. Well. Most certainly." He flicked his fingers again, and the string reset. He started on the next shape that he could remember. "You say that as though it's a bad thing. We all do love an audience here. You'll be like that soon enough, when you accept that you're going to be a performer."

"I don't know. I…still can't really accept that any of this is real. It hasn't sunk in yet."

He looked up at her and honestly sympathized. He didn't sympathize with anyone. Ever. He winced. He pushed it away. *No, no, just unfulfilled lust. That's all.*

And now I'm lying to myself.

"I understand, Cora dear. I really do. It will take time to come to accept where you are and who you've become. But...have you had an ounce of pain since this all transpired? Your illness is gone, isn't it?"

She looked thoughtful for a moment then nodded. She turned her gaze out to the tent in front of them. "It's so strange. I lived with it every day of my life for so long, and now it's just...gone. You'd think I would be ecstatic. That'd I'd be thrilled. But I barely notice. It's only when I wake up and realize that I've slept well. Or when I can sit on the stage like this for hours and not be in agony."

"See? This place isn't all bad. It cured your pain. You'll have time to perfect all the hobbies you've ever wanted to try. There's no rent to pay, no bills, and everything you want will be provided for you." He turned his head to kiss her knee. "Even me."

She picked up her other leg to clonk him in the head.

He laughed. He should be in his workshop, creating a sketch for a new backdrop. But he was enjoying this. It was... nice to talk to her. He wanted her here with him. It was *fun.*

That was why it had stung when he believed she was going to kill them all. *Goodness me, I really do have a crush, don't I?*

He laughed.

"What's funny?" Cora asked.

"Nothing." He grinned and kept his eyes shut. He had been resting on her for another hour since he had toyed with her last, and they had sat in silence for largely that entire span of time. He knew she was likely churning over the idea of him in her mind. Debating the *should shes* and *shouldn't shes* of her situation.

Oh, she very much shouldn't, but he wasn't about to tell her that.

The notion of having to babysit someone for nine hours would have normally revolted him. He would have screamed and thrown things at Ringmaster for imposing on him in such a fashion. The giant ball of lard would have regretted ever stepping over such a line with him.

But Cora was different. Cora was entertaining. She was beautiful. And the act of slowly seducing her to his side was immensely enjoyable.

When her stomach rumbled, he laughed again. "Hungry, cupcake?"

"I guess so. Bastard stomach likes to speak for me." She smiled. It was that little lopsided half-smile that he had come to look forward to a little too much. The one that didn't want to enjoy his banter but had to admit that she did anyway.

He sat up smoothly and pushed his sunglasses up his nose with the press of his ring finger. He glanced at the clock that sat backstage, out of the view of the audience. Eight o'clock. Four hours to go until midnight and broaching past dinner time.

Hopping up to his feet, he fetched his vest, his tie, and his coat. There would be no strolling around the park half-dressed. Dignity must be preserved. "I'll go fetch us something to eat."

"Can you let me go? Please?"

"You can keep asking, darling. It just makes this better for me." He winked at her as he finished buttoning his vest and slung on his coat. "I do think I like it when you beg."

She shot him that withering glare again. Too bad she

didn't realize how much he enjoyed it. *Show me all the fire and spite you have, cupcake. I think it turns me on.* "You're a pervert and an asshole."

"We've covered both of these things." He jumped off the front lip of the stage and headed to the exit. "I'll be back before you know it. Don't go anywhere!"

At her frustrated growl behind him, he cackled.

It wasn't how he had expected his night to go. He had been preparing to add her to his collection of dolls. Instead, he was fetching them dinner. He tucked his hands into his pockets and whistled an aimless tune as he headed to the cafeteria.

It was hamburger night. Hm. That was going to be problematic for his handless houseguest. He would have to let her go so she could eat. With a small, private, and wicked smile, he stole a bunch of grapes from the bowl of fruit and plopped it on the tray. He had a plan for those.

"Where's Cora, you sick piece of shit?"

He looked up and blinked. He hadn't even noticed that he had been approached. "Oh, hello, Aaron." He smiled at Barker and the man beside him. Ever the travel companions. Ever the bedmates. "And hello, Jackie-boy. I'm just fetching dinner for us, in fact."

"Where is she?" Aaron glowered at him. He was likely still bitter about getting torn to shreds. He really did hold on to his moods for far too long.

"We've been training. I've been teaching her the extents of what her body is capable of." He grinned viciously, letting the inuendo sit thick in his words. "And she is...quite talented. She just needs practice." He grunted in his throat, remembering the image of her in a stag-legged split in a handstand. His view had been...delicious. He didn't need to fake the dark lust that must have come over him. The sincerity of it was far more effective than any lie could have ever been. "Practice I'm eager to give her."

Their expressions of disgust and anger were too perfect. "You pig," Jack growled at him.

First a ham, and now a pig. Have I put on weight?

He laughed. "What, boys? Sad that she picked someone debonair and charismatic over the world's most disappointing sandwich? Please. Give her some more respect than that." He snorted and sauntered away with a shake of his head. "I recommend you amuse yourselves tonight. She won't be joining you."

"Where is she?"

He debated his choices for a moment before he shrugged idly. For once, telling the truth gave him the more powerful position. "She's tied to a post in my tent."

"You *what—*" Aaron shouted, and all other conversation in the tent ceased. Heads swiveled to watch them.

"If you hurt her—" Jack began.

Simon didn't let him finish. "You'll what, Rigger?" Simon turned to face the two men. He knew he hardly made the most intimidating sight, holding a cafeteria tray heaped with food, but he would make do. "Jackie-boy. Dear, sweet, toothless Jackie." He shook his head and *tsked.* "Remember the last time you wanted to tango with me? How did that go, precisely?" He remembered how much fun it had been to strangle the man slowly as he dangled from his strings. That had been a good Thursday. He clicked his tongue. "Stop your constant griping at me. She's mine, whether you like it or not."

"You can't keep her prisoner. Ringmaster—"

"Ringmaster knows! It was at his direction that she's there until midnight. At which point, I assure you, she will go free. But go whine to him all you want. Now, if you'll both kindly excuse me, I need to go feed my hungry guest. She's worked up an appetite already." He grinned, flashing his teeth dangerously at them, and turned to leave. He whistled cheerfully. He would have skipped if it wouldn't have spilled the food.

Let them go and fuss at Ringmaster if they wanted. Let them wonder why she was his temporary prisoner. Whatever reason they invented in their heads was far more entertaining than the truth. They were likely conjuring a mental image of Cora strung up from the rafters, legs wrapped around his waist, weeping in pleasure and begging for mercy as he plundered her. Sadly, that was not in his cards for tonight.

Oh, well. He wanted it to be.

He very much wanted it to be.

But, alas.

His shadow snaked along the ground beside him, grinning like the fool that he was. "Don't look so pleased with yourself. You had nothing to do with this. I made the decision to spare her, not you."

The shadow stung its tongue out at him. Simon rolled his eyes. "You're worse than Clown."

His reflection cackled silently. His grin quieted down to a satisfied, happy smile. His shadow stretched out far ahead of him, eager to return to his tent. And to Cora.

Simon sighed.

He wasn't the only one with a crush.

Why do I get the feeling this is going to cause me nothing but trouble?

Cora squeaked in shock as Simon's shadow suddenly appeared on wall of the tent next to her. He shot up out of nowhere, towering over her. He was grinning from ear to ear like a jack o' lantern.

She could only sit there and watch as he began to pet her own shadow, stroking her hair. When he rolled a comically large tongue out of his mouth to lick up the face of her silhouette, she thrashed and kicked. "Gah! Stop that!"

The shadow laughed silently and licked her again. Slower. She couldn't feel anything. It wasn't like the shadow was touching her, but it was the principle of the thing. She made her shadow kick at his, but it didn't seem to do any good. "Knock it off, you pervert!"

The shadow cackled again. And licked her.

"I hate it when you do that." She glared at him.

But the shadow just smiled, as if to say, *"Do you really?"* And licked her another time.

She let out a heavy sigh.

"Oh, leave her be, will you?"

She turned to watch Simon walk into the tent, a tray with two plates of food in his hands. "He can go places you aren't. That's still weird to me."

"Mmhm. He can go wherever he likes. Unfortunately." He glared at his shadow on the wall. "Stop bothering her. You know it makes her uncomfortable when you do that."

"I can't decide who's the bigger pervert. You or your shadow." She glared over at the offending silhouette. The shadow laughed silently, and then sank into the darkness. At least he had stopped shadow-licking her. For the moment.

"I promise you we're equally matched in that regard." Simon put the tray of food down on the stage next to her and sat beside it. "If I didn't think you'd break my nose again, I'd love to lick every inch of your body."

She shot him a look meant to set him on fire with her mind.

He only chuckled. "Now, I'm not terribly thrilled by the idea of hand-feeding you a hamburger. I'll do it if I have to. Instead, I thought perhaps we could work out a deal. I'll free your arms, but..." He picked up a small bunch of grapes from the plate and pulled one of the pieces of fruit from the stem with a quiet snap. "You have to earn it first."

"I hate you. I hate you *so* much. Do you know that?" She really wished she could set him on fire with her mind. She didn't get any cool super-powers with her immortality. Bendy, great. But nothing else that she could figure out how to use.

"Yes, yes. Complain all you like." He held the grape close to her lips. "Eat."

She felt her jaw twitch as she glared at him. She was not going to eat grapes out of his goddamn hand.

"Six. That's all you have to do. Eat six, and I'll set your arms free for the rest of the night." He looked so pleased with himself, she wanted to slap him.

Being able to move her arms sounded amazing. Not having to be fed a burger by a madman also sounded amazing. She couldn't begin to imagine how humiliating that would be. "One."

"Ah! And now we have it. The deal is sound, we're just haggling on a price. Five."

She hated when he was right. She really, really hated it. Sadly, he was right more often than not. *I guess the devil would be, wouldn't he?* "Two."

He moved in closer to her, holding the grape nearer to her lips. "Let's jump to the end. Three."

"Do you know how badly I want to set you on fire right now?" She tried to sound threatening. She failed.

"Mmhm."

She tilted as close as she possibly could, straining against the strings that held her wrists bound behind her back. "Do you know how badly I want to slap that stupid goddamn grin off your fucking face?"

He inched closer to match her. He called her bluff. *"Mmhm."*

Cora tilted her head back and growled loudly. She thumped her head against the post a few times. "Fine! Fine. Three."

"Fantastic. We have an accord. Now, be a good girl. One."

She knew why he was doing this. She knew. It was bizarre, it was cruel, it was torture...and it was undoubtedly more than a little erotic. It triggered in her things she had long since suspected had curled up and died. She shot him another withering stare even as she leaned forward to take the grape from his fingers.

The look on his face was no longer smug. Well, no longer *just* smug. She was pretty certain he only came in "smug" mode. It was just what was layered on top of it. And what was layered there now was the same hungry, dark desire she had seen from him when he was kissing her hand.

He wanted her. That much was very clear. He had said as much outright. And his body language, his expression, and...well, the outline of him against his clothing, displayed that was very much true.

But as her mouth closed around his fingers, taking the piece of fruit from him, she knew she wanted him. That was becoming *painfully* clear.

But it wasn't going to happen.

"One," he counted off, his voice a little choked as he reached for a second grape. She took it from him without a fuss, trying to get this over with as fast as possible. "Two." He reached for the third. He held it out to her, this time trapped between the sides of his pointer and middle finger. She would have to take his fingers into her mouth to eat it.

"Simon," she warned him.

"We had a deal. You didn't specify how I was to feed you the grapes. You should be more careful in your contracts. Especially with me." He scooched close to her, a wry smile across his face. "Be glad it isn't in my mouth."

Two can play at this game, you egotistical shit.

She opened her mouth and licked her lips, making a slow show of it, just for him. He grunted low in his throat, a sound of pure need. She ran her lower lip between her teeth then pouted her lips. If he was going to torture her? She was going to torture him.

He touched the grape to her lower lip, waiting for her. He clearly wanted her to finish the deed.

She took his fingers into her mouth. She took the grape with her tongue, letting it brush along his pointer finger. He moaned quietly.

The moan turned to a surprised yelp as she bit down hard on his fingers.

He yanked his fingers out of her mouth and waved his hand. "You little hellcat!"

She chewed on the grape and eyed him with her own level of smug satisfaction. "That's what you get, dick-bag."

She expected him to be angry. She wanted him to be angry. If he turned on her, hit her for biting him, and snapped at her, it would make it easier to truly hate him. She wanted him to smack her. It'd shatter the strange heat that built in her whenever he was around. *Show me you're just another abusive piece of trash. Please.* It was what she would expect from someone like him.

But Simon was anything but expected.

He laughed loudly, looked down at his fingers to see if she had broken the skin, then waved them again to cool the sting. "Well played, Cora dear. Very well played." He gestured with his other hand, and the strings holding her hands behind the post let go.

She pulled her arms in front of her and rubbed her shoulders. She knew better than to get up and make a break for it. He was trusting her not to do anything too stupid, and she was trusting him not to rip her limbs off.

And the burger did look really good.

"A well-earned meal, I'd say." He picked up his plate from the tray and sat back to balance it on his thigh. He paused to shake off his hand again. "Ow."

"Remember that if you ever try to stick anything in my mouth without permission again."

He paled. Just a little. His eyes went wide. "You wouldn't."

She grinned at *him* for once. "Try me."

She watched his Adam's apple bob as he swallowed nervously. "Noted. Duly and thoroughly noted."

20

Cora had to admit the burger was pretty damn good. And knowing she didn't have to watch her weight was a huge benefit. She didn't feel bad about eating the fries Simon had heaped on her plate.

Once more, she found herself pondering Simon Waite, the Puppeteer. The madman, the artist, and the murderer. The one who had twice now contemplated making her into one of his terrible puppets by force.

And the one she was sitting next to, eating a burger and fries, as if they were on a date at a drive-in movie. It felt natural. It felt exciting.

She had half a mind to cup the bulge between his legs and tell him to be a good boy.

No! Holy shit, what's wrong with me?

But he really wasn't so bad. He wasn't, once she saw through all his malice. Well, when it wasn't pointed at her. She sat on the edge of the stage with him, her knees dangling off the edge. His feet almost touched the ground, and hers weren't even close. "How tall are you, anyway?"

"Six-five." He munched on one of the fries. From somewhere in the tent, he had had fetched a couple of beers in unlabeled, brown glass bottles. He drank from his. Hers was on the wood surface next to her. "Doors can be irritating."

She snickered. "At least you don't have to worry about buying a car, huh? I bet you wouldn't fit in most of them."

He chuckled. "Probably not. How is the outside world? Still crippled with xenophobia, tribalistic racism, sexism, homophobia, war, and disease?"

"Pretty much. But now we have the internet that lets us hate all sorts of fun, new, and interesting people. Oh, and watch lots of stupid cat videos."

"The internet?" His brows furrowed in curiosity. "What's that?"

"It's a digital way of connecting devices around the world. It lets us communicate with each other. For better or worse. I could talk to somebody in South Africa or New Zealand right now and tell them all about our weather and how much I hate their politics."

He made a face. "That sounds terrible."

"Oh, it's not all bad. I had a great online friend from Tibet who I used to talk to all the time and another from Germany when I was going for my photography degree. I liked doing journalism, so I traveled a bit after college before my illness got particularly bad."

"You could have done studio photography, no? Is that still a thing?"

"There wasn't regular money in it. Everybody has cameras on their phones and can snap as many selfies as they want. I had to resort to working at the bank."

He paused as he dipped a fry into a puddle of ketchup. He was one of those kinds of people who drowned his fries in them. More proof he was a hedonist. "What's a selfie?"

She held out her arm at full length and mimed taking a

photo of herself. "Up the nose from two and a half feet away."

"That's hideous." He cringed. "People think that's attractive?"

"No. They're terrible. Then when people decided that their arms weren't long enough, they started making long sticks you could put your phone on." She mimed extending the telescoping selfie-stick out to a greater length.

"Humanity deserves to die a slow and painful death." His comment was so dry it made her laugh. He put the fry in his mouth and talked as he chewed. "For that reason alone, if no other."

She smiled and nudged his arm. "It's not that bad. We get to laugh with and at each other more now than we ever used to. Funny videos on the internet and the like. Humanity's connected in ways they never used to be able to. It still causes problems, but hey. That's life."

"Please see previous comment about humanity needing to die." He picked up another fry and swirled it in the puddle of ketchup.

Cora looked over at the clock. It was almost eleven. One hour to go before it was over. "You're going to let me go when it's midnight, right?"

"Well...I mean, I suppose I don't *have* to, now, do I?" He grinned even as he was chewing on a fry. It made him a little less frightening. "I could think of other things we could do with our late-evening, early-morning hours."

She suspected he was teasing her. And she also suspected he wasn't teasing her at the same time. "Ringmaster'd be pissed."

"That fat man is always meddling in my affairs and ruining my fun."

She shook her head. They sat in silence for a long time. "I don't know what this is between us, Simon."

"I can tell you what I want it to be. It mostly involves you hanging from strings. Naked."

She tried not to laugh at his crass and blunt statement but did anyway. "At least you're honest." *I can't tell if that makes him more or less offensive.* "A lot of guys would pretend they were after more than just a quick fuck if they thought it got them what they wanted."

Murmuring into his beer, she almost missed what he said. "Who said I was going to make it quick?"

She slapped him hard in the chest, and he almost sprayed beer.

He coughed. "Rude."

She slapped him in the chest again. "I don't think you ever get to call anybody rude, Simon. You're the king."

"Am not."

"Are too." She didn't miss his shadow sticking his tongue out at her. She rolled her eyes and laughed. She lay back on the stage, eager to stretch out after being stuck tied to a post for so long.

"The fact of the matter, Cora dear, is that I seem to find you less insufferable than all the other idiots who make up this park. Perhaps I'm simply tired of talking to myself"—he gestured at his shadow aimlessly—"but I...enjoy being around you. That is before you factor in that I'd very much like to tie you up and rut you so hard you cry out your *own* name." She smacked him hard in the arm again. He chuckled. "I'll take that as a 'maybe later.'"

"You're a pervert."

"And you still aren't saying no." That time she kicked him. He laughed and lifted his arm to defend himself. "Such a violent little spitfire! I deserve none of this bodily harm."

"You deserve this and more." She kicked him again playfully. She wasn't hitting him hard anymore. Not too hard, at any rate.

"Woe be unto the Puppeteer, long-suffering, long-abused, and tragic creature that I am! It's such a travesty." He put the back of his hand to his forehead in mock dismay.

She laughed again. At least he found strange ways to cheer her up. Even if it was because she was kicking him. She looked up at the roof of the tent and the way the stripes converged into a single point overhead. "What happens at midnight? Or do you think Mr. Harrow was just being cryptic?"

"He was likely just being cryptic." The playfulness was gone from his voice.

"Likely, or? Or what, Simon? What do you think happens at midnight?" She lifted her head to look at him as he took a sip of his beer. His expression told her everything. He had a theory. And his theories had all been proven correct so far.

He shrugged. "It's hard to say."

"What aren't you telling me, Simon?"

"A great many things." He put the bottle down on the stage. "And I only have my suspicions."

Sitting up, she watched him, trying to uncover anything she could from his faintest twitch. Fear, her familiar friend as of late, began to creep back into her. "Suspicions about what, Simon?"

"I could lie to you. But what good would it do? You won't understand what I'm saying, anyway." He looked at her with a wide smile. "I think we're about to Invert. We have what we came for. We've gathered plenty of seity from the crowds, and now we have you. It's time to go back into hibernation before we draw too much suspicion." He shrugged a shoulder. "That, and I can almost feel it, like the air before a storm hits."

"Invert?" She didn't know what it meant. But she knew it wasn't good. "No—" She hopped up from the stage. "I'm not going to—"

He snatched her with his strings before she had even made it two steps toward the entrance of the tent. He yanked her to him, her back against his chest. She was standing between his knees. He wrapped his arms around her casually. "Cora, Cora, Cora..." His hot breath washed against her cheek. "Silly thing. Did you forget so soon?"

"I don't want to be trapped in whatever parallel universe this place goes to!"

"You've changed your mind, then? You'll kill us all instead?" He held her tighter to him. "On second thought, don't answer that. I'd rather not know."

She struggled, but it was useless. Between his strings and his arms around her, she wasn't going anywhere. "Simon, please, let me go."

"No. Not now, not ever. And it really isn't a universe so much as it's a...eh...bubble. But there's an upside to all this. If I'm right and we do Invert, you'll finally get to leave the Faire." He chuckled darkly. "You just may not be glad you did."

"Please..."

He kissed her shoulder. He took his time. His hand splayed out against her stomach, pressing into the fabric of her tank top. His lips wandered up a notch toward her neck, and he placed another slow, gentle kiss against her skin. Then a third, just a little closer. She shivered and felt her skin explode in goosebumps.

He wrapped his other arm higher, his hand resting on her shoulder, fingers pressing into her skin as he slowly kissed his way to her throat. He groaned low. She felt it vibrate through her more than she heard the noise.

When he spoke, his voice was thick and quiet. "I don't think I've ever wanted someone so badly as I want you, Cora. And I mean that with all my past taken into account." He finally reached the spot where her neck and shoulder met, and he began to feather soft, teasing kisses where he seemed to know she was the most sensitive.

She jolted at the contact. Her skin rushed with goosebumps.

But still, he didn't stop. "Your heart is racing. Your breath is short and fast. You can't even form words."

"I—" she stammered. He was right. Everything she tried to say seemed to die in her throat. He nipped at her, little more than scraping his teeth over her. She needed to get out of here, but to where?

I can't stay here. But I can't leave either. The cost is too high. But the idea of being stuck in the "Inversion"—or whatever the fuck it was—terrified her. The urgency of her situation warred with the urgency of the man who was at her back, holding her against him. She could feel the strength in his frame, kneading his fingers into her shoulder and her stomach, caressing her. She felt him at her back, taut muscle and warm strength.

"Let go, Cora. Let go of your old life. It's gone to you. You have nowhere to go, nowhere to be...no one to help you. No one to hold you. No one but *me*." He pulled her tighter to him at his words. "Let go..."

She was trembling and shaking like a leaf in his hands. He slid his fingers from her shoulder toward her neck. His fingers brushing against her felt like firebrands. Everything in her felt like it was electric. He took her chin his grasp and tilted it away from him, making more room for him to wander his lips up toward her ear, trailing kisses the whole way there.

Her eyes slipped shut.

This felt too good.

Let go. It'd be so easy.

He turned her head to face him, and she opened her eyes to see him hovering near, his lips a hair's breadth away. He whispered to her quietly. "I released you from my strings quite a while ago, Cora. Now it's your turn to let go."

Let go.

She wanted to. Oh, she wanted to. She went to face him, to wrap her arms around his neck. She wanted to kiss him. She would end the feeling that stretched between them like a piano wire, ready to snap. But she never got that far.

"Puppeteer!"

Simon turned his head and swore. He looked up and glowered at the entrance of the tent.

She turned and saw two men standing there. Jack and Aaron. Her face exploded in crimson as she realized what she must look like. What this position looked like, standing between Simon's knees, his arms around her.

It looked exactly like what it was.

She squeaked and scrambled out of Simon's arms. He let her out from between his legs but caught her wrist and yanked her close to him. "Run away, and you won't have to wait until midnight as a conscious creature. You'll be spending it healing from having your legs torn off."

She felt her eyes turn into saucers at his threat. He meant it. She shivered and nodded weakly. He let go of her wrist, and she took a step to the side and away from him. She couldn't look at any of the men in the room. She was too embarrassed.

"Let her go, you monster! What've you done to her?"

Jack shouted. The two men stormed farther into the tent until they were ten feet away.

"Nothing she hasn't enjoyed. Secretly. Deep inside." He chuckled sinfully. "And here we have the two jealous cowboys, riding into town to save the damsel in distress. Well, I hate to tell you, my dear knights in shining armor, but your princess prefers the dragon."

"Cora, come here." Jack held out his hand to her.

"Do it, and you all will end up as mincemeat." Simon stood and tugged on his coat. Like the flick of a light switch, all playfulness in his demeanor was gone. He was once again the vicious, cruel demon.

Cora hesitated. She shook her head. "It's okay Jack. It really is. It's...it's fine. He's not hurting me."

"What're you holding against her?" Jack glared at Simon, clearly not believing her. "What the hell kind of blackmail do you have?"

Simon shrugged dismissively. "I needn't explain myself to the likes of you. Now, leave my tent immediately." He flicked his hand, and she watched as the air seemed to shimmer with a thousand crisscrossing threads. She could only see them in just the right lighting, and they came and went like spider's silk. "You interrupted a very important conversation between me and the lady."

"You wouldn't know what to do with a lady if one smacked you in the face with a skillet," Aaron cracked. "Oh, wait."

Simon laughed dryly. Humorlessly. "Am I going to have to eviscerate you twice in one week, Barker? I'm tempted. But I received an earful from our fat father-in-law already. Now, *get out.*" His words were hissed between clenched teeth.

"Not without Cora." Jack took a step forward, squaring

his shoulders. The man was built. But Simon had a thousand little knives in the air already. She didn't know what "The Rigger" could do, but she didn't know as it could stand against the Puppeteer. She didn't know if anybody could, except for Ringmaster.

"Jack, please, it's not worth it. Don't do this." Cora moved to step in between Jack and the Puppeteer. "It's all right. He's not hurting me, I promise."

The Rigger looked at her and furrowed his brow. "Then, why? Why him? Don't you see what he's like? What he does to people? Hernandez—"

"Hernandez asked me to free him from his misery!" Simon snarled from behind her. He put a hand on her shoulder and yanked her back against his chest. She let him. There wasn't any point in fighting him. Not now. Not like this. "And is it so hard to fathom that she might want me instead of you, Rigger?"

"I'm not here because I'm jealous, Simon," Jack ground out through his teeth. "I'm here because you're a manipulative, violent, *evil* sack of shit, and—"

The argument was broken off when a loud *gong* rang from outside the tent. It was like the single chime of a gigantic church bell. Cora looked at the clock, and...it was midnight. Her window of escape was over. She hadn't planned on scrambling through said window, but now that it was shut, she once more felt like a guillotine had been dropped on her.

But why had there been a bell? It had never tolled midnight before. The three men groaned audibly in joint dismay.

"I was right." Simon sighed. His threads vanished from the air.

Cora's ears popped. It was like there was a sudden pressure shift. She had gone scuba diving once, and when she had gone under the water, descending through the depths, she had to pop her ears. It felt kind of like that. She staggered a bit at the sudden sensation. Simon reached out and put a hand on her back to steady her. "What the—"

"Easy, now," he urged her quietly. "It's all right. It's done. It's all right. Sit down, and I'll explain—"

What was done? Her chance for freedom was gone, but —oh. Oh, no. She took a step away from Simon. "I...please, no. What did you do?"

"Once more, I had nothing to do with this. Welcome to the Inversion, Cora. You can leave the Faire now. Go see for yourself." His smile was somehow both sick and sympathetic at the same time.

It felt like spiders were crawling over her. Something felt wrong. Very, very wrong. Her ears were ringing from the change in pressure. She took another step away, then another, and then turned and ran. She brushed passed Jack and Aaron without a single glance at them.

And once more, as seemed to be her curse and her new lot in life, she ran away from Simon to the tune of his laughter.

She had to escape.

She had to get *out*.

At the very least, she had to try.

21

Cora flew out of the tent and almost immediately ate the pavement as she tripped over herself. She staggered to a halt and stared up at the sky. It wasn't what she had been expecting.

She didn't know what she was looking at. It always looked like something. Sunny, clouds, raining, or swirling gray. She had even seen some crazy colors during a storm on a trip to the Midwest. It was midnight, so it was supposed to be dark. She expected to see stars, a moon, or just a gray overcast.

The sky always predictably looked like *something.* She had never seen it look like *nothing.*

Nothing was overhead. No clouds, no stars, no moon... nothing. Literally nothing. Just an inky black void that somehow seemed closer than it should be. It looked like fabric had been stretched over the Faire, just out of reach of the observation tower.

She had never considered herself to be claustrophobic until that moment. She had to look away from it. Its nearness, or rather the fact that she couldn't tell how near or far away it was, gave her vertigo. Her stomach lurched angrily, and she had to struggle to breathe for a moment.

But the rest of Harrow Faire seemed normal—as normal as it could be, anyway. All the lights in the Faire were off save for the few that were always on to illuminate the paths. The rides were unlit. No music hung in the air. Only the tower still had its bulbs glowing.

But something felt too quiet. Too empty. It took her a second to realize what it was. The last few nights she had spent in the Faire, she had seen the ghostly employees of the park wandering around this late cleaning or shutting things down. But there was no one. She shuddered and wished she hadn't left her coat inside Simon's tent. She felt cold, even if the air was perfectly still.

The silence was deafening. There were no insects. There was no wind. There was nothing at all. To make up for the lack of noise, her ears began to ring. She half-ran and half-jogged to the entrance of the park and stopped when she was a few feet away.

Everything just kept going from bad to worse.

Her heart fell a thousand feet. It landed in a dark well somewhere with a heavy *splat.* She didn't know if her soul was ever going to come back out of whatever hole it just tumbled into. There was no getting to her car and speeding away.

There was no going home.

Home was missing.

Because the world was missing. Replaced with...she didn't know what she was looking at.

Right on the other side of the archway with its three upward pointing swords should have been a stretch of tarmac. Instead, there was a forest.

Kind of.

It had trees. Rows and rows of them stretched on into the darkness. They were dimly lit, like there was an ambient light filling the woods. But she couldn't see any source of it. It was like they just existed, and that was enough. Like the laws of light, and existence, no longer applied.

But it wasn't just the presence of the trees that killed all the hope she had left in her heart. It was their color.

The forest wasn't normal. Tree trunks were usually a dark brown or umber. These were gray, with a pale blue hue to them. They looked like evergreens that stretched high up overhead, the lower branches having died and snapped off from lack of useful sunlight. Only rows of their nubs remained, jutting out at odd angles, scars left behind by life and time.

There was a funny thing about people and colors, she had discovered. It was fascinating. People were taught from a young age about what colors things are. The sky is "blue," grass is "green," and dirt is "brown."

It wasn't. At least, not always. The sky was cyan. And grass was rarely a pure green, but generally, at least in New England, it had a yellowy tone, more of a chartreuse than a pure green. That was what ran through her head as she tried to understand what she was looking at.

Colors are funny.

But the grass wasn't green, or chartreuse, or anywhere close to what it should be.

What she was looking at was *purple.* So were the pine needles up overhead.

Purple wasn't even a real color, anyway. But the fact that the human mind tricked her into seeing a color was the least of her worries. Because she was staring at a forest which had its colors perfectly backward.

She had gone to college for an art degree. She had a BFA

in photography. She had spent enough time living and dying in Photoshop to know what she was looking at. Someone had taken a picture of a forest and had clicked *invert* on the color spectrum.

Just like Simon's eyes. White was black, black was white, and cyan was red.

Dark brown was a pale, grayish-blue. The grass and pine needles were purple.

And everything just seemed to glow with its own light.

Toto, I don't think we're in Kansas anymore.

Wasn't this what Simon had said? That the Faire was about to "Invert?" Well, he had warned her. She'd give him that much credit. She'd admit that no, she wouldn't have believed this if he had tried to explain.

She didn't know if she wanted to go out there. But she needed to know if she could. Reaching out her hand, she stepped forward. She expected to hit the invisible barrier that kept her locked inside Harrow Faire. Instead, her hand passed through the border. She blinked. She took another step. And then another.

And then she was on the other side of the gate. Looking around, all she could see was the forest in three directions and the Faire at her back.

Maybe there was a world out there. Weird and inverted, sure. But maybe this was some kind of alternate place, and she was free! Maybe there was someone out there who could help her. Who could help her escape Harrow Faire.

It could be dangerous to leave. But it was also dangerous to stay.

Hope was what drove her forward. Hope for freedom, and the desperate need to understand what had happened. She started off into the woods in a straight line, just in case she went too far and needed to turn back. There was a faint path in the woods, and it looked straight as a rail like a road.

Hope continued to spur her on. There might be a world out here. A world where she wasn't stuck inside the Faire.

The forest was silent. Nothing rustled the branches or the needles overhead. The only sound was her shoes on the sticks and grass underneath, crunching the little bits of forest debris as she passed. No animals called overhead or in the shrubs. No crickets or insects. She didn't see any flowers or shrubs, just grass and trees.

This is unnatural. It felt fake, like a Wild West façade propped up by planks of wood. She felt like if she shoved on a tree, it would just all topple over, or fall to the ground like one of Simon's painted backdrops.

It felt like the ghosts that haunted the Faire selling cotton candy and funnel cake.

It made her skin crawl. But maybe, just maybe, there was something out there.

She walked for ten minutes before she saw light straight ahead of her. *Yes! There is something out here!* Smiling, she began to jog. The forest was dark but had just enough coming-from-nowhere ambient light to let her see where she was going, but whatever was up ahead was bright enough to stand out against the gloom.

When she got a little closer, she slowed.

No.

No, that's not possible!

She looked behind herself and at the way she came and saw nothing but forest and a path in a straight line. Gray tree after gray tree, and mottled purple grass. Turning back to what she had seen as the source of light...she saw the gate of Harrow Faire. Its three swords sticking up into the empty void that was the night sky.

And there, leaning against the painted surface, was Simon. He had his shoulder against the post of the gate. His arms were folded across his chest, and he had one ankle over the other. He was casually waiting, and she knew it was for her.

He knew this was going to happen.

With a wail, she turned around and ran back into the forest. No! She must have just gotten turned around. She ran for a solid thirty seconds into the rows of trees before she saw light up ahead. She knew she hadn't turned—she knew it!

But there was the Faire. And Simon.

She turned and repeated the pattern a third time. Now she was shaking and out of breath. No matter how hard she ran, how certain she was that she had gone in a straight line, she wound up right back at the gate of the Faire.

She was sweating. She was exhausted. And she was trapped. No matter how hard she ran, no matter how straight she knew she went, she wound up here. At the Faire. With *him.*

"You can go all night if you want, it won't change the outcome," Simon called to her.

She stormed up to him, feeling her hands shaking again. "No. This doesn't make any sense."

"It makes perfect sense. Isn't that the definition of insanity? To do the same thing twice and expect a different response?"

"I can't...this isn't real. This isn't possible."

He sighed. "You're caught up on that again?" He scratched at his chest as if he had an itch over his heart. "Calm down, Cora. You're going to give me indigestion with this cramp you're giving me."

Right. He could feel her pain. She winced and tried to swallow down her panic. "What...where are we?"

"I don't rightly know for sure. Nobody does. Think of this as a...pocket in reality, I suppose. A little bubble stuck to the outside of a bigger one. You can run through those trees for as long as you want, cupcake, but it won't do you any good. Sometimes it'll let you go for five minutes. Sometimes for fifty. One day I went for a stroll to clear my head, and I ended up being stuck out there for a week." He grimaced. "Mr. Harrow can control it, but the Faire has a sick sense of humor of its own. And that's coming from me."

She couldn't take it anymore. She put her head in her hands and lost the battle with her tears. She was trapped. This was worse than being stuck on Earth in the Faire. Now there wasn't even a world outside anymore.

"Oh, fantastic. More waterworks." He grunted, clearly irritated and bored. "Well, you've gone from weeping at the gate to weeping five feet outside the gate. What remarkable progress you've made in the past three days!"

That was it.

That was the last straw.

She flew at him in a rage. He yelped in surprise as she slammed him up against the wall of the gate. She punched at him as hard as she could, pounding her fists into his chest.

Now she was crying in frustration and anger and taking it all out on him. She kept hitting him, again and again. It took her a long time to realize he wasn't stopping her. He was holding on to her shoulders, but not to push her away.

"That's it, cupcake, let it all out," he urged. "Keep going."

She pummeled him, useless as it was, letting out a strangled cry as she slammed her fists into his chest. She went to hit him in the face—to try to break his nose for a second time—and her resolve cracked. Her anger burned out like a firecracker. Hot, bright, loud, and brief. All that was left was the hollowness that came after.

She felt empty.

Shutting her eyes, the last of her tears flowed down her cheeks. He pulled her into him, and she didn't have the strength left to fight. She let him pull her against him in a hug. He cradled the back of her head in his hand and tucked her under his chin.

Shushing her, he held her. "It's all right, Cora...it's going to be all right."

"No. I don't think it is."

The smell of an antique store washed over her. Dust, and age, and that old-fashioned cologne he wore, and the hint of sawdust and paint. "You can punch me some more if it'll make you feel better."

"It kinda did." She chuckled weakly. "Simon..."

She didn't even know what she was asking for. Pity. Freedom. Anything, really. Something to hold on to. Any shining light of hope that she could cling to.

"You're home. You have us. You're Family." He slowly let her go and reached to take her hand. "You've had a long day, and it's late." He began to lead her away, pulling her along by her hand. She followed him, still feeling like she had been emptied out. Like someone had pulled her heart straight out of her chest and splattered it on the ground.

The bullet had hurt less.

She glanced back at the bizarre forest and had to look away. She moved closer to him, and he squeezed her hand a little tighter.

They walked through the silent Faire. As they got to the staff-only area, she saw a few people gathered around outside their boxcars. They all stopped to stare at her as

Simon led her patiently along the path. As they passed Jack's car, the Rigger stood from the stairs to approach them.

Simon shot him a glare. "Not now. Have some respect."

Jack hesitated then nodded once and backed off.

Then they were back at her boxcar. It really was hers now. There was no leaving...no going home. The world was gone. "How long does this last?"

"Sometimes it feels like a week. Sometimes a month, sometimes a year." Simon opened the door to her car and flicked the lights on, leading her in and shutting the door behind them.

"Feels like?"

"Time passes slower here than it does on Earth. It might be five, ten, twenty years before we return to the park as you saw us." He gently urged her to the bed, and she would have panicked if she didn't feel so dead inside.

"Twenty years...?"

"The longest we've gone is forty." He sat her down on the bed and knelt, taking her shoes off and tossing them aside.

He placed his hands on her knees and stayed where he was, kneeling there, looking up at her without any trace of malice or his usual sadism. The shadow on the wall behind her looked utterly heartbroken. It reached out to comfort her but couldn't touch her. It settled for petting her own shadow.

I don't know what I would do without you, Simon. She couldn't say the words out loud. She had come to rely on him. On his fiendish playfulness. Seeing him like this—concerned for her—made her want to curl into a ball and cease to exist. "What happens now?"

"Whatever you like." Simon sighed. "There's no sun here. No moon, no weather, no nothing. It can get...gloomy. There are no patrons to entertain and...nothing to do. The others play games, watch their movies, and practice new routines for when we come back. They do all they can to stay sane. I build new dolls, paint scenery, and pass the time until the Inversion ends. You'll soon realize that performing on stage for a crowd of mortals is all we have to look forward to."

"You're not helping." She cringed and buried her head in her hands.

He carefully took them in his and lowered them back to her lap. He leaned down and placed a kiss against her fingers. "We have the Faire. Out there are nineteen people who care about you. That want you to be happy, and part of the Family. And here, kneeling at your feet like a fool, is someone who has come to value you highly enough to refuse the idea of turning you into one of his dolls. Twice. That is no small feat."

She felt a bit of warmth creep into her cheeks.

He kissed her fingers again. "Tomorrow, you'll wake up, and your new life with us can truly start. Say goodbye to who you thought you were, Cora Glass. Tomorrow you are the Contortionist, once and for all." He stood and reached down to stroke his hand over her hair. "Sleep. Sleep, and let it all go. Let go of your old life."

He moved to leave, and she reached for him. She was scared. She didn't know if she could take the silence if he left. He cradled her face in his palms, and leaning down, captured her in a kiss. It was...sweet. Soothing, and devoid of the fiery passion she had felt from him every other time.

She let her fingers curl into his clothing, and when he broke the embrace, she kissed him back. It was a shy gesture. Furtive, confused, and a little desperate. But it was all she could think of to do to thank him.

He rested his forehead against hers and stroked her

cheek with his thumb. They stayed like that for a long time before she found the nerve to whisper her fears to him. "I feel so alone."

"You are anything but. You're tired, you're overwrought, and you're caught in a nightmare. But tomorrow, you will wake from this fear. Don't think of this place as a gilded cage. Think of it as the freedom to be who you were meant to be, free of pain and a world that sought to break you down." He straightened and stroked his hand over her hair again, combing his fingers through the strands. "Sleep, Cora dear."

She didn't want him to leave. She didn't know what to do if he stayed. Caught in the middle of the war between her need and her fear, she let her hands fall from where they clung to his coat. She nodded once.

Simon left her there and crossed the boxcar. He opened the door and, before leaving, turned to look at her. He smiled. Just a little flicker of his devilishness returned. "Goodnight, Cora. Today has been great fun."

He shut the door quietly behind him, and she felt like it had slammed shut on her life. She lay back on the bed. She expected to be flooded with tears again, but nothing came. She was all cried out for once.

Simon was right. She hated it, but he was. She wouldn't ever tell him—his ego was a disaster enough as it was.

Cora Glass wasn't dead. She hadn't ever existed.

She closed the curtains so she didn't have to see the empty sky outside. It was the final nail in the coffin on the truth she had been refusing to accept for three days.

There was no escape.

There was no bargain to be made.

Mr. Harrow couldn't, or wouldn't, release her now. Even if she were willing to make a deal at such a terrible price, she knew he meant his words that no other offer would ever be extended. It was time to let go of the teddy bear she had been clinging to in the dark. This nightmare was her reality now. It was up to her to survive it.

Taking in a slow breath, she let it out as equally measured. The lid had closed on the coffin, it had been nailed shut, and it finally sank in that there would be no clawing her way through the wood planks.

Trent. Emily. Lisa. Her stupid job at the bank. All her family. Her college years. All of them were nothing more than a memory for her now. They might as well have been nothing more than a dream.

A dream of Cora Glass.

And tomorrow, she would wake up from that dream into another life. The Faire was her home now.

She was Family.

She was the Contortionist.

Shutting her eyes, she let it happen.

Cora let go.

We live all our lives in cages.

Each of us, be we a slave or be we a king, call a prison our home. The prison is that which gives us shelter. It is our society.

We answer to the call of our peers, and we take our place within the structures of humanity around us. We are the ticking cogs within a machine that contains us. We are protected by its housings, even as we are driven forward by the gears about us through no choice of our own.

There is no such thing as freedom.

We rely upon others of our species too strongly for it to be any other way. We are born into a life that is chosen for us by the product of our context. How much money is at our disposal? Do we have shelter? Do we have a Family to love us? Are we born into a country that hates us for the color of our skin or for which God we worship, or are we meant to become a king? These things are chosen for us and declared at the start.

Even if we assail those facts and rise above them or sink beneath them, it matters little. We merely change one cage for another. A slave who leads a rebellion is still a truth within the confines of his context. A tyrant overthrown is the same.

The most to which we can ever aspire is not to break free from the cage that sits around us as some may believe, but that instead we might choose one that best suits our needs. A home for a captive lizard is not suitable for a bird. A gorilla is displeased by an environment that would be bliss for a snake.

Do not mistake me—it is better to hate your cage and search for something more than to be complacent. That we might find our cage a Heaven or a Hell is far more preferable to wanting nothing at all. Ants care not whose dirt they dwell in.

Hate your cage. Find another. Build it with your own bare hands if you must—but understand that it is a cage all the same. Embrace it. Fashion it with pride. Make it your home.

There is no such thing as freedom for our species.

Take these words to your soul, and happiness will follow.

-M. L. Harrow

To be continued in Harrow Faire: Book Three
"The Clown"
Order Here

ALSO BY KATHRYN ANN KINGSLEY

Harrow Faire:

The Contortionist

The Puppeteer

The Clown

The Ringmaster

The Faire

Immortal Soul:

Heart of Dracula

Curse of Dracula

The Impossible Julian Strande:

Illusions of Grandeur

Ghosts & Liars

The Cardinal Winds:

Steel Rose

Burning Hope

The Masks of Under:

King of Flames

King of Shadows

Queen of Dreams

King of Blood

King of None

Queen of All

Halfway Between:

Shadow of Angels

Blood of Angels

Fall of Angels

ABOUT THE AUTHOR

Kat has always been a storyteller.

With ten years in script-writing for performances on both the stage and for tourism, she has always been writing in one form or another. When she isn't penning down fiction, she works as Creative Director for a company that designs and builds large-scale interactive adventure games. There, she is the lead concept designer, handling everything from game and set design, to audio and lighting, to illustration and script writing.

Also on her list of skills are artistic direction, scenic painting and props, special effects, and electronics. A graduate of Boston University with a BFA in Theatre Design, she has a passion for unique, creative, and unconventional experiences.

Printed in Great Britain
by Amazon

73116717R00166